THISTLES
and
THIEVES

Also available from Pegasus Crime:

Plaid and Plagiarism
Scones and Scoundrels

BOOKS ONE AND TWO OF
THE HIGHLAND BOOKSHOP MYSTERY SERIES

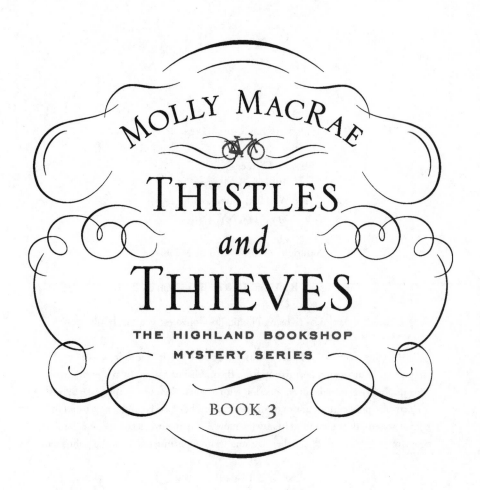

MOLLY MACRAE

THISTLES
and
THIEVES

THE HIGHLAND BOOKSHOP
MYSTERY SERIES

BOOK 3

PEGASUS CRIME
NEW YORK LONDON

THISTLES AND THIEVES

Pegasus Crime is an imprint of
Pegasus Books, Ltd.
148 West 37th Street, 13th Fl.
New York, NY 10018

First Pegasus Books hardcover edition January 2020

Interior design by Sabrina Plomitallo-González, Pegasus Books

ISBN: 978-1-64313-321-8

10 9 8 7 6 5 4 3 2 1

Printed in the United States of America
Distributed by W. W. Norton & Company, Inc.
www.pegasusbooks.us

For the real Ranger, who lost his best friend,
but found two more.

". . . for the decoction of the thistle in wine being drank, expels superfluous melancholy out of the body, and makes a man as merry as a cricket; . . . my opinion is, that it is the best remedy against all melancholy diseases."

—from *The Complete Herbal*
by Nicholas Culpeper (1653)

1

Janet Marsh pedaled for the rise ahead, wondering if shifting bicycle gears would come back to her as easily as riding. After how many years? Fifteen? Twenty? All right, since she'd ridden with her youngest on the back of the bike in graduate school. Could it really be thirty years? But she felt fit, despite the years and extra pounds. She'd been walking up and down hills every day since moving to the Highlands. Almost every day.

Her initial plan for her maiden bike ride had been too easy—sticking to the somewhat level streets running parallel to Inversgail's High Street and working her way, zig by zag, down toward the harbor and her shop, Yon Bonnie Books. That hardly gave her and the sleek new bike—or the striped yoga leggings—a workout. She'd sailed past the bookshop, singing, *"By yon bonnie banks and by yon bonnie books,"* with more than enough time to pedal back home, shower, change, and arrive to help her daughter and their business partners open the shop and tearoom at ten. Too much time.

No, if she wanted to be ready for the next Haggis Half-Hundred Ride—her *first* Half-Hundred—she needed more of a challenge. And if the hill she'd started up proved to be too much, then all she had to do was turn around and coast back down.

Janet pictured herself gaining speed on the downward glide, wind streaming off her gleaming blue-and-black helmet. Like a carapace. An aerodynamic exoskeleton. *Empowering.* The shell's color scheme went well with her graying hair, too; she'd noted that when she tried the helmet on in front of the mirror before stepping out into the chilly fall morning. She adjusted the helmet's chin strap, glad she'd adjusted the bike's brakes before setting out, too. And that she'd tested them. Twice. She tested them again, then put her mind and her thighs into the climb ahead, up into the hills that embraced her new town, her new life.

She sang a few lines from an old favorite, *"I'm goin' up the country, baby don't you want to go? I'm goin' to some place I've never been before."* But she put the brakes on that song pretty quickly. The twang in that one didn't work in this landscape of banks and braes. She looked at the autumn-browned bracken covering the hills around her and imagined a cold wind rattling corn stubble in a field back home in Illinois. Home but not home. Not anymore.

What's this? A wee bit homesick? Janet examined that unexpected twinge of emotion and decided there was nothing wrong with it. But as the road took a sharper incline, she countered her twinge with a burst from a more appropriate favorite: *"On the steep, steep side o' Ben Lomond."*

Breath for singing soon failed. Janet pressed the pedals grimly onward, muttering altered words to another favorite. *"But I would ride 500 miles, and I would ride 500 more, just to be the lass who rides a thousand miles, to fall down dead at her own door."*

And I'd . . . like to see, she thought between gasps, *the bloody . . . Proclaimers . . . do . . . a better job . . . of singing . . . while pedaling . . . up this . . . bloody . . . hill.*

She ground to a halt. Straddled the bike. Gulped air. Leaned her forehead against the cool metal of the handlebars. Maybe she'd proved enough for one morning. The downward glide toward home was calling.

She straightened and looked behind her—the *view*! She felt it in her heart. *And no, this is not a heart attack. It's love.* Undulant hills rose to the left and right, with the slate rooftops and chimneys of Inversgail nestled in their laps. The tide was out in the harbor, but that didn't matter. Even the colors of the harbor muck were picturesque at this distance. Could she see the islands? Just barely. And the sea—cerulean shades all the way out to where they blended into the sky. *A view to die for.*

If she could make herself go a little farther, she could turn again and stretch her arms to hold it all in her embrace. *If I can gasp my way to that bridge . . .*

By the time Janet reached the ancient stone bridge, she didn't think she'd stay standing if she got off the bike. Her legs felt like a quivering blancmange. But the bridge looked just wide enough for a car to pass her safely. She stopped at the crown of the span, close to the lichen-covered wall, and leaned herself and her bike against it. The top of the wall was a perfect height for her to rest her elbow on, and she was glad for the strength of the rough, cool granite.

She pondered "bridge" and "strength" as her breath caught up with her. Age had nothing and everything to do with the strength of this bridge. *Built by whose hands,* she wondered, *and how long ago? Made of stones, the bones of the earth.* Not like the abandoned bridge she'd walked across with a group of birders back in Illinois. She hadn't enjoyed that experience, didn't like heights with poorly guarded edges. Remembering the creaking and groaning of the arthritic planks as they'd skirted holes in the deck of that bridge, Janet shuddered. Not the smartest thing she'd ever done. That poor stretch of wood and iron was barely more than a century old and already left to rust and rot.

She patted the side of this stout fellow, like patting the flank of a trusty steed. *Your strength has been, it is, and it will continue to be.* It was also the only thing keeping her from toppling into the burn below. She chanced a look over the side to see where she would go if she did topple. Headfirst onto rocks the size of Shetland ponies and Highland cattle, by the looks of it.

Janet shuddered again and made herself focus instead on the gurgling water, letting her eyes follow the burn wending its whisky-colored way beyond the rocks and between banks of frost-killed thistles. There were more rocks farther along. But rocks on their own weren't threatening. Except—what was that?

On the nearside of the burn, near the largest nonthreatening rock—what was that in the thistles? A bike wheel? And beyond the wheel, half in the burn—plastic? A bag? Cloth. A sleeve, an arm. Not moving.

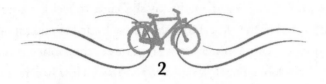

2

Aburn and a bed of dry thistles was no place for a nap.

Janet cupped her hands to her mouth and called, "Hello along the burn!" There was no answer, no movement. She thought for a moment and then climbed off her bike, her legs not at all like jelly. Maybe she'd exaggerated their distress. She walked the bike back off the bridge, losing sight of the sleeve and the other bike's wheel, and looked along the embankment for a way down to the creek.

It's steep, but not a bluff, Janet thought. *There is no edge and the world is not waiting to tip me off of one.* There was no clear path, either, but the verge was wide enough for a car to have pulled off the roadway, at least to get two wheels off the pavement, anyway. She stepped over tire ruts to study the slope. It didn't immediately strike terror, so she leaned her bike against the bridge, and made sure her helmet sat straight and firm on her head.

"I can do this," she said out loud and then, calling, "Hello! Hello!" even louder, she picked her way downward. The burn continued its gurgle. A curlew cried. No one answered her calls. When she reached the burn and started along its bank, Janet took her phone from the pack at her waist.

She came upon the bike first, its rear mudguard knocked sideways. Then the man—crumpled. She didn't know him. He'd been wearing a helmet, too. It hadn't saved his neck, though, and it was clear he would never be able to tell her how he came to be there.

She said, "Hello," again, softly, as she knelt to feel for a pulse. His skin was as cold as the rock she stumbled backward to and sat down on.

She pressed three nines on her phone—the police emergency number—and looked back up toward the road. How had he managed to lose control so completely and end up all the way down here?

"A man," she said when the dispatcher answered. "Older, but not elderly. He and his bike came off the road." She held back tears, wondering where they'd come from, and answered the dispatcher's questions about where and who and how. "He must have *flown* down the bank and then came off his bike. And then the rocks. Or first the rocks. I don't know which, but he hit his head or broke his neck. Or both. Yes, I am sure. He is dead. Yes, I can do that. I'll stand by the bridge—the Beaton Bridge? I'll stand there so you'll see where."

Before she climbed up to the road, Janet went back to stand over the man whose tweed blended in with the thistles. *He's dead. Thistles are dead. A natural and unnatural bed.* One of his hands lay in the burn palm upward, fingers curled and cupping the water like an offering.

She made another call on her way up the bank. Constable Norman Hobbs answered. "Norman, I've just called 9-9-9. It's Janet. Marsh. To report a fatality. In case you haven't already heard." She knew she was babbling.

"I have heard, Mrs. Marsh. Are you safe?"

She hadn't considered that. She stopped, listened, scanned the area with all its possible hiding places. *Hiding what? Who?*

Hobbs cut into her thoughts. "Janet?"

"I think so?" She hadn't meant it to sound like a question. And of course he'd heard about her call. As local constable, he would be first on the scene, if she'd stop delaying him. "Yes, I'm perfectly fine. I'll be standing by the bridge."

"I'll see you shortly."

When Hobbs disconnected, Janet debated calling her daughter to let her know she might be late to the shop. But Tallie was the one who'd asked her if she was trying to prove something by getting back on a bike after all these years.

Janet called their business partner Christine instead. She and Christine Robertson, a Scot transplanted to Illinois and now replanted in her hometown, had been friends since Tallie was in grade school. Christine, a retired social worker, knew a thing or two about people proving themselves. Janet pressed Christine's number, meaning to remain calm and give only the basic facts. The climb up the steep bank got to her, though, and the facts became even more basic.

"It's me," she said. "I've found a body."

Christine's response was more basic yet. "*Again?*"

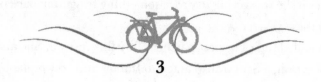

3

N orman was very fussy and wouldn't let me show him where to find the body," Janet said.

"Norman's always been *perjinkly*. He's an old plod. As stodgy as the porridge he probably eats for breakfast." Christine set a cozy-covered teapot from their adjoining tearoom on the bookshop sales counter. "There. Let it steep and that should set you right."

Being back in the shop and surrounded by books was all it took for Janet to feel right. After she'd thanked Hobbs for arriving quickly—*and why wouldn't he? I didn't get that far from Inversgail in my slow as treacle uphill ride*—she'd pedaled back home, showered, and changed into her bookseller's khakis. Then to prove something, *again*, she got back on her bike and rode to Yon Bonnie Books. She'd wheeled the bike into the storeroom, taken over for Tallie at the cash register, and spent the next hour in bibliotherapy—selling, recommending, and being soothed by the presence and weight of books. During a lull, she'd told Tallie and Christine her story.

"If Norman's an old plod, what does that make you?" Tallie asked Christine. "You're always telling us you used to change Norman's nappies." At a look from her mother, she backtracked. "Not that I think either of *you* are old. I just like saying 'Norman's nappies.' He was right to make you stay back, though, Mom. There wasn't any chance he'd miss the body, was there?"

"No."

"Then it's his job to preserve the scene until they determine cause of death. The fewer feet, the better."

Tallie had left a burnt-out career teaching law when she joined her mother, Christine, and her own former college roommate, Summer Jacobs, in the move from Illinois to Inversgail.

"Did you think I was speaking ill of Norman?" Christine asked. "Perish the thought. He's perfect for his job. He was an old plod as a wean, as well."

"Did you *want* to go back and see the body again?" Tallie asked.

"No and yes," Janet said. "The man was alone with no one to wake him." She shook her head. "That didn't sound the way I meant it. I didn't mean prod him awake."

Tallie put her arm around her mother's waist. "I wonder who he was?"

"An older man. Probably older than we are, Christine. I couldn't really tell, but his skin had that thin, papery feel."

Christine nodded. "Fragile. Like the backs of Mum's hands."

"Bicycle clips," Janet said. "He wore a tweed suit and had bicycle clips at his ankles. They made him look old-fashioned. But it wasn't an old-fashioned bike, now that I think of it. It was something serious enough for the hills. I wonder if he was one of the Haggis riders yesterday?"

"Wearing a wool suit?" Christine asked.

"It isn't a race," Janet said. "It's a challenge. More of a fun ride, with haggis when you finish. But he would have been riding with a group, or they would have reported him missing."

"A wild animal could have startled him," Christine said. "Or run in front of him."

"What kind of wild animal?" Janet asked. "Do deer come down from the hills this close to town? One of those beautiful red stags?"

"I was thinking more of cattle," Christine said. "Or sheep."

"Your feelings toward sheep are completely uncalled for," Janet said. "They're sheep. They're placid."

"And, technically speaking, they aren't wild," Christine agreed. "But they smell and they gather in mobs."

"They're called flocks and they only smell if you get too close," Janet said. "That's why I avoid them."

"Any animal could startle someone," Tallie said. Then, heading for the children's reading nook, she called over her shoulder, "Dog, rabbit, fox. Can you imagine if an eagle swooped down at you?"

"Terrifying," Christine said. "It was more likely a hairy coo, though, or one of the larger sheep. The beast startled him, he came off the road, and he couldn't stop once he started down the bank. It's a horrifying thought, but yes, it could have happened that way."

Tallie came back with a stuffed toy cradled in her arms. "Did you see sheep this morning, Mom? Or a coo like Hamish?" She held the toy, a red-haired, long-horned highland cow, up to her cheek. "Look at that face. How could anyone be afraid of him?"

"Aye, people think they're cute," Christine said. "They think the *Outlander* lad is cute, too. Romantic fancies are always in vogue."

"We make good money off those fancies," Janet said.

"And nothing wrong with that," Christine said, giving the cow and Tallie pats on their cheeks. "Good for us. Here's another theory. Maybe the cyclist was riding solo, traveling through, and unfamiliar with the road. There's a turn before that bridge, isn't there? He might have missed it. Gone off the road in the fog. It was a murky one last night."

"Why would he be out riding an unfamiliar road in the dark and the fog?" Tallie asked.

"Senile," Christine said. "Lost in the fog, inside and out. Why do you think we don't let Mum get on her old bike?"

"Norman knew him, though," Janet said. Judging by their raised eyebrows, she'd left that part out of her story. "Sorry. He wouldn't tell me the name."

"Next of kin and all that. We'll know soon enough." Christine sighed. "And now I've been gone long enough. I honestly don't know how

Summer puts up with my wandering ways. Have your cuppa, Janet. Raise it in the old fellow's honor." She waved a hand over her shoulder and disappeared down the aisle with the tallest bookshelves toward the clinking of teacups and cutlery in the tearoom.

"*Does* Summer think Christine wanders out here too much?" Janet asked.

"I haven't heard her say anything, and Summer does her share of wandering over to the paper."

Summer wrote a weekly advice column for the *Inversgail Guardian*.

"True," Janet said. "Do you think she and James are turning into a bit of a thing over there?"

"You could always ask her these questions if you really want to know."

"Mm. But it seems so nosy."

Janet had gone over to the natural history shelf, and so made that comment more to the books than to Tallie. She found the guide she was looking for and took it back to the counter. "They actually seem to get along quite well, don't they? I'm talking about Summer and Christine."

"Did you have your doubts?"

Janet ignored the teacup Tallie put in front of her and leafed through the book. "Well, you know how Christine is. She can come across as prickly. Somewhat."

"Somewhat? Sort of the way you come across as absentminded when you have your nose in a book? Somewhat."

"Hmm. What?"

"Anyway, you're learning how Summer is, too."

"She has a passion for baking and an excellent work ethic. Beyond that?"

"No need to go beyond. She was a reporter longer than I was a lawyer. Her nose for news is just as good at sniffing out bull. She saw through Christine's prickles the first time they met."

"They share that passion for baking, too," Janet said. "A match made in heaven. Or in an oven."

"Or made in a patch of thistles. Summer can prickle right back if Christine gets to her."

"That poor old guy died in a patch of thistles."

Tallie pushed the teacup closer to Janet.

"It must be beautiful along there when they're blooming," Janet said. "The bank is covered with them. I'd like to know what kind they are, but I wasn't really looking at *them* this morning."

"Ask Rab. That's the kind of thing he might know."

"Almost anything is. Unless you ask him when he's coming in to work this week."

Rab MacGregor, who didn't often have much to say, worked part-time in the bookshop and tearoom. They hadn't actually hired him, but just as he might be anywhere from a weather-worn forty to a youthful sixty, he showed up anywhere from one to four days a week and seemed to know what needed doing, so they paid him. His dog came to work, too. Ranger, a seemingly self-trained cairn terrier, had claimed one of the chairs by the bookshop's fireplace as his own. On workdays, he sat or dozed in the chair, like an indulgent spouse waiting for his love to finish shopping.

"Do we know if they're coming in today?" Janet asked. "Rab and Ranger, I mean." She looked at the front door, as if it would give her the answer. Someone else was just coming in. "Oh, bloody—hello, Ian."

Janet bared her teeth, not caring if it looked more like a grimace than a smile. Ian Atkinson, her next-door neighbor, who also happened to be an internationally bestselling crime writer, was the thistle in her side. He'd told Janet that people often mistook him for Alan Rickman in his *Sense and Sensibility* phase. Janet admired the late actor and adored Jane Austen, and she wondered how either of them would feel about Ian's reduction of *Sense and Sensibility* to a "phase."

"Good morning, Janet. Nice to see you, Tallie." Ian approached the counter, stopping halfway to flip glossy, lank hair off his forehead. "Janet, I can't help but notice that you've changed."

"I beg your pardon?"

"Your clothes." He smirked. "I saw you get on your bicycle this morning."

Tallie, with her back to Ian, made discreet gagging noises as she edged past her mother. "I'll go put Hamish back with his friends then unpack the order in the storeroom. Sorry, but if you call, I might not hear."

"So kind of you, dear." Janet flashed the same rictus for Tallie that she'd used on Ian.

The short interruption didn't jog Ian loose from his conversational track. "You were wearing something quite a bit more revea—" At that point, possibly noticing Janet's teeth, he cleared his throat. "Where were you off to?"

"Getting some fresh air and exercise."

"Relaxed, that's what I meant to say. And now you look properly businesslike and bookish."

"What can we do for you today, Ian?"

"Just stopped in to say hello. But while I'm here, is there anything for me to sign?"

"We have five copies of *The Claymore in the Cloister* coming in sometime next week. I'll give you a call. How's the new book coming?"

"Beginning to gel." He gave a quick smile. "Either that or it's turned to sludge. Sometimes it's hard to tell."

"Do you have a title yet?"

"The editor and I are batting around a couple of them. Tell you what, though. I value your opinion as one who knows books. Which do you like best, *The Dirk in the Distillery* or *The Chib in the Cheddar*? Ah! I can see the answer on your face. We've already had two Cs, with claymore and cloister. That's exactly what I said. Dirk and distillery are new. Different. Fresh. I couldn't agree with you more. I'll hold out for dirk and distillery. I'll make a note . . ."

Ian's part of the conversation turned into a muttered soliloquy and Janet didn't hear any more. She watched him wander off into the fiction section. *Probably to stand in front of his shelf of books and stare in awe.*

As soon as Ian left the counter, Tallie reappeared. "Sorry to abandon you."

"Survival of the fittest in action. You can run faster." Janet spoke softly; Ian wasn't above eavesdropping, claiming it gave him fodder for plots.

"Survival of Ian and the business, too. I can't go around smacking every irritating author or customer. You're all right?"

"Oh, sure."

"Except for how it ended, how was your ride?"

Janet thought back on the wheeze-inducing hill. "My knees and thighs might have something to say about it later, but the view was worth it. Do you know what I thought when I looked out over Inversgail and the harbor, though? 'To die for.' I never should have."

"But he was already gone. You know that, right?"

Janet picked up the plant guide and flipped through it without focusing on any of the pages.

"Saying what you did—something anyone who visits the Highlands might think or say—didn't make it happen," Tallie said.

"Of course not."

"What were you doing way out there? *Up* there? I thought we agreed you'd start out slowly."

"We did. Then I tested my capability, reassessed the terrain, calculated risks and possibilities, and amended the agreement. Level roads? Not a problem. A few gentle grades? Took them like a champ. The first hill of the Half-Hundred? Trust me; a haggis would have gone up that hill faster than I did. I'll go up it again, too, because other than blowing like a belabored beluga by the time I reached the Beaton Bridge, I made it without embarrassing myself." Janet's voice rose just as surely as she'd ridden up the hill. "And I *am* going to ride in the next Haggis Half-Hundred."

"*You?*" Ian stuck his head around the corner of a bookshelf.

"Why not?" Janet asked.

Ian stepped out into the open, hands raised, palms out. "Not what I meant. I've complete faith in you and your—" He waved a hand vaguely up and down his thigh. "Yes, well, what I meant to ask is, if you rode to the Beaton Bridge this morning, were you there for the excitement?"

"*Excitement?*" Janet said, wondering anew how Ian managed to write international blockbusters but so often clunked when it came to real life. She'd asked Christine if it were a British versus American disconnect, with the fault being on her end for misinterpreting. Christine, proud Scot, had scoffed. *He's English*, she'd said, *and a twit. There's your disconnect.*

"The excitement about Dr. Murray," Ian said. "Found dead under the bridge. He was out bicycling, too. Had a heart attack, I suppose. You haven't got a heart condition, have you, Janet? Even so, you should be careful."

"He wasn't found under the bridge," Janet said. "You should be careful, too, Ian. Get your facts straight before you spread them or a load of misinformation and suppositions around." She'd let the accumulation of his clunks get to her. Again. A deep breath didn't quite clear the irritation from her voice. "When did they release the name?"

"Well, if you're going to take that tone, I might just as easily ask how you appear to have insider—*oh!*" Ian bounced the heel of his hand off his forehead. "I should have known. *You* found him. Is this like a hobby for you? How many bodies have you've stumbled across since landing in our once peaceful Highland village? But I thought you were out for a bike ride. What were you doing under the bridge?"

"*Not* under the bridge," Janet snapped.

Tallie jumped into an uncomfortable silence. "You knew the man? Was he local?"

"Doc Murray? He was about as local as you can get. A GP, retired for several years now. Stayed here when he closed up his surgery. Quite distinguished looking. Think Patrick Stewart or Ian McKellen. Or Peter O'Toole. Long, tall, and patrician. Although, depending on his condition when you found him, perhaps that wasn't the case this morning. Was he much disfig—"

"He looked sad and alone," Janet said. Then, remembering the cupped hand, with its offering of water, she added, "Oddly enough, he looked at peace."

"I do realize I ask what sound like callous and inappropriate questions," Ian said. "Occupational hazard of the crime writing life. But Dr. Murray was well-loved. It's a sad loss to the community." He sighed in a way that made Janet believe he meant it.

"When *was* the name released?" she asked.

"Oh, you know, I must have heard it at some point this morning, the way one does. It must have been after they let his housekeeper know."

Now he fiddled with a button, a thread coming loose on one of his leather elbow patches, the corner of an eyebrow—the targets random and none of his fiddling necessary as far as Janet could tell, and she didn't believe him.

Tallie didn't seem to, either. "*Where* did you hear it?" she asked.

Ian waved a hand and shook his head. Janet couldn't tell if he was dismissing the question or hoping they'd believe it could have been anywhere and wasn't important. Maybe it wasn't.

"I wonder what happens to the housekeeper, now?" he said instead. "I wish I could afford a live-in, I'd offer her a job. Or maybe not. She's a bit laughable, really, and I'd have her constantly dabbling around underfoot. A doddery old duck."

"Don't be rude," Janet said.

"By calling her an old duck?"

"Or laughable or doddery," Tallie said.

"They aren't *my* words. Malcolm the great and good doctor called her that. 'Florrie, you doddery old duck,' he'd say, 'you make me laugh. Stop quacking.' It wasn't meant to be rude, I'm quite sure. More a term of endearment."

"Not really," Tallie said. "No more than calling you an old dic—"

"Thank you, Ian," Janet said over Tallie. "Thanks for taking time out of your busy day to stop in to see us, and thank you for letting us know about Dr. Murray. You mustn't let us keep you, though." She walked ahead of him to the door and held it for him. "We'll see you later. Maybe next week. I'll call you when your books come in." When the door closed behind him, she muttered, "Or maybe I won't. Tone-deaf twit."

Back at the counter, she patted Tallie's shoulder and said, "Sorry for interrupting you, dear. I agree with you completely. I'd say go ahead and finish that astute remark now, but I see children coming through from the tearoom."

"No problem. It'll keep."

4

N ow," Janet said as she locked the door behind the last customer late that afternoon, "what were you dying to say about Ian?"

"Nah, that's okay." Tallie started counting down the cash drawer.

"Really? You bottled it up long enough. It might do you good to get it off your chest."

"Or it might do me good to be more mature."

"There's my darling lawyer daughter."

"Or I'll get Summer to come up with a better insult," Tallie said. "She has a wicked way with words."

"Wicked words will have to wait," Summer said, coming through from Cakes and Tales, followed by Christine. "Darts practice."

"She made the *Guardian* team," Christine said, rubbing Summer's shoulders as though she were a boxing coach loosening up her champion's trapezii.

"*Barely* made the team," Summer said. "Part of it's psychological. James thinks we can give the competition a false sense of security and superiority with the whole blond Barbie American thing."

"You're okay with that?" Tallie asked.

"Sure." Summer removed the clips keeping her hair in a neat bun and shook out honey blond hair that fell to her elbows. "I see myself more as Boudicca than Barbie. But I have to practice. I can't trade on my warrior good looks and not deliver. Want to come, Tallie? James hung a dartboard in the old press room. Top secret."

"I won't breathe a word," Tallie said. "And on the way over, I'll tell you about the wicked words."

"See you at Nev's later?" Janet asked.

The younger women waved and let themselves out the front door. Janet relocked it behind them and asked Christine, "Does Summer know Boudicca's uprising wasn't successful?"

"And that she poisoned herself afterwards? I didn't want to bring her down. She's that chuffed over making the team that it was all I could do to keep her from practicing with the leeks we got in for the vichyssoise."

"Are you going ahead with adding soup to the menu, then?" Janet asked.

"No, we came to our senses. Tea and basic baked goods are enough to deal with. We're doing well enough with them and they're more practical for our space. So the leeks were, in fact, expendable, but Summer kept herself under control. We announced the soup decision this morning in the doorway."

It had been Christine's suggestion that the four of them meet for a few minutes before they opened each morning, "so we're all on the same page or sipping from the same blend." They shared information about the featured tea and scone of the day, new book displays, titles of particular interest, comments from or about customers, sometimes a joke or inspirational quote, and any concerns from the third branch of their business—Bedtime Stories, the bed and breakfast located in the rooms above the bookshop and tearoom. Janet chose the place for the meetings—*between a teapot and a bookshelf*—the interior doorway between Cakes and Tales and Yon Bonnie Books.

"Did I miss anything else this morning?" Janet asked.

"We were more concerned about you and what you were going through with the poor, wee man," Christine said.

"Not wee, according to Ian."

"What would that great numpty know about him?"

"He was vague about how he knew," Janet said, "but you might have known the man—a local GP, Malcolm Murray."

"Good lord. Of course I knew him. You must have known him, too."

"I don't think I ever met him."

"How could you not have? You must have needed him at some point during your summers here. You have children. Children are always scraping or bumping or coming down with something."

"That's a stereotype," Janet said.

"Tallie broke her arm once. I distinctly remember that."

"Slipping and falling after an ice storm in Champaign."

"Are you sure?"

"It was three years ago. She was thirty-five."

"Good lord," Christine said again. "You see what the shock has done to my head." With a hand to the brow of her shocked head, she trailed over to the chairs in front of the fireplace and dropped into one. "Malcolm Murray. It's a sad loss."

"I'm so sorry," Janet said, sitting more gingerly in Ranger's favorite chair. "I'm never sure if Ian's being sincere, but he said that, too, and for once I believed him."

"If he said it, then I wish I'd put it differently," Christine said. "I meant that Malcolm's death is a loss to Inversgail. Not to me, personally. Not really. Tony and I were gone for so many years that I didn't know Malcolm professionally. I knew his reputation, though. I knew him growing up, too, but only from a distance. You were right. He *was* older than we are. Seven or eight years."

"Wow. Seventy and still biking up and down these hills?" Janet said. "More power to him—oh dear."

"Oh dear." Christine nodded. "It's that sudden absence, isn't it? A life erased. Even if you didn't know someone, a sudden death can take some getting used to. And for many people, this one will take a lot of getting used to. If you're talking stereotypes, Malcolm Murray might have set the stereotype for 'good doctor.'"

"Ian said something like *that* this morning, too," Janet said. "And then he said something that made me wonder if I'd like the good doctor so much after all. Or like Ian, ever."

"Wondering about Ian is a given. What did he say?"

"He claimed he was quoting Dr. Murray talking about his house-keeper, calling her old, laughable, and doddery. Maybe, just *maybe*, we can cut your good doctor some slack for saying that, but Ian gets out in the world. Literally. He does book tours all over Europe and in the States. He should know better. Tallie was ready to flay him. There's no telling what Boudicca would do."

"Why give Malcolm a pass?"

"Consideration for his upbringing and generation?" Janet shrugged. "I didn't know the man or his background. Ian said the words were a form of endearment, and maybe for Malcolm they were. Ian laughed, though, and I told him it was rude."

"And I'll tell *you* something, Janet Marsh."

Rising up inside Christine, snapping like blue lightning in her eyes and chilling her voice, came a phenomenon Christine seemed wholly unaware of. Janet had only witnessed it since their move to Scotland; she thought of it as the release of Christine's inner Queen Elizabeth II.

"You and I are of Malcolm Murray's generation, or close enough, and *I* am of this place," the Queen said. "And though it's true that I spent the past thirty years rubbing up against the rarefied and progressive attitudes of the state of Illinois's flagship university and its vaunted, pancake-flat environs, my parents are of an even older generation, and they stayed right here in this place, and you'll not hear them *ever* laughing at or ridiculing an old woman just because she's old, nor will you find them treating her in a condescending manner. Neither will you hear them maligning old men."

"I apologize, Christine."

"Not everyone in a village is an idiot." The Queen and Christine rolled their *R*s and wore their dudgeon like ermine-edged robes.

"I know. Believe me, having grown up on a pig farm in those pancake flats, I do know that. I'm appalled that I was just as obtuse and rude as I accused Ian of being. That's why he made us so mad this morning, though. Tallie came *this* close to being vulgar about him in front of the customers."

"He has that effect." The Queen began to retreat and Christine reached over to pat Janet's knee. "I don't blame you."

"*I* do. I hold librarians to a higher standard. Just because I retired from lending books and started selling them doesn't mean I can slip. But do you want to hear how awful Ian really was? This is the tone-deaf twit thinking he's funny by imitating Dr. Murray."

Janet got up and went to the fireplace where she propped her elbow on the mantelpiece. She flipped imaginary lank hair from her forehead, and in a plummier accent than Ian's said, "Florrie, you doddery old duck, you make me laugh. Stop quacking."

QE II vanished in an instant and a baffled Christine asked, "What did he call her?"

"Doddery old duck."

"No, her name. *Florrie.* Janet, she isn't his housekeeper; she's his sister. Oh, I've not thought of Florrie in years. How did I not know she's living back in Inversgail?"

"It could be a coincidence. There must be more than one Florrie in the area."

"But a Florrie that Malcolm called 'old duck'? Her mam couldn't keep her out of puddles when she was a wean and so they called her Ducks."

"Oh, please, no," Janet said. "I can't stand it. Ian was right? 'Old duck' *is* an endearment?"

"Stand firm, Janet. Doddery isn't complimentary *or* endearing. You don't need to forgive Ian for anything."

"It didn't stop there. He wondered what will happen to her now that Malcolm's gone, which sounded surprisingly human, considering it came from Ian. But then he ruined it by joking about hiring her as his own live-in and having to put up with her dabbling around underfoot. He's a good mimic, Christine. He might have picked up that attitude from Malcolm."

"I'd hate to think it. But, oh, if it's Florrie. She's our age, Janet. We were at school together. We weren't grand pals, but I knew she went up to St. Andrews when I went to Edinburgh. Last I heard she'd married and stayed in Aberdeen. If Ian could mistake her for a fussing, fretful . . . I've not heard anyone speak of her since I've been back."

"You've been busy and it's been a long time since you've known her," Janet said. "Life happens."

"She adored Malcolm. She'll be devastated by this."

"Are there other relatives? You said she married. Does she have family of her own?"

"A husband. Beyond that, I don't know. There was another brother, though. Gerald. A year younger than Malcolm—Malcolm's shadow. He didn't follow him into medicine, though. He went into the military. Florrie said that was the opposite of medicine. I've no idea where he's living. Or if."

"We don't know if Ian's right about *her* living here," Janet said. "Norman will know."

"We can't ask him."

"Why not?"

"Because I called him an old plod this morning, after telling you we don't laugh at old people."

"You called him an old plod *before* you said that. You slipped, I slipped, we all do."

"—and if I talk to him, I'll do it again. That isn't fair to other plods or to Norman. I need to rise above that kind of thing. I can't do it on such short notice, though, but I do have a better idea. Are you all right getting home on the bike?"

"Of course."

"Good. I'll pop home and check on my own oldies and be round to pick you up in half an hour."

"For?"

"A condolence call."

"Oh, I don't know, Christine. It sounds so awkward. She doesn't know me. I don't know her."

"That makes a level playing field. She and I don't know each other, either. Not anymore."

∽

Janet almost gave in and walked her bike home. Instead, reprising her groaning imitation of the Proclaimers with, "*I would ride 500 miles,*" muttered under her labored breath, she made it up the stair-step hill to Argyll Terrace and to the third stone cottage along on the right. Four snug rooms down and two up, built of granite as sturdy as the Beaton Bridge, and more durable than her marriage had been.

She turned in at the drive and glanced at a lamplit window upstairs in Ian's house next door. That was his writing room, he'd told her. She often caught a furtive movement at the window when she arrived home, as though he'd just slipped out of view. *If staring out the window is part of your secret creative process, Ian, don't let my comings and goings interrupt. And if you're just keeping tabs, that's fine, too.* She'd rather have a nosy neighbor than one who grumped and turned a blind eye.

Smirr and Butter, a rain gray tom and a butter pat of a kitten, noticed everything, too. They appeared from the family room as Janet came in the back door. Smirr advanced a few paces before flopping on his side. He yawned like a pensioner woken from a nap. Butter pounced on Smirr's twitching tail then rubbed his forehead under Smirr's chin. New additions to the Marsh household, the "lads" came from different backgrounds and experiences, and had become instant best mates.

Janet scooped up Butter on her way to the kitchen. Smirr reached a paw to pat at her foot as she passed, then followed her and leapt with nimble grace to the kitchen counter.

"Smirr, dear," Janet said with mild reproof.

She put Butter on the floor and Smirr leapt back down to supervise the kitten while she organized a light evening meal for them. They tucked in and she went upstairs to exchange her khakis for black slacks. As she put on the matching black jacket, the cats came in to offer thanks with a few turns around her ankles. She looked down at the gray and yellow hairs they left behind. The kitten met her eye and mewed.

"You're right," she said. "A touch more color won't hurt."

She hung the jacket back in the wardrobe and slipped into a deep purple cardigan. Then she went to watch for the Vauxhall Christine drove. Christine's parents still owned the car, but since moving in with them to be the extra pair of hands they needed, her father seemed content to borrow the keys from her rather than the other way around.

"You look proper, Janet," Christine said when she got in the car.

"Thank you."

"For knowing how to dress?"

"For coming with me."

"Did you ask your mum and dad what they know about Florrie?"

"Oh, aye, and Mum was right on top of it. Said she saw Florrie Friday last, at the school prize-giving. Florrie looked *feart*, but she did a grand job of reciting 'To a Wee Mousie.'"

"That's—"

"We would have been eight or nine at the time."

"At least it's a sweet memory. What about your dad?"

"He saw someone who reminded him of her in Inverness a few years back, but only in passing. By the time he realized who she might be and turned around to call hello, she'd turned a corner or gone into a shop. I don't think they've heard about Malcolm. I didn't say anything and Dad didn't bring it up. I left it that way, for now, and left Dad fixing salmon for their tea."

"Will we pick them up for Nev's after we see Florrie?"

"Mum has a bit of a cold so Dad thought they'd stay in tonight."

"Probably best, but I'm sorry I won't see them. Do you know where we're going?"

"Not far."

"Not far" didn't mean much, because Janet hadn't paid attention to the turns Christine made and she didn't recognize the neighborhood. Bigger front gardens with walls and gates. They might all have had live-in housekeepers once. Or still. Christine slowed and turned in at house Janet thought might be Georgian. Symmetrical. Stuffy rather than cozy. All the downstairs lights appeared to be on and spilling from windows not yet draped for the night.

"At least someone's home," Janet said as they got out of the car.

"You're not expecting much from this visit, are you? You keep saying 'at least.'"

"At least it isn't raining, the wind isn't blowing, and at least I came with you."

Christine pushed the bell then took Janet's arm in hers. They waited together, then heard a single bark somewhere inside and a lock turn and the latch snick. The door opened only wide enough for a woman to look out at them, expressionless.

"Florrie," Christine said. "It's Christine MacLean. I brought my friend Janet Marsh. We heard about Malcolm and we've come to offer our sympathy."

Florrie looked at Christine and then Janet. "Why? What's the point?" she asked, and closed the door in their faces.

5

F lorrie! Wait!" Christine stared at the closed door, then turned a distraught face to Janet. Before Janet could think what to say, determination overtook the distress. "She didn't slam it," Christine said, and she reached toward the bell again.

Janet put a hand on Christine's arm to stop her. "Wait," she whispered. "I didn't hear her relock it." She tried the knob. It turned and she gently pushed the door open.

Florrie hadn't moved. The blank expression on her face hadn't budged, either.

As gently as she'd opened the door, Janet said, "Sorry for the intrusion, Florrie. I'm Janet. Sorry, too, for the reason we're here, but I'm glad to meet you." She did a quick search through her mental card catalog of people she'd met since arriving in Inversgail. The woman standing in front of her, appearing as rumpled and soft as her faded jeans and sweater, didn't match anyone in the imaginary cards.

Florrie said nothing.

Has she even blinked? Janet wondered. She and Florrie were an even height, both shorter than Christine. Janet looked into Florrie's eyes for any sign that she'd heard her, or if she had, that she cared; she didn't find anything that gave her a clue. *That's not a vacant look, though. Someone's definitely home behind those eyes, but* that *door is locked and bolted.* Temptation pulled at Janet, goading her to turn around and search the dark behind her for whatever held Florrie's gaze. Instead, she nudged Christine into action.

"Is there anyone we can call for you, Florrie?" Christine asked. "Have you had your tea?"

Christine took a half step forward. Florrie tilted her chin up a few degrees. Janet wondered if Florrie was finally making eye contact with Christine.

Christine took another half step.

Florrie took two back. "So it's Christine, is it? I mind how we played together a summer or two."

"It's been a long time," Christine said. "It's good to see you, Florrie. I think Janet and I should come in and make you a cup of tea. What do you say to that, eh?"

"It's Florence." She turned and walked into the house, leaving them at the still open door.

"Did she ask us in?" Christine asked.

"No," Janet said.

"We'll go anyway."

Janet tried too late to stop Christine; Christine had already started after Florence, and Janet decided not to make a scene by arguing with her. *Because if we can do something to ease that woman's pain . . .* She closed the door, and at the click of the latch wondered, *But is it pain?* She tried to soothe her own unease by smoothing a furrow settling between her eyebrows. It didn't help.

She hurried after the others, past a carpeted stair to the first floor, and along a dim, flagged hall. She caught a glimpse of an ornate frame hanging at the first landing up the stair and pictured a kilted ancestor keeping a watchful eye on the comings and goings in this dour place. Hers were the only footsteps she heard now, Christine having followed Florence into a room on the right, at the end of the hall. Only Christine looked around when Janet entered.

They stood in a room that made any discomfort the rest of the house held worthwhile. The walls were book lined, the space lit by a table lamp and crackling fire. An old spaniel lay on the hearthrug, nose toward the warmth. He lifted his head with a soft woof when Janet held her hands to that warmth. He didn't challenge her right to be there, though, and went back to a dream of rabbits or grouse.

"What a lovely room," Janet said. "I'd want to spend all my time here."

"She's a retired librarian," Christine said to Florence. "Gets misty-eyed whenever a dozen or more books gather in one place. She's right, though; the room's as cozy as a snug. I'll make the tea and bring it in here, shall I?"

"Don't bother."

"It's no bother. I'm happy to do it."

"If I want it, I'll get it myself."

"That's all right, then. The fire's lovely," Christine said. "Shall we sit?"

Janet thought Christine must not have noticed the three chairs in the room—one pulled near the fire, a second over by the window to catch the light, the third at a delicate desk. *Arranged for the pleasure of a single person.*

"If I'd wanted company, I'd have said come *ben.*"

"But Florrie—"

"Florence."

"You left the front door open," Christine said. "Left it open and walked away."

"Did I? I am competent, you know, despite . . ."

Florence's voice trailed away as she turned to look at—what? Janet couldn't tell if she was looking at the dog, the photograph on the end table beside the lone fireplace chair, the books on the shelf behind, or nothing at all.

"Will there be family here to help you with arrangements?" Janet asked. "There are so many details at a time like this."

"I am competent," Florence repeated, her voice thin but steady.

"We *ken* that," Christine said. "It can be a comfort, though, to have someone else. Someone to lean on a little. Have you called anyone? Did Constable Hobbs call someone for you?"

"I laughed at him," Florence said. "At Norman, when he came to the door. I thought it was fancy dress. Guising in something he bought at Oxfam."

"Oh dear. Poor Norman," Janet murmured.

"How was I to know that weedy Norman Hobbs grew up and joined the *polis*," Florence said. "He surprised me, is all."

"*Dinnae fash*," Christine said. "He must be used to all sorts of remarks."

"I didn't believe him when he said Malcolm wasn't here. He said he'd had an accident. Went off the road with his bike. Dead by the burn at the Beaton Bridge. But how can that be? He didn't say goodbye." Florence shook her head, as though to worry from it a reason for that lapse.

Christine moved closer to put an arm around her. "Without a goodbye makes it even harder, doesn't it? But how was Malcolm to know?"

"That he was leaving the house?" Florence pulled away. "Why *wouldn't* he know?"

"That's not what I meant," Christine said.

Janet, feeling less awkward than simply out of her depth, tried to smooth over the misunderstanding. "I thought Malcolm might have joined the Haggis Half-Hundred bike ride yesterday."

"Oh, aye," Florence said. "He'd no time for me if *I* wanted a chat, but he blethered on about that for weeks."

"So maybe he went for the ride and that's when he left the house," Janet said. "But if he did, I wonder why none of the other riders reported him missing?"

"Why would they?" Florence said. "He wasn't missing."

Janet looked at Christine, hoping for guidance through the murk of this conversation.

Christine nodded that she understood and adopted her professional social worker voice. "You say he wasn't missing, Florence. How do you square that with what happened? He went out and didn't come back."

"But he did. He came home after the ride. You can't be any less missing than that. I spoke to him. I don't know when he went out again, but he did, without saying a word. No 'I'm going out for another ride, and I'll see you after.' No 'Don't bother getting my tea, and ta for all the times you do.' No 'Lock the door behind me. I'll not be back.'"

"Did you tell Norman this?" Christine asked.

"What was he doing sneaking out like that? Again? And me standing here not even knowing he'd gone."

"How awful for you," Janet said. "Florence, there must be something we can do for you."

"You can leave me in peace to get on with *not* mourning him."

"You don't mean that," Christine said. "That's the stress and all the emotions talking. I know how it can be. How hard it is to lose someone and say goodbye."

"Easier to say good riddance."

∽

Janet waited until she heard the door locked behind them and they'd gone down the steps before saying, "Again? She said he was sneaking out *again*. What kind of good doctor does that? *Again*. I don't like that word anymore. I don't trust it or any of its implications."

"Do you feel right, leaving Florrie here alone?" Christine looked back at the door as though weighing its strength against her determination if she decided to go back in.

"She said she's competent," Janet said. "Let's not worry her by standing here, in case she's watching."

"She's not. She'll have gone back to her snug room to turn inward and beat down on herself and Malcolm."

"Did you see any books in that snug library that looked like they were being read? There weren't any lying around open. I didn't see any obvious bookmarks. None of them were waiting for a reader to return and pick them up again."

"I didn't notice," Christine said. "I watched her."

"As one who gets misty-eyed wherever a dozen or more books gather, I did notice. There wasn't a throw anywhere for a chilly evening, either." Janet looked at the front of the house, the blank face of uncurtained windows staring into the dark. "The whole house is watching us. Get in the car, Christine. We can pull over farther down the street and talk more, but get us away."

"How reliable do you think she is?" Christine asked as she backed out of the drive.

"I'm not sure what you're asking and I'm not sure I can tell anyway. We stopped in unannounced at a very stressful time for her. And we were there all of five minutes."

"Fifteen or twenty."

"Ten tops. Aren't you going to pull over?"

Christine didn't answer. She turned a corner, gripping the steering wheel so her knuckles looked ready to pop.

"I'm not sure you're safe to drive, Christine. I know how you get. You'll worry over this until you're completely distracted. *And* there's a fog moving in."

The Vauxhall took a corner too fast for Janet's nerves.

"Honest to Pete!" She risked distracting Christine further by turning the full force of a scowl on her. "And you wonder if Florence is reliable."

"But I never wonder about Nev's. It's aye reliable."

∾

"I didn't know you needed a drink this badly," Janet said as Christine parked in the closest space they could find near Nev's.

"We arrived in one piece, didn't we? And we've our standing date with the girls here later, so consider this just us being a wee bit early. It's not a drink I need, anyway. It's food. Anything fried."

"That might not qualify as food."

"Not such a terrible coping mechanism or vice, though. Will you join me?"

"Oh, aye." Janet opened the door for Christine, and they left a creeping fog outside for the swirl of voices and pub smells—ale and battered fish with a twist of damp dog.

"Heaven," Christine said.

Most of Nev's clientele were locals, the pub's exterior holding no appeal for passing tourists. It occupied a narrow building squeezed shoulder to shoulder between the *Inversgail Guardian* and Smith Funerals. Hardware for a sign hung above the door, empty for the past decade. Or two or three. In the basement, with its face to a corner, stood a sign with the faded words "Chamberlain's Arms." Anyone with a memory of the sign hanging out front knew it didn't refer to Sir Neville. No one working at the pub claimed to know where the name Nev's came from.

"How's the evening's *dreich*?" Danny, the barman, asked went they stopped to order their food.

"I'd like to bury it under a plate of whatever you have on special," Christine said.

"One of those days?"

"And the day's not over," Janet said. "I'll have what she's having."

"Fried haggis." Danny said. "You're sure?"

"Bring it on."

"Comes with chips."

"Brilliant. And bring the brown sauce."

"Forget the sauce," Christine said, "and we'll hope it hasn't been as bad as that, but bring two halves of the Selkie's. We'll be at our usual."

"You're early," Danny said. "Seamus still has it."

"No matter. We'll find another."

Nev's had more interior corners than seemed natural for what appeared, from the outside, to be a rectangular building. The bar and small kitchen along the left side only took up space halfway down that long wall, though, and the room opened up beyond them. And the wall between Nev's and Smith Funerals took two interesting jogs. The "Smithward" jog, on the street end of the businesses, gave Nev's a room for darts. The corresponding "Nevward" jog, beyond the darts room, created the corner where Janet and Christine's "usual" table sat. No one liked to speculate what Smith's did with their bonus room.

The table had become their usual on Monday nights soon after they'd settled into their routine at Yon Bonnie Books. "Nev's is a perfect place for us to go for a quality of life check," Janet had said. Christine agreed, calling Nev's neutral ground, an honest place where they could be honest with each other, "which isn't always possible in front of customers in the shop." Summer had liked the idea and offered a toast: "To whisky and unwinding." Tallie had answered with one of her own: "Drams to drown the occasional *dreich*."

With their table taken on this Monday evening, Janet and Christine looked for a next best place.

"The nearer one will do for now," Janet said, nodding at a small table closer to the bar.

"Is that you, Christine?" Seamus called from "their" table as they sat. "Here, now." The elderly man struggled to rise. "I've just been keeping it warm."

"No rush, Seamus. We're grand right here."

"I'm away home the noo. Màiri won't have heard about Malcolm Murray."

"A sad day," Christine said. "We've just been to see Florrie."

"Eh? You're sorry?" Seamus fiddled with a hearing aid as he passed them. "Aye, we're all sorry. He'd aye a kind word. A great heart. Cheers to your mum and dad."

"Thanks, Seamus. Mind how you go."

They watched him make his way to the door, a hand on the back of a chair here and a shoulder there to steady himself.

"A bit squiffed?" Janet asked as they relocated to their table.

"Seamus? He's teetotal. He's just older and deafer. *We're* not deaf, though. What can you hear? Is anyone at the other tables talking about Malcolm? Or Florrie?"

"I might hear something if I went and hovered," Janet said.

"Good idea. Try over at that one—"

"No. And don't you do it either. We'll wait and ask Danny what he knows when he brings the food."

Christine dropped into a chair and Janet saw Queen Elizabeth flicker in her eyes—a woman thwarted and sinking into the dumps. *But does the real Elizabeth allow herself to feel so low?* Janet wondered. *In London, possibly, but certainly never at Balmoral. How interesting, though. Now that we have Boudicca with us, we have two queens on our hands.* She wondered if this might be the right time to ask Christine if she was aware of the Elizabeth phenomenon.

"What's that sly smile for, then, Janet?" Danny asked. He set two plates of deep-fried haggis and chips on the table, then two half pints of Selkie's Tears, the house special ale.

"Not sly at all, Danny. Anticipatory. This looks and smells delicious."

"Ta, Janet. Looks like I might need to bring the other half to get a smile out of you tonight, Chrissie. Why don't you tell me what's eating at you before you start eating this?"

"You've heard about Malcolm Murray?" Christine asked.

"Hard to believe, isn't it? He hardly seemed to age. Like the Beaton Bridge itself."

"A fixture," Christine agreed.

"For decades, and he did a lot of good over those years. He'll be missed."

"Janet found him."

"Did you, hen? I'm sorry. I wouldn't wish that on anyone. It isn't something you soon forget." Danny had found a young man dead behind Nev's earlier in the fall. "People are saying it was Malcolm's heart or a stroke. Medical emergency of some kind." He quirked an eyebrow at Janet.

"It could've been something like that. Something made him lose control and leave the road, but I don't know anything more."

"Rhona and her lot are feeling it." He nodded at a table in the area beyond the bar and kitchen. "They rode yesterday, too."

"What do you hear about Florrie these days?" Christine asked.

"Me?" Danny said. "Not much. I heard she came back to live at the house. I don't know when or why, and I've not seen her. Never saw much of Malcolm. Never at all in here. Will Tallie and Summer be joining you?"

"They'll be along later," Janet said.

"And your mum and dad, Chrissie?"

"Staying in tonight. Mum's a bit *peely-wally*. Dad says it's a cold."

"It's that time of year. Can I get you anything else? I need to—" He nodded toward the bar. "I'll stop back later."

Janet couldn't think of Christine as Chrissie, any more than she could think of Queen Elizabeth as Lizzie or Betsy. But when Danny called her Chrissie, it suited her. He was the only one who did. They'd known each other since childhood and fallen into a comfortable, uncluttered relationship since her return.

When he'd gone back to the bar, Christine picked up one of her chips and immediately dropped it. "Too hot. Don't touch the haggis; it'll be sizzling."

Janet snatched her hand back from her own plate.

"So." Christine stood. "While we let them cool, we'll go extend our condolences to Rhona for the loss of a fellow half-hundred rider."

"Oh, now," Janet said, but she got up with an irritated *tchah* when Christine ignored her and plowed straight toward the far table where Rhona McNeish sat with two other women. Janet put a fingertip on one of her chips—hot, but hardly dangerous. She snapped up the chip and ate it. Then, with a more resigned *tchah*, she followed Christine.

Janet didn't know Rhona well and hadn't known she was involved with the Haggis Half-Hundred, but it didn't surprise her. She'd first met Rhona as the leader of an environmental group that had worked tirelessly to restore a local wildlife area—Glen Sgail. Rhona, with her brush of red hair, reminded Janet of a Highland pony ready to winter outside. If Rhona were caught in the rain, Janet would expect her to shake herself off with a few efficient twitches and carry on.

"Here she is," Christine said when Janet caught up to her at Rhona's table. "I was just telling them you plan to join them on the next Half-Hundred."

"That's my goal, anyway," Janet said. "We'll see if I make it."

"Of course, you will," Rhona said. "If you're looking to get in shape for it, you should join us on some of our shorter rides. Do you know Isla and Lynsey?" She nodded at one and then the other of the women at the table as she made her scant introductions.

"Pull a couple of chairs around," Isla said.

Lynsey moved her chair over to make room.

If Rhona was a pony, Lynsey was a whippet—lean, alert, and eager to race. Janet thought she must be a few years younger than Tallie and Summer, maybe early- to mid-thirties. *And Isla? She's a . . .* But Janet didn't see a resemblance to any particular animal in the fifty-something woman watching her.

"We'll join you another time," Christine said. "Our food's growing cold, but we wanted to come tell you how sorry we are about the way the ride ended for Malcolm Murray yesterday."

Lynsey looked down at her hands clasped in front of her on the table. "I don't want to believe it. Lachy doesn't believe it."

"Her husband," Rhona said to Christine and Janet, "but it goes for all of us. We've never required riders to stay with a group or to ride in pairs. We might be rethinking that now."

"We *will* be," Lynsey said.

"Aye, we will," Rhona agreed. "It makes sense."

"Any idea what happened?" Christine asked.

"I said it would happen."

Lynsey spoke so quietly that Janet wasn't sure she'd heard right. And maybe she hadn't; neither Rhona nor Isla reacted. Christine, though, looking both sympathetic and intrigued, put a hand on Lynsey's shoulder and started to say something.

But Isla spoke first, looking at Janet, and cutting Christine off. "You're the incomer who took over the bookshop. The American."

"Guilty," Janet said with a light laugh she hoped was disarming. "Incomer" wasn't the friendliest word for someone who'd transplanted herself to Scotland, but it was true enough. "I didn't take over the shop all by myself, though. Christine's in it with me, and my daughter and another American."

"And I'm more of a repatriate," Christine said, rolling her *R*s to good effect.

"Don't mind Isla," Rhona said. Then she pointed at Janet and Christine and said, "Did you know these two had something to do with solving the murders a month back? Never underestimate the power of a couple of canny women. We're happy to have you in Inversgail and glad to have the shop still open and in good hands."

"True enough," Isla said. She raised her glass to Janet. "Better a canny incomer than another T-shirt shop."

"*Wheesht*, Isla. Don't mind her," Rhona said again. "Come out for a ride with us, Janet. You, too, Christine. I'll give you a call."

They thanked her and returned to their haggis and chips, now barely tepid. Christine didn't seem to mind. Janet decided she didn't, either.

"What were you going to say to Lynsey?" she asked Christine.

Christine raised an eyebrow.

"When Lynsey said, 'I said it would happen.' You put your hand on her shoulder and started to say something."

"Did I?" Christine thought, then shook her head. "Something helpful, like 'don't be a dafty,' no doubt. I honestly don't remember, though. Isla's *incomer* nonsense drove it straight out of my head."

"Then let me ask you this. You're so anxious to ask about Malcolm, and to hover and listen in; what do you expect to hear? Or what do you *hope* to hear?"

"Not just about Malcolm," Christine said. "Florrie, too." Then she shook her head. "I honestly don't know that, either. It might be that I'm trying to hold onto something, because I'm losing people, and the losses begin to add up. And Mum has a cold. But is it just a cold? Someday it won't be."

"You're right. Someday it won't, but not yet."

"We don't know that. We don't know that at all." Christine took up the salt shaker and shook it over her chips. Aggressively.

Janet took the shaker away from her. "They're beyond help at this point. And I've been *no* help. I've been grousing at you and making things worse. I'm sorry, Christine."

"Not worse. The opposite. Your jabs help. They give me something sharp, like a shard of glass, to focus on. It's amazing how a few jabs with a shard keep you in the moment instead of drifting off into self-pity."

"Lovely. I've always wanted people to think of me like jagged, broken glass. But if it helps, I'm happy to oblige." Janet picked up her fork. "Are we going to be able to eat all this?"

Christine popped a chip in her mouth, chewed, swallowed, and lifted her glass for a toast. "Och, aye, for tomorrow we die."

Janet put her fork back on the plate.

"Too sharp? Too dark?" Christine asked. "See if this is better. Lift your glass.

May those who love us love us,
and those that don't love us,
may God turn their hearts.

And if He doesn't turn their hearts,
may He turn their ankles,
so we'll know them by their limping."

"That's Irish, isn't it?" Janet said. "Not Scottish."

"I've heard otherwise, but who's to say? It's also meant for drinking whisky, but in the end does it really matter?"

"Not if it helps us see them coming."

They touched glasses, and drank, and Christine, who had a view of the door, said, "Don't look now, but guess who just came in."

6

Norman or Ian," Janet said. "Has to be."

"No fair hedging your bets."

"Ian, then. Unless—" She watched Christine's face. "Unless it *is* Norman, and you're going to try to pump him for information. And now you look disappointed, because it *isn't* Norman and you just realized you *want* to pump him for information. Ha." Janet crossed her arms in triumph. "It's Ian."

Her answer sounded louder than she'd expected, and she realized the room had grown quieter. Not silent, as tables toward the back still chatted and laughed. Nearer, she heard the sibilance of whispers. A few people stared toward the bar. Several others either stared into their glasses or had bowed their heads. Janet, arms still crossed and shoulders drawing in, leaned toward Christine and added her own whisper. "*Not* Ian. Who is it?"

"Gerald," Christine whispered back.

"Who?" Janet mouthed, but Christine's attention had also turned to the bar. Janet picked up her glass, for casual cover, swiveled halfway around, and almost dropped the glass.

The man she'd seen dead that morning, now wearing a field jacket and jeans, stood at the bar, silent, nursing a glass of whisky, with a book under his arm. Tall and thin, the nose and the cheekbones were unmistakable. Ian had said patrician. Janet thought raw, gaunt. Like a grizzled wolf losing ground in a lean year.

Danny stood across the bar from the man, wiping a glass and surveying his other customers with a look that clearly said, *Nothing to see here. Leave the man be.*

Janet swiveled back around and made Christine look at her. "The other brother?" she whispered.

"Malcolm's shadow."

They raised their eyebrows at each other and went back to eating. *With something hanging over us, watching,* Janet thought. *Like a vulture.*

Talk around them resumed at an almost normal level, then hushed again so that Janet heard the door swing shut.

"Gone?" she asked, and when Christine nodded, she added, "Why didn't anyone say anything to him? If Malcolm is such a loss, why didn't anyone offer the man their sympathy?"

"If I'd known that's what would happen, I wouldn't have started that silly guessing game about who came in."

"What went on behind my back when he did come in?" Janet asked.

"He walked in and walked to the bar. The rest of the place, any of us, might not have existed. He didn't look around, didn't seem to care that people whispered or stopped talking."

"Maybe he's hard of hearing or deaf," Janet said.

"I didn't think of that. He walked straight to the bar and stopped in front of Danny. He nodded. Danny nodded. Danny got down a bottle, poured a dram, and handed it to him. You could be right. Neither of them said a word. No money passed between them, either. Gerald drank up, set the glass on the bar, and walked out. Tell me, Janet, did you get the feeling we were in the presence of a ghost?"

"Oh, believe me, when I first saw him, I thought he was Malcolm. So yes. And if everyone else felt the same way, maybe that's why no one said anything."

"I'm not overly shy," Christine said. "But—"

"Maybe he is."

"Maybe. Deaf, shy, antisocial. Dangerous? I can't put my finger on it, but it felt like something was going on that wasn't for me to interfere in.

That's not a situation I find myself in very often." Christine raised her empty glass toward the bar. "Let's see what nodding Danny can tell us."

They waited while Danny tended to the other patrons who'd suddenly discovered their glasses were empty when Gerald left. Then he called a young man from the kitchen to take a turn at the bar, and he brought two more half pints to the table and sat next to Christine.

"He comes in two or three times a year," Danny said. "I can't think when was the last time. A dram and he's gone again. Only the one."

"Always on the house?" Christine asked.

"The first time he came in, he drank up, and turned for the door just like that. I started to call after him, but I didn't. I was more interested that he came and went the way he did than a loss from the till. And that's the way it goes each time." He shrugged. "For me it's only a dram two or three times a year. For him? I don't know, but I do the same and more for you and others from time to time."

"Is he living here or hereabouts?" Christine asked.

"No idea. He might just pass through from time to time."

"I wondered if he might be deaf," Janet said.

They watched Danny think about that, his eyes perhaps tracking the path of Gerald's other visits—moving from the door, glancing at the darts room, the jukebox. He shook his head. "Runrig came on the jukebox one of those visits. 'Alba.' And I got a second nod out of him. Selectively deaf, maybe. Keeps himself to himself."

"With a wee bit of help from you," Christine said. "You were like a sheepdog standing there, watching over him and his dram, and wiping that one glass the entire time. You're a good man, Danny Macquarrie. A good dog, too."

"Good dog should get back to his bar." He leaned over and gave Christine a peck on the cheek. "Woof."

"Before you go, Danny," Janet said, "did you happen to see what the book was?" She tucked a hand in her armpit. "Under his arm. Big enough to see from here, but it looked comfortable, so nothing too thick or hard.

He might have held it too close, but did you get a look at the spine or any part of the cover?"

"I can't say I paid much attention to it," Danny said. "Could have been dark green. Or that might be his jacket I'm remembering. That's how I picture him—with a book under his arm. He's never put one down on the bar. I've never asked what he's reading. Why?"

Christine pointed at Janet. "Licensed book snoop."

Danny saluted Janet and went back to the bar.

Christine said, "His book. I'd say I'm surprised you chose that detail to focus on—"

"But you're not, because you have your own peculiarities."

"Which I like to think of as strengths."

They toasted their strengths with the fresh half pints Danny had brought.

"Have you ever seen Gerald in Yon Bonnie Books?" Christine asked.

"I don't think so. Not Malcolm either. I don't know about Malcolm, but Gerald doesn't strike you as much of a shopper, does he?"

"Do you think it's interesting that Florrie didn't mention him? She had plenty to say about Malcolm."

"Not plenty, really," Janet said. "What she did say left a lot to the imagination."

"Shall I tell you what I don't like? I don't like worrying about someone when I don't know how to go about helping them."

"What if they don't want your help?"

"You're the certified book snoop, and I trust you to do that properly," Christine said. "I'm the certified social work snoop, so please trust me, as well."

"Certified or certifiable?" Janet asked.

"Whatever. But I don't often let what someone wants or doesn't want stop me."

"One of your more endearing strengths."

As they drank another toast to their strengths, Janet saw Rab Mac-Gregor coming from the darts room. He might have been feigning interest in his phone, so that he missed her wave, but Ranger, trotting by his side, stopped to say hello.

"I sat in your chair in the shop for a wee while this evening, Ranger," Janet said. "I hope you don't mind. Rab, will you be in this week?"

Rab appeared to consult the phone, then a corner of the ceiling, then Ranger before answering. "Aye, I reckon that's a good idea. I was sorry to hear about your experience this morning, finding Dr. Murray. It must have been a terrible shock."

"It was. Thank you, Rab."

He nodded. "Best we don't intrude, then."

"Thank you. Good night. Good night, Ranger." Janet turned to Christine as man and dog walked off. "That was sweet. Oh, but wait—" They watched Ranger's tail disappearing out the pub door behind Rab. "I didn't ask him *when* he'd be in."

"He wouldn't have answered anyway," Christine said. "Here come Tallie and Boudicca. How do you think Summer would like it if we started calling her Boud?"

"It's a *secret* identity; don't blow it. Look, a hound's following them, too."

James Haviland, newshound and editor of the *Inversgail Guardian*, came in behind Tallie and Summer. He'd recruited Summer to write the paper's advice column soon after the women arrived in Inversgail. He played fiddle in a ceilidh band and captained the *Guardian*'s darts team. And he and Summer might, as Janet had wondered to Tallie that morning, be something of an item. As a journalism student he'd spent time in the States interning at the *New York Times*, and he often reminisced about the garlic dill pickles he'd loved and left behind.

"Evening, lasses," Christine said when Tallie and Summer joined them.

"How's your project?" Janet asked.

"Steady and on target," Tallie said.

"A ways to go, though." Summer asked a couple at a neighboring table if she could take an empty chair and pulled it over next to Janet's.

James brought three pints from the bar. Before sitting, he pointed at Christine's and Janet's glasses. "Another round for you?"

They declined and he sat, but not in his usual Nev's pose—fingers knit across his stomach and looking like a favorite uncle about to doze after a good meal. Janet had never thought of him as birdlike, but the way he glanced around the room now, tipping his head one way then another as he listened, reminded her of a robin in the back garden.

"What is it?" she asked.

James tipped his head toward her. "I was listening for Death, but I don't hear him."

Summer bumped him with her shoulder. "You're being metaphorical. I hope."

"Sorry," James said. "Sorry, Janet. I assumed folk would be drinking to Malcolm Murray the *nicht*, but this feels like a different level of energy."

"We reached another level a wee while ago," Christine said. "And by 'we' I mean"—she swirled a finger over her head—"the room. We had a visitor."

"Almost a ghostly visitation," Janet added. "Gerald Murray."

"Ghostly, is it?" James smiled. "You've a bit of the storyteller in you, Janet. But, aye, the shock of losing his brother could do that, I reckon."

"You've met him?" Summer asked.

"We ran an article about him when he demobbed. Years ago, now. He was a Sapper. Royal Engineers."

"Do you have any current information about him?" Christine asked. "Where he lives, by chance?"

"Or about their sister, Florence?" Janet asked.

James looked less like a robin and more like the newshound he was. "Why?"

"As a concerned friend," Christine said. "As you say, considering the shock."

James shook his head. "I only met him the once and never knew about a sister. You're kind to think of them. Malcolm did a lot of good in the community. Quiet good. He didn't put himself forward, but he was there when needed."

"What happens next concerning his death? Officially?" Tallie asked. "Who investigates?"

"A Road Policing Unit out of Fort William is looking into it. They've made an appeal for witnesses. You can find it on their Twitter feed."

Janet and Christine raised their eyebrows.

"Are you not on Twitter?" James asked. "You hear all the latest there. No matter; we posted the appeal in our online edition as well."

"I didn't hear anything about that," Summer said.

"You were busy." James mimed throwing a dart. "It's all routine, anyway—the investigation, the appeal to the public."

James took his phone from the breast pocket of his coat, tapped and scrolled and tapped again, then handed it to Janet. Christine leaned in to read over her shoulder. Tallie and Summer took out their own phones. The appeal read:

> Regarding the death of Dr. Malcolm Murray, by collision, while riding his bicycle October 4 near the Beaton Bridge outside Inversgail. We need to hear from anyone who was in the area of the bridge that afternoon. Did you see a motorist before, during, or after the collision? Our enquiries into this tragic incident are ongoing, and we would appeal for anyone who saw Dr. Murray the afternoon of October 4, who has not already spoken to police, to contact us on 101. Our thoughts

are with Dr. Murray's family and friends at this difficult time
and we ask that their privacy is respected.

"Standard stuff," James said when Janet handed his phone back.

"But a collision," Janet said. "And a motorist. What evidence did they
find that makes them think a car was involved?"

"That's the reason for the appeal, isn't it?" Tallie said. "They don't
know that a motorist was involved. They're still looking for evidence."

Janet pictured the side of the road that morning. "I stepped over ruts
when I looked for a way down the bank. I wonder if the ruts from a
moving car are different. You know, different from ruts left by a parked
car. I suppose they use—What are those things people use to measure
small things very precisely?"

"Calipers," Tallie said.

"I imagine measuring ruts and treads is precise work," Janet continued.
"I wish I'd taken pictures of the ruts."

"Why?" Tallie asked.

"Because once you get past how awful it was to find him, it's interesting," Janet said.

"And how on earth do they manage to photograph and measure tire
tracks and such with some of the roadside vegetation we have around
here?" Christine said. "That was a wee bit of a pun, there. How on *earth*
and the ruts being in the mud or soil."

"Very wee," Janet said. "But the vegetation is a good point. The
bracken at the edge of the road was flattened."

"People might stop there for the view," James said.

"It's worth it," Janet agreed. "But not much room to pull over safely."

"A bit dicey, I agree, but when has that stopped anyone?"

"The view might be the problem," Summer said. "It was a beautiful
day yesterday. Distracted driving."

"Could well be," James said. "I can show you statistics. There are more
wingdings on bonny days."

"How many riders were there?" Summer asked. "Didn't they block the road off in some way for safety?"

"Sixty-three riders," Danny said, coming around to pick up empties. "And no, they didn't block the road. They bought the haggis from me and I delivered it to the finish. I drove past Isla rounding up stragglers, but no one near the Beaton Bridge."

"Did you see Dr. Murray?" Janet asked. "Did you know any of the others?"

"No. Had my eyes on the road, didn't I. Skintight kit on some of them, but I didn't get a good look."

"What color was the skintight kit?" Christine asked.

"Absolutely *brilliant* shade of pink." Danny glanced at her. "But my eyes were on the road. Strictly forward. I only happened to notice the kit along the periphery." On his way back to the bar, Danny called over his shoulder, "Mind, my peripheral vision is *excellent*."

"They've closed roads for races in the past," James said. "Never that road, though, that I recall. And this was more of a ramble and ride at your own peril. I spoke with Norman Hobbs earlier; he's received a bit of abuse over closing the road for the scene of collision investigation."

"Scene of collision," Janet echoed. "Distracted driving." She felt she was having trouble getting past those points. "Has anyone come forward?"

"No word on that."

"James, do you have bike statistics?" Tallie asked. "Maybe there are more bicycle accidents on bonny days, too."

"It isn't such a busy road, is it?" Janet asked. "It wasn't this morning. No one passed me."

"Not so busy, but an artery," James said. "You were out that way this morning, Janet?"

"I found him."

James took a long pull on his ale, looking at her over the rim. She saw wheels of some sort turning in his head. *Focused wheels, though, not distracted,* she thought, and immediately tried to wipe the image from her brain.

"You didn't know Janet found him?" Christine asked.

"Not all the details are out there for public or journalist consumption," he said. "It could be that Norman wanted to spare her endless calls and questions from the likes of me." He looked at the phone still in his hand, tapped and swiped, and then slipped it back into his pocket.

Janet only tentatively believed him about missing out on the details. Then she wondered why, and if she was going to start being suspicious of everyone.

A fiddle tune started dancing in James's phone pocket. He pulled the phone out again and looked at it. "Sorry, I should take this. And I'll be back for that." He pointed at his ale and then pivoted, phone to his ear, and went out the door.

Janet glanced at Tallie and Summer. They'd bent their heads to their phones again, so she tapped Christine's elbow and beckoned her closer. "Did you notice the discrepancy in the police appeal? They're asking for people near the bridge, or who saw him, yesterday afternoon, but Florence says he came home after the ride and didn't go out again until later."

"Can we trust her to know what time he went out again?" Christine asked.

"Can we trust that she told the police he came home after the ride?"

"Surely she did," Christine said.

"Then why isn't the appeal for a wider time range?"

"Evidence?" Christine said. "Maybe that's a detail amongst those not for public or journalist consumption."

Janet sipped her Selkie's Tears and wondered what those details might be and how she could find out. Ask Norman Hobbs? He'd want to know why she wanted to know. Or maybe not. By now he knew her nosy ways. *No*, she told herself. *Being interested, because I'm involved, isn't the same thing as being nosy.*

"Janet? Are you away with the selkies?" James sat back down, looking at her as though she'd missed something.

"Sorry, what?" She started to take another sip of ale, but put the glass down and pushed it away.

"I meant the creatures, not the ale," James said. "You looked thoughtful. But I was saying we might want to interview you about the accident. Background details, that kind of thing. Have the police interviewed you yet?"

"I talked to Norman when he got to the scene. He said there was no telling how long it would take for the Road Unit to arrive, so he let me go on."

"No doubt they'll get round to you," James said. "If they need you, they know where to find you."

∽

"You've missed the turn," Janet said later as Christine drove her home, "but you can turn at the next corner."

Christine didn't make the turn at the next corner. Unlike the white-knuckle trip between the Murray house and Nev's, she drove sedately on.

"What is this, Christine? If you had too much to drink, then why don't you pull over and let me drive?"

Christine said nothing.

"I should've gone with Tallie. I should've had her drive *you* home. This isn't funny, Christine. Really. What are we doing?"

"I had no more to drink than you did. I'm taking no chances."

"Then what are we doing?"

Christine made a turn onto a road that climbed steadily into the hills as it left Inversgail. "We're on a mission. Trust me."

"Hmph," Janet said, but only as a matter of principle, because she did trust Christine. And then she thought she knew the road they were on. "It's different in the dark, but the bridge should be just up ahead."

Christine slowed and the Beaton Bridge appeared in her headlights. "I'll cross over and stop on the other side."

"But you will *not* get me to walk down to the burn in the dark," Janet said. "And don't you try to go down there, either. I really do mean that, Christine. We'll break our necks."

"And we're not reckless fools, so put that notion right out of your head. There's a large torch in the boot. Come on."

"Don't you want your emergency flashers on?"

"No. Bring your mobile."

A cold wind scurried around them as they got out of the Vauxhall and closed the doors. Christine took the flashlight from the trunk, but left it off, and they walked to the middle of the bridge.

"As I rode up this hill, thinking I'd never make it to the bridge, I made up new words to that song by the Proclaimers," Janet said. "About riding five-hundred miles, instead of walking like the guy in their song, and riding five-hundred more just to fall down dead at my front door. I wish I hadn't."

"They're identical twins, did you know that? The Proclaimers."

"That's a fun tidbit. No, I didn't know. I was standing here, looking out like this, when I saw his arm in the burn. The thought of him lying there all through the night—" Janet shivered and looked away, then looked up. "How many more stars we can see here than back home."

"I hope he's up there somewhere among them," Christine said.

"Malcolm?"

"Mm. And I hope there *is* a somewhere, somewhere up there." She flicked on the flashlight and leaned over to hold it low to the ground. "Look how the pebbles and bits of debris on the road cast shadows. It makes them stand out more. Tire tracks and ruts should do the same. Let's get those pictures you wished you'd taken this morning."

"Brilliant."

∽

It was easy enough to find the Murray house the next morning—the online British Telephone phone book gave Janet the address. Her thighs encouraged her to skip riding two mornings in a row, and she was tempted to go along with them, but her willpower prevailed. So she and her thighs, with the promise of gentle pedaling through a posh neighborhood and no steep hills, set out.

She didn't know what she expected to see when she rode past the house. It looked smaller in the daylight than it had loomed the night before or in her imagination. At the end of the street, she turned around and rode back for another look. A pleasant street, a garden put to bed for winter, a quiet house. She was glad she'd be able to tell Christine . . . tell her what? That she didn't see anything malevolent seeping out the windows? *What utter rot.*

Janet pedaled faster on the way home. Tallie had gone out earlier for a run and hadn't returned by the time Janet got in. After a shower and change into work clothes, she was glad to be heading for Yon Bonnie Books.

And there she found a cardboard box—a whisky carton large enough to hold a half-dozen bottles—sitting at the front door, a folded note taped to its lid.

7

J anet pulled the note off the box and looked up and down the street, as though whoever had left it on the steps might be watching. She wouldn't put it past Ian to pull a stunt like that, except she knew he was too cheap to leave a bottle of whisky, much less an entire carton. *Who, then? The ghost of Malcolm Murray? Ridiculous fancy.* She opened the note and read, *"Please look after these books. Thank you."*

Well, of course it was books. And if she'd looked more closely to begin with, she'd have seen the worn condition of the box, showing that it was probably recycled. She hoped this wasn't a precedent. While the shop did carry a selection of rare and antique editions, they didn't accept the bags and boxes and stacks of used books people offered them. Finding books on the stoop, like an abandoned baby, was a first.

Janet looked up and down the street again and saw nothing more unusual than the third sunny morning in as many days. The harbor was beginning to sparkle with the incoming tide. Seagulls rode the breeze, biding their time for unsuspecting fish to follow the tide. Some mornings she'd see Rab and Ranger sitting on the harbor wall, but only one of the harbor cats lounged there today. Too bad. Rab could have carried the carton inside for her. She unlocked the front door, tested the weight of the box, and hefted it inside herself.

"I wondered how long you were going to stand out there," Christine said. Coffee mug in one hand and scone in the other, she stepped out of Janet's way. "What were you looking for? The long-lost MacGregor?"

She watched as Janet maneuvered to push the door closed with her backside and then grunted the box over to the sales counter. "Oh, sorry, did you want help with that? Did you get a deal on all that whisky?"

Janet pulled her glasses halfway down her nose and looked at Christine.

"Tallie does that with her specs," Christine said. "But you don't pull off severe as well as she does. Something to do with her smoother cheeks and lack of gray. You're so cozy-looking, people want to sit on your lap."

When Christine stopped for a breath and a sip of coffee, Janet thought her uncharacteristic prattling had ended. It hadn't.

"Of course, I'd have brought it in if I'd seen it," Christine ran on, "but I came in through the other door and didn't give this door a minute's thought. But why wasn't Tallie here to bring the box in for you? It looked awfully heavy. Oh, right, she probably went running. These young women and their energy. It's a marvel. Were we like that when we were their age?" She stared, bright-eyed, at Janet.

"How much coffee have you had this morning?" Janet asked.

"Mum spent a bad night and I sat up with her, so rather a lot. Why? Have I strayed into small dog territory? Am I yapping?"

"Rather a lot. To answer one of your questions, it's a box of books, not whisky." Janet handed Christine the note she'd found, and then tried to open the box. When she realized the flaps had been glued shut, she complained to the absent donor. "Really? It isn't enough to be anonymous? You can't even use tape like a normal person?"

"Your Anonymous is a Paddington Bear aficionado, judging from the note," Christine said. "To quote the original, 'Please look after this bear. Thank you.'"

"Isn't that just so sweet." Janet wrestled to get enough grip on a glued flap to yank it free.

Christine stopped her. "Frustration brings out your sarcastic streak. Shift over and let me have a go."

Janet stood aside and Christine wrenched the flaps open.

"That's what a caffeine overload and superior leverage, thanks to my natural advantage in height, brings to the table. I wouldn't be surprised if I don't have a bit more brawn, as well. But here, you can have first look."

"You're very kind and oh so strong and tall. Please accept that as a compliment unsullied by sarcasm; I'm much less frustrated now. Oh, well." Janet lifted one of the books out. Smaller than a modern mass-market paperback, it was leather bound with gilt embellishments—thistles all down the spine. "This might actually be worth the frustration and associated sarcasm. This truly is sweet."

"What is it?"

"An adorable little edition of *Kidnapped*."

As Janet took more books from the box and laid them on the counter, Summer came downstairs from Bedtime Stories. In exchange for being the on-premises host for their bed-and-breakfast guests, she had a gratis bedsit of two small rooms there. Tallie let herself in the front door as Summer began to ooh and ahh over the doorstep discovery.

"Does anyone have anything more interesting than these books to discuss before we open?" Christine asked.

"Tell us where they came from and I'm good," Tallie said.

Janet told them about finding the box. Christine recited the note.

Tallie picked up a faded green clothbound book the size of the leather-bound *Kidnapped*. "*The Little Minister* by J. M. Barrie. I haven't read this one. I should get it from the library, though. This one's kind of fragile."

"You're one up on me," Summer said. "I haven't heard of it." She took the book from Tallie and opened it carefully. "No wonder. Published in 1911. I'd be fragile, too."

"The Stevenson and the Barrie might be worth some money," Tallie said. "How many more in the box?"

Janet peered in. "At a guess, more than a dozen. Maybe two."

"And another dozen on the counter," Christine said. "But what exactly does 'look after these books' mean? Is Anonymous coming back for them? Are we being asked to store them? Indefinitely?'"

"The note might not mean anything more than 'here,'" Summer said. "But we could look for inscriptions."

Janet heard a knock at the front door. "There's Norman. I wonder what he wants." She motioned for him to wait a moment. "All right, lasses, enough fun and games, we have businesses to open and run."

"Aye-aye." Christine put her arm around Summer's shoulders. "If you don't mind getting the tearoom underway, Boudicca, I'll have a wee word with the constable and be along directly. And then I'll tell you all about how lucky you are to have me on top of my game and on your team today."

"What's Christine on about?" Tallie asked Janet as Christine went to unlock the door.

"Too little sleep and too much caffeine."

"Lucky Summer."

"Nice to see you, Norman," Christine said, opening the door. "You're bright and early. Are you official or un this morning?"

Constable Norman Hobbs, peaked cap tucked under his arm, greeted the women, and ran a hand over his close-clipped hair. "A bit of both. Making my usual rounds and thought I'd check in, see how you're faring after yesterday."

"Thank you, Norman," Janet said. "I'm okay."

"Brilliant." Hobbs flashed a smile at Janet and then went back to craning his neck for a better look at the books spread across the counter.

Janet, feeling protective of the foundlings, slid over so that she stood in front of them. "The Road Police—is that what they're called?"

"The Road Policing Unit, aye."

"Will they be in touch?"

"They haven't been?" Hobbs asked. "Och, well, they're the experts and they'll have their priorities. I don't presume to know their methods and how they operate. I expect you'll hear from them sooner or later, as they'll want to dot *i*s and cross *t*s. You'll be familiar with that kind of thorough work from your experience with the local constabulary." Norman Hobbs *was* the local constabulary. "Or not. Depending on what they've found, they might not think it's necessary to interview you further. Unless you have anything to add that you didn't tell me at the time?"

"No."

"I'll just make a note to ask them about getting in touch, shall I?"

"Do you know what they *have* found?" Janet asked.

"I've not received the latest word from the RPU specialists," Hobbs said.

Janet thought he managed to sound both cagey and just the least bit put out that she'd reminded him of that snub. *So if he hasn't heard the latest word, did he hear the next latest? And what isn't he telling us?*

"Tell me, Norman, are they satisfied Dr. Murray's death was an accident?" she asked.

"They've made no official statement as I'm aware." He brought out a sparkly purple notebook and pen.

"New notebook from your great-niece?" Tallie asked.

Hobbs held the pen and notebook so they glinted. "She's a generous wee lassie."

"Want me to take a picture so she can see you using it?"

"Brilliant. I'll move over here for a better background." He went to stand beside Janet.

"To make it look more realistic, why don't you look at the notebook instead of what's on the counter," Janet suggested. "Maybe even write something in it."

Hobbs adjusted his gaze appropriately and Tallie snapped the picture.

"She'll love it. I probably shouldn't send it to your work email, though." She handed him her phone. "Go ahead and send it to yourself."

He looked at the photo, smiled, and tapped his number on the screen. When he returned the phone, he moved his tapping finger so that it hovered over the leather-bound *Kidnapped*. "May I take a wee *keek*?"

Janet felt suddenly possessive as well as protective, but made herself say yes. Hobbs picked up the small volume, running a finger down the thistles on the spine. He opened it carefully and turned the first few Bible-thin pages until he reached the beginning of the story. Janet watched his eyes track the lines of text as he read.

"Will you be selling it?" he asked. He closed the book and held it as though he might clasp it to his heart.

"We don't know yet," Janet said. "The books are a mystery. They were in a box I found at the front door this morning."

"Just the box? No note or explanation?" He sounded aghast at such cavalier treatment.

Tallie handed him the note and he read it.

"That's disappointing," he said. "Raises more questions than it answers."

"Book lovers do have their quirks," Janet said. "Maybe the note's a riddle or a joke, and we'll hear from the owner sometime today. If we find out they're ours to sell, we'll let you know." She held out her hand, and when Hobbs put the book in it, she felt just the least bit of resistance, as though he might not let it go.

"Was it your job, as constable, to notify Dr. Murray's next of kin?" she asked. "That must be an awfully hard part of your duty."

If the resistance had been real, it disappeared at her question and commiseration. Hobbs made solemn noises in response.

"Did you have trouble locating the brother?" Christine asked. "We saw Gerald briefly last night at Nev's, and wondered if he'd traveled here after hearing the news."

"Had he been away?" Hobbs asked. "I wasn't aware. He gave no indication of that when I called on him at home."

"That's good, then. It must have made it easier for everyone," Christine said. "It's been so long since I've thought of him. Is he still out there along the Mull Eigg Road?"

"You must be thinking of someone else. Gerald has a croft on Achnamuck."

"I wonder who I'm confusing him with," Christine said. "And Achnamuck, you say. What's that in your road sign Gaelic?"

"Something akin to field of pigs," Hobbs said.

"So he left the Royal Engineers and took up farming. As more of a hobby, do you think?" Christine asked. "Or did he go whole hog and jump into the muck with both feet?"

"Mrs. Robertson," Hobbs said with mild reproof. "The man lost his brother yesterday."

Christine, smiling and beginning to look glassy-eyed, seemed to have missed the reproof. Janet nudged her and she jumped. "Forgive me, Norman. My remark was flip and insensitive. I'm not quite myself today."

"She was up all night with her mum," Janet said.

"I'm sorry to hear that. I hope it's nothing serious."

"Very kind of you, Norman. I'll tell her you asked after her. In the meantime, I'm operating in a fog of fatigue and caffeine. Tell me, did you also notify Malcolm's sister?"

"Aye."

"How did she seem to you?" Christine asked.

"Much as you might expect."

Janet was sure, judging by the twitch at the corner of Christine's eye, that Hobbs's circumspect answer hadn't satisfied her. Before Christine said anything else she might regret, Janet slipped into the gap left after Hobbs's answer.

"The alert they sent out yesterday—"

"Appeal," Hobbs corrected.

"Yes, sorry. The appeal is why I asked if you know what they've found. They asked for people who saw Dr. Murray, or who'd been in the vicinity of the bridge, Sunday afternoon. That makes it sound like they found something pinpointing the time of death."

"As I understand it, the Haggis Half-Hundred took place in the afternoon, and Dr. Murray was one of the riders," Hobbs said.

"We know that," Christine said. "But did Florrie—"

"Florence," said Janet.

"Did *Florence* not tell you that Malcolm came home *after* the ride?" Christine made a show of studying his face. "You have the impassive constabulary face down pat, Norman. I hope your superiors are well aware of such dedicated talent. Of course, if this information is new, it might change the course of an otherwise routine investigation. It might possibly do the same for your career."

Hobbs took out his pen and notebook again and made another note.

"So then, Norman, back to Florence," Christine said. "Do you have any idea how long she's been living here, or what her situation is? Has she other family? Has *Gerald* other family? There now, I'm blethering on again. Too many questions. But I'm concerned about her. Do you know what became of her husband?"

"It's not my place to spread gossip, Mrs. Robertson," Hobbs said. He placed his cap on his head, making that an official Constable Hobbs statement. "I'll let you get on with your business."

"Thanks for stopping in," Janet said. "We'll let you know about the books."

When he'd gone, Christine congratulated herself. "Did you notice how savvy I was asking questions? Testing the Norman waters, as it were, to see how much he'd tell us."

"You were very skillful and the picture of innocence," Janet said. "Too bad he didn't cooperate better."

"And imagine him trying on that rubbish about not spreading gossip. That's exactly why I called him stodgy porridge yesterday."

"Were you watching his face, though?" Tallie asked. "I think he used that line about gossip not just because he shouldn't answer your questions, but because he couldn't."

Christine squinted at the place where Hobbs had stood, as though bringing the memory of his face into better focus. "Very helpful. You're an astute member of the team, Tallie. Now I'd best go earn my keep. We can't have our future darts champion overwhelmed." She waved and headed for the tearoom.

Tallie squinted after her, the way Christine had squinted at the memory of Hobbs. "What did she mean by 'very helpful' and 'astute member of the team'?" she asked. "What team?"

"I'm sure that was just the caffeine talking. *She* might overwhelm Summer before the customers do. Don't be so suspicious, dear; it does funny things to your eyebrows. Besides, you know how Christine is."

"I do. That's why my eyebrows and I are being so funny."

"Put it this way," Janet said. "While we know that Christine is the opposite of stodgy porridge, we also know that, in the end, she's eminently sensible. So what do you and your eyebrows even begin to imagine she's thinking of getting us into?"

"It's not *our* imaginations my eyebrows and I worry about."

8

Mornings that came with spates and splashes of sunshine tended to be quiet ones in Yon Bonnie Books. This one gave them time for the tasks that always needed attention. Tallie went to inventory postcards. Janet rearranged the window displays, a task she enjoyed that also gave her spare room in her head to consider all the questions she planned to ask the Road Police should they come to call. Rather, the questions she'd *like* to ask, depending on how approachable and responsive they were, and how willing to share information with a concerned, well-meaning, citizen who was not without skills.

In other words, a nosy, rank amateur, Janet thought. *Or did I say that out loud? Oh dear.* She went back to composing her questions, addressing the RPU specialists in her mind. How *did* you narrow the time frame for your appeal? What time did Dr. Murray come home? *Aha!* Did you *know* he came home after the ride? Did you ask Florence to make a guess at what time he went out again? Back to my first question about narrowing the time frame, did you find something like a watch broken at the time of impact? Notes to self: Don't think about the word "impact." Don't use the word "interview" about our visit to Florence. *Don't* get carried away.

Janet patted a stack of books in the window display and gave herself a shake. Then she grabbed a cleaning cloth and set to polishing the glass in the front door. Although she couldn't help also looking for seals in the harbor—or Rab MacGregor sitting on the harbor wall.

"I hate to wish for a rainy day," she said when Tallie wandered over, "but at least the sun helps me see the smudges Rab missed the last time he cleaned."

"They might be new smudges *since* the last time."

"Innocent until proven guilty. You see, as eminently sensible as Christine is, you, with your legal brain, are more so."

"Thank you. Are you buttering me up for something? Sorry, that sounded suspicious again, didn't it?"

"Do you miss teaching law?"

"Look at me and my eyebrows now." Tallie closed her eyes and lolled her head with a sleepy smile. "That's my imitation of Smirr and Butter living the good life, and the way I feel about it, too."

"All three of you are charming."

"We aren't expecting any deliveries today, are we?"

"No stock. A day coach or two, maybe."

"Let's hope for three." Tallie came and took the cloth from her mother. "But while it's quiet, why don't you take the foundling books into the office and look through them more carefully?"

"Foundlings. That's how I think of them, too."

"And you're itching to discover their parentage, yet here you are washing windows. I can clean glass with the best of them, because I'm a very helpful member of Christine's team of something or other, so go on. I put the box in the office for you, and the computer's on."

"A very helpful and *astute* member of Christine's something or other. Call me if you need me."

"Call me if you find treasure."

No one actually spent much time in the office, "office" being more of a euphemism. The room, a narrow slice partitioned from the space behind the sales counter, reminded Janet of a galley kitchen without windows. It was useful for getting work done out of the public eye, though, and as Christine said, they could be thankful it didn't smell of a morning fry-up. At some unspecified future date, they planned to "do something" with the office. They'd bought the business from a couple who'd apparently gotten along better by each having their own desk—facing opposite walls so they'd sit with their backs to each other. One recent morning, Rab had surprised the women by moving the three-drawer filing cabinets, previously flanking the desks like twin bulwarks, to the wall at the far end so they stood next to the lone bookcase. He'd also moved the desks so they sat side by side along the wall with the door.

"Opens up the vista," he'd said by way of explanation, and he'd been right. Those two changes made a comfortable difference. Now when you entered, you saw a clean expanse of cream-colored wall straight ahead and slightly more floor space. No one sat with her back to the door, and the bookcase at the far end somehow looked less lonely and less like a second thought.

The computer sat on the desk farther from the door. Janet logged in and then turned to the box of books. Tallie had thoughtfully set the box on the chair at the other desk so there was room on the desktop to spread and sort the books to her heart's content. Janet patted that heart and then folded back the box flaps. The leather-bound edition of *Kidnapped* sat on top.

She took the book out and looked over the exterior, checking spine, edges, corners, and cover for wear, stains, dirt, and damage. Wear was minimal and she found none of the rest. The three embossed thistles down the spine—done in gold leaf—glinted as she turned the book. Each thistle was slightly different. She stroked the middle one with a fingertip and then opened the book to look at the endpapers—marbled—and to check the binding—intact and tight. Janet understood completely why Norman Hobbs yearned to own the little gem. She might not let him. *She* might want it.

Her disappointment came when she looked at the publication information and realized the book was only one volume in a set. And if it was the only volume they had, it wouldn't be nearly so valuable. But maybe the others were still in the box.

She set *Kidnapped* in the upper left corner of the desk. Then she unpacked the rest of the books, counting them as she did and laying them out in neat rows. Thirty-seven in all. Six rows of six plus *Kidnapped* sitting alone in its corner.

"Well, pshaw," she said to it. "Are your buddies missing or are *you* missing?"

Tallie poked her head in. "Talking back to the books?"

"Always."

"Anything interesting yet?"

"It's an odd bunch of books to find together in one box."

"It's a whisky box. Maybe they all got drunk and went home together," Tallie said.

"Stranger things have happened. Norman's going to be happy, though. *Kidnapped* is one of a set, but the *only* one of the set."

"You mean *it* was kidnapped?"

"I didn't think of it that way. I hope not. But coming from a broken set, it isn't worth as much. If Norman doesn't care that it's an orphan, and if it's ours to sell, then that should make him happy."

"Unless you decide to keep it. I see book lust in your eye."

"I don't *need* another book," Janet said.

"It's only a small one. Any clue yet about who brought them?"

"That's my next step. Look for names, inscriptions, bookmarks, stray hundred-pound notes. You know. Typical stuff."

"I could use a good bookmark," Tallie said. "You go ahead and keep the hundred-pound notes. Oops, customers need me. See you."

Looking for the names, inscriptions, and ownership marks didn't take long. Janet didn't find any at all. Then she fanned through each book, looking for any of the at-hand objects people used to mark their places. Over her years as a librarian she'd found photographs, birthday cards, receipts, toothpicks, recipes, prescriptions, credit cards, once a flattened toothpaste tube, once a double-edged razor blade, and sometimes money. But all she saw while flipping through the foundlings was an occasional margin note. No tangible surprises, not even a real bookmark.

The more recently published books were in decent shape, if a bit dusty, but ten- and twenty-year-old fiction and reference books weren't anything they'd bother giving shelf space to. The shop's trade in used books was high end, skewing toward the antiquarian and rare. Their limited selection lived safely in a locked case.

A handful of the foundlings, including *Kidnapped* and *The Little Minister*, were old enough to be interesting. Just in her quick flip through each of them, though, Janet saw that their condition would best be described as well-handled and well-loved. Still, some of them were first editions and they might be worth a bit of research. She stacked them on her lap, rolled her chair to the computer desk, and opened a new document where she recorded the books' vital statistics—title, author, publisher, publication date.

She was intrigued by each of these older books. She'd never held such early editions of T. H. White's *The Sword in the Stone* or Arthur Ransome's *Swallows and Amazons*. And although *Kidnapped* was the only volume of the Stevenson set, the box might have come from a one-time Stevenson fan. Another of the books on her lap was *Records of a Family of Engineers*, a posthumously published family history by Stevenson. Another was an abridged edition of a book by his grandfather.

And one of the books Janet loved immediately, as much as she loved the copy of *Kidnapped*. It was an edition of *The Complete Herbal* by Nicholas Culpeper, MD, published in 1850, and it almost qualified as the treasure Tallie wanted her to find. In her cursory internet search, she learned it was one of many editions since Culpeper published the original in 1653. This one was such a plain-faced, utilitarian chunk of a thing, covered in uninspired brown cloth, that Janet could picture someone looking at it, shrugging, and using it to replace a missing doorstop.

Judging from the number of stained pages in the *Herbal*, and the pencil and ink notes in *its* margins, she doubted that anyone had reduced it to

such a lowly position. More likely the book had passed through generations of grateful hands as people searched Culpeper's wisdom for their
troubling symptoms, looking for relief and a reason to hope. But Janet
decided she loved the book even more to think it would, in its unassuming
way, shrug in return and dedicate itself to holding a door open if asked.

In addition to the stained and marked pages, the *Herbal*'s front and
back boards were loose. And though the spine was intact, the text block
had begun to split, with the first half of the pages separating from the
second half and several pages in the middle coming loose. If someone
weren't careful when opening the book, the two halves might pull the
brittle spine apart. And it looked as though someone had either caused
that split or helped it along by tucking something between the pages in the
middle of the book. Something much more substantial than a bookmark
or bookmark-like substitute—Janet could make out the faint depression
it had left in the pages—about the size of a thick envelope. A chapbook,
maybe? Or a slim paperback. The damage might have been accidental.
Janet had seen that kind of thing happen at the library, when a child
tried to fit a book back on a shelf, and the book opened just enough to
engulf a smaller one already there. This intruder had stayed tucked in
the *Herbal* for quite some time, though. Long enough to leave its mark.

"So, no, Dr. Culpeper, I'm sorry," Janet said to the book. "You aren't
the kind of treasure we can sell for a fortune. If you're even ours to sell.
You're old and used and a little bit abused, but I think you're pretty cool,
even with your warts and scars." She set the Culpeper and others back
on the other desk.

"Mom?" Tallie looked around the door. "Coach."

For the next several hours the bookshop and tearoom kept busy as
one day coach after another out of Fort William, Glasgow, and Inverness
arrived in Inversgail. The daily *Outlander* onslaught, Christine called it,
named for the many trippers who were fans of the wildly popular *Outlander*
books and television series. The trippers were a mix of Europeans, Amer-
icans, and an increasing number of Chinese, many of them on a quest to

find the "real" Highlands. Yon Bonnie Books attracted them by looking like a "real" bookshop. Built of granite blocks, like so many of the shops on the High Street, Kate Greenaway might have drawn up the plans herself and painted the trim its charming dark green. Inside, to a mix of lilts, airs, and classical music floating down from the overhead sound system, the questers discovered poetry, stories, books of photographs, and guides for any type of "real" Highland adventure they cared to experience.

Customers were sometimes disappointed by the three American women's accents. But they were delighted by Christine and Rab (if he happened to be in). And Ranger would allow selfies, up to a point, before turning his back and closing his eyes. Summer's "real" short-bread and scones universally left customers in good humor.

Just as Janet had hoped to find a treasure among the foundling books, she lived in hope with each new onslaught that one of the pilgrims drawn to the locked case of antiquarian books would become smitten, unable to live without *A Hundred Years in the Highlands* by Osgood Hanbury Mackenzie. Theirs was an excellent and rare 1921 first edition, first impression, signed by the author to Colonel Stuart Farquhar, who'd opened Yon Bonnie Books after returning from the Great War in 1919. She held her breath that afternoon as a young couple from Shanghai held the book between them with reverence and dewy eyes. But it wasn't to be.

"Sorry, Mom," Tallie said after putting the book back and relocking the case. "Smitten, but not enough to break their budget."

"I'll keep dreaming."

"It's bound to happen, just like I'm bound to get my chance to call Ian an old dic—"

"Customers, dear," Janet broke in. "Has he been in again?"

"No. I'm just having a flashback to yesterday."

"He *is* the gift that keeps on giving. We're in a lull between *Outlander* storms. Why don't you take a break?"

"Do you think there's time for a fast walk around the block and a cup of tea?"

"Go for it."

Christine had decided to take a break, too, sipping from a mug as she came from the tearoom.

"Sleep catching up with you yet?" Janet asked.

"What? No. Not that I've noticed. Why do you ask?" Christine set the mug on the sales counter and drummed her fingertips beside it.

Janet hadn't really thought sleep was about to overtake Christine. One look at her jittery pupils would tell anyone that.

"Did you find a name?" Christine asked. "In the box of books? Do you know who left them?"

"Not yet." Janet figured that answer covered all three questions well enough.

"Wouldn't prove anything anyway," Christine said. "Who owned them once, aye. Not who owned them since. Not who left them."

"You're right."

"I'll look at a few. Help you out. Over there." Christine waved toward the fireplace. "Leave the counter free for customers."

"Thank you. On both counts. Go grab one of the chairs before someone else does." Janet waved her hand toward the fireplace, too—as a distraction. Christine, focusing her jittery eyes on Janet's fluttering hand, missed Janet sliding the mug quietly aside. "I'll bring you some of the more interesting books," Janet said.

Maybe if Christine sat long enough in one of those very comfortable chairs she *would* fall asleep. Her absence from the tearoom might be hard on Summer, but Tallie wouldn't mind helping out there. Janet slipped into the office and grabbed the two closest books. Then the Culpeper caught her eye and she took it, too.

Christine's eyes had slid to half-mast but she roused when she saw Janet peering at her. "What have you brought?"

"*Records of a Family of Engineers,*" Janet said, "and *The Bell Rock Lighthouse,* part of something called the Craftsman Series."

"Good Lord." Christine scowled and sank deeper into the chair.

"You're probably right, but what about this?" Janet held up the *Herbal*.

"Looks better. What is it?" Christine held out her hand.

"First, listen," Janet said.

Christine made an annoyed sound but settled back again.

Janet read the *Herbal's* full title and impressive, exhaustive subtitle—read it soft and slow and lilting. Like a croon. Like a lullaby:

> "The Complete Herbal: To which is now added, upwards of one hundred additional herbs, with a display of their medicinal and occult qualities physically applied to the cure of all disorders incident to mankind: to which are now first annexed, the English physician enlarged, and key to Physic. With rules for compounding medicine according to the true system of nature. Forming a complete family dispensatory and natural system of physic. To which is also added, upwards of fifty choice receipts, selected from the author's last legacy to his wife. A new edition, with a list of the principal diseases to which the human body is liable, and a general index."

And whether it was the immensity or density of the subtitle, or Janet's melodious croon, the result was Christine sound asleep. Janet tiptoed back to the sales counter with the books. When the bell on the door jingled, she was sorely tempted to issue a good, old-fashioned librarian's *shhh*.

But it was Rab and Ranger arriving as unceremoniously—and quietly—as they usually did. Man and dog looked over at Christine.

"Aye," Rab said, and nodded toward the tearoom. "I'll give a hand, shall I?"

"That would be great," Janet said. "Oh, before you do, though, do you know anything about a box of used books I found on the doorstep this morning?"

"Sorry, no." Rab took a folded tea towel from a pocket of his coat, unfolded it and gave it to Ranger. "Be a good lad," he said to the dog, and then he took himself off to the tearoom and Ranger, good lad that he was, took himself to his favorite chair. He jumped into the chair, arranged the tea towel to his satisfaction, looked again at Christine, and then settled down for his own nap. As Janet hid a sympathetic yawn, Tallie and Summer came from the tearoom.

Tallie handed a cup of tea to Janet. Summer looked at Christine's mug on the counter and then at Christine.

"So much for her claim that caffeine replaced all the blood in her system," Summer said. "She actually did pretty well, considering. Did you send Rab in when she fell asleep?"

Janet shook her head. "He's Rab. He just . . . arrived."

"He's an Inversgailian Jeeves," Tallie said. "He shimmers in when needed. Hey, maybe he knows something about the box of books."

Janet shook her head. "Even Jeeves is fallible."

⁂

One trio of customers seemed disappointed that afternoon to find only two of the four comfy fireplace chairs available. They were quiet and polite about it, though, and snapped pictures of Ranger before heading for the tearoom.

"I wonder if I would've said anything if they'd taken pictures of Christine, too," Janet said to Tallie.

"I'm sure you'll make the right decision if you get another great opportunity." The bell at the door jingled. "Road Policing Unit, I think," Tallie said. "Looks like Norman followed through with his call. Be right back."

Without explanation, Tallie slipped from behind the counter. She disappeared down an aisle toward the tearoom, leaving Janet to face two dour members of Police Scotland alone.

9

The female and male, walking in lockstep, stopped short of the counter, stopped short of making eye contact, and surveyed the area of the shop they could see. Janet thought it mildly interesting that they stood shoulder to shoulder and appeared to be the same height—neither of them as tall as Constable Norman Hobbs, both of them possibly no older than thirty. Definitely under thirty-five.

From her years as a public librarian, Janet was a strong adherent to the ten and five rule of customer service—smile and make eye contact with anyone within ten feet; warmly greet anyone within five. If Police Scotland went in for the rule, these two hadn't yet internalized it. Hobbs, stodgy porridge though he might be, always had a pleasant way of dealing with the public. But maybe she'd judged the young duo too quickly. When they finished their perusal of the shop, for whatever it told them, and approached the counter, Janet threw the rule's ten and five feet together into one, welcoming go. She made eye contact, smiled, *and* greeted them warmly. The duo returned only the eye contact.

"We're looking for Janet Marsh," said the female—S. Carmichael, according to her name badge.

"Do you know where we can find her?" the male—F. Macleod—asked.

"And who might you be?" Janet asked, eyes still making contact, smile still in place. Neither of them answered. She felt her warmth ebbing, and although she hadn't originally thought of offering them tea, she decided now she *might* have, but wouldn't.

Tallie returned, then, with Rab in tow. While Rab took a detour to look at Ranger and Christine, Tallie came behind the counter to stand beside her mother and offer her own warm greeting to Carmichael and Macleod. Janet enjoyed the visual of mother and daughter standing shoulder to shoulder across the counter from the police, the more so because she and Tallie were also a similar height. She felt certain that if she asked Tallie about it later, Tallie would have noticed. She didn't think the duo across from them would be amused.

The napper's comfort must have satisfied Rab and suggested his own. He came behind the counter, moved the stool closer to the back counter, sat, crossed one leg over the other, and leaned an elbow on the counter behind.

"I'll watch the till, shall I?" he said.

S. Carmichael's eyes, having followed the bookshop staff and their various maneuvers, settled their focus on Tallie. "Ms. Marsh?"

Tallie acknowledged that with a nod and a "Yes?"

"Is there a place we can speak to you away from the public?"

"Sure. The office is right here."

"We only need to speak with Ms. Marsh," F. Macleod said when Tallie and Janet both started for the office.

"Aye, I know," Janet said with a smile over her shoulder and without slowing.

Carmichael and Macleod hurried after them. Macleod closed the door.

"We're Ms. Marsh and Ms. Marsh," Janet said apologetically. She was beginning to feel sorry for Macleod. He looked less like a policeman and more like a newly minted schoolteacher not used to unruly pupils. "This is my daughter, Tallie. I'm Janet Marsh. Would you like to sit?"

She offered the two desk chairs. The officers remained standing.

"Sorry for the confusion," Tallie said, hiking herself up to sit on the desk next to the box of foundling books. "But you didn't specify."

"We *specifically* asked for Janet Marsh when we came into the shop," Carmichael said.

"Oh my goodness no," Janet said, pouring on the warm, fuzzy, and slightly condescending. "You didn't *ask*. You said you were *looking* for Janet Marsh, but when I asked who *you* were you didn't identify yourselves or tell me why you're here. I assume you're from the Road Policing Unit of Police Scotland, but I don't know that, so what was I to think?"

"We're here concerning the road accident involving Mr. Malcolm Murray on Sunday last," Macleod said.

They produced their warrant cards. S. Carmichael and F. Macleod were Sandra and Fergus.

The names suited them, Janet decided, and their awkwardness was growing on her. She wanted to say, *Now was that really so hard?* But there was no point in turning awkward into antagonized. Or more antagonized, if she'd misread the awkward.

"Thank you," she said, as warmly as she'd first welcomed them. "Now, how's your investigation going, and how can I help you?"

Rather than answer, Sandra Carmichael pulled out a notebook and read from it. "According to the report filed by P. C. Hobbs, you saw Mr. Murray's body from the bridge—"

"I didn't know it was a body, at the time, and I didn't know it was Dr. Murray. I'd never met him." *And darn it, why didn't I write down my list of questions?* "You do know he was a doctor, don't you, and quite well-thought-of in Inversgail?"

"If you'll let me finish," Carmichael said.

"Of course. And I know perfectly well you must know who Malcolm Murray was. But you *do* want my impressions as the first person on the scene, don't you? Because it didn't look right, even from the bridge. I saw the bike in the thistles and then his arm in the water. So I went down to see if he needed help. He didn't. It looked like a sad, lonely way to die, although maybe he died doing what he liked. Presuming he liked riding his bike and eating haggis. Why do you suppose he wore a tweed jacket and trousers for riding that kind of distance? Too warm and a bit fussy, I'd have thought." She knew she was blethering like a caffeinated Christine, but the memory of finding Malcolm Murray dead had rattled her. "Have you found out what happened?"

"The investigation is ongoing," Macleod said.

"The tire ruts at the side of the road," Janet said.

"What about them?" Carmichael asked.

"Given the right conditions, can you read them like, well, like animal tracks? For instance, can you tell, from a set of tracks or ruts if a car stood in one place for a time or if it just sort of veered onto the verge and then back onto the road again without stopping?"

"What information do you have?" Carmichael asked.

"About tire tracks and ruts in general? Oh no, I see! You mean specifically about the ruts beside the road at the Beaton Bridge." Janet shook her head. "No, I'm sorry. I don't know anything specific at all. I'm just curious in general."

"Did you pick up or move anything?" Carmichael said.

"Where? What sort of thing?" Janet asked.

"At any time from the point you stopped on the bridge until P. C. Hobbs arrived," Macleod said.

"Or after," said Carmichael. "If he didn't notice you doing so or didn't put it in his report."

"I haven't read his report," Janet said.

"So you did pick something up?" Macleod asked.

"No. I'm just trying to help, which would be easier if I knew what you're looking for and why."

"She's big on knowing why," Tallie said to the officers. "But, Mom? It probably isn't the time for that."

"Ah. I see." Janet looked at Carmichael. "Just the facts, ma'am?"

Carmichael's expression didn't change. *A pity,* Janet thought, *but she's probably too young for* Dragnet *references.*

"I'm afraid I can't help you with that, then," Janet continued. "I felt for a pulse, but tried not to touch or move anything, and I don't remember picking anything up."

"We should warn you that we expect full and honest cooperation," Macleod said.

"That sounds ominous and official. Do you—"

"Mom?" Tallie interrupted.

"Sorry, dear." Janet turned back to the two officers. "I am sorry for running on. Honestly, it's just nerves. I do wonder one more thing, though."

"What's that, Ms. Marsh?"

"It hasn't even been thirty-six hours since I found Dr. Murray, and less than that since you started your investigation. I want you to know I realize that. But if your question about moving or picking something up—or the answer to it—is important or integral to making a determination as to what happened, then why didn't you come ask me sooner? Or does that gap in time indicate new information and the investigation moving in a new direction?"

"Thank you for your time, Mrs. Marsh," Carmichael said without answering Janet's question. Macleod apparently had nothing to add, either. The two left, and Janet turned to Tallie.

"Did I come on too strong at the end?" Janet asked. "Was I too officious?"

"A tad," Tallie said, "but I wouldn't worry about it."

"They aren't exactly chummy, are they? And it was a waste of time, frankly. They wouldn't answer my questions and they didn't like my answer to theirs. I did get the feeling, though, that Sandra hoped I *had* found or moved something, and thought I really might have but had decided not to tell them. Also, that they didn't need my answer anyway."

"That's a fairly involved and complicated feeling to come away with," Tallie said. "I hope, for your sake, it isn't true. You probably don't want cranky road police out there waiting for a missed turn signal or a faulty taillight."

"I don't imagine they're vindictive like that. I'm sure that only happens in the movies, or Chicago. But didn't you get the feeling they were disappointed when they left?"

"They were hard to read," Tallie said. "When I went to get Rab, he said in his very quiet way that he recognized them, even from behind. He's seen them off the clock, and off their patch, in a pub in Dornie. They're seeing each other and trying hard to keep it a secret until one or the other can get a transfer."

"That was rather a lot to tell you between the tearoom and book counter."

"He's the Jeeves of Inversgail *and* Dornie," Tallie said.

"Oh, but now I hope we don't see them again, because I'll never be able to keep myself from saying something. If they're working so hard at keeping that a secret, though, I wonder if they're at the top of their game on the investigation?"

"The *ongoing* investigation," Tallie said.

"True. So how long do you think an investigation like this typically takes?"

"It might not be officially closed until autopsy results are available."

"That implies waiting. Sandra and Fergus weren't waiting. They were here asking questions."

"Actually, just that specific question," Tallie said.

"And that implies there's a hole or a gap in the information they've collected. A hole or a gap that's keeping them from closing the investigation. What's missing that could be so important?"

"Norman said they'd be dotting *i*s and crossing *t*s if they came. That really might be all they're doing."

"But what item is small enough that Norman wouldn't notice me pick it up, and presumably take away with me—?"

"Or toss in the nearest bin," Tallie said, "if you'd only picked it up because you're keen on a green Scotland."

"What could I move, again without Norman noticing—unless I did either of those things before he arrived? But why would I do *any* of those things? It does leave one wondering what needs dotting and crossing."

"And you love to wonder as much as you love to ask why."

"I do. So I'd been wondering about their *i*s and *t*s in general. The way I've been wondering about tire tracks in general. But now I'm wondering about a specific set of *i*s and *t*s—two of each. They're in the word 'intentional,' and I wonder how long before the Road Policing Unit will feel confident enough about those *i*s and *t*s to issue their official statement using it?"

༄

The two cyclists Janet and Christine had met at Nev's the night before came in toward the end of the day—the lean whippet and the other who hadn't provided an easy comparison. Today she made it easy. She wore the cornflower blue tunic, marked with the National Health Service Scotland insignia, and navy trousers of a district nurse.

"Nice to see you again," Janet said when they came to the counter. "Lynsey and Isla, isn't it?

"Guilty," Isla said.

Janet thought Isla's smile and tone might be considered mocking, but as a new businesswoman in town—and the incomer who might be highly suspect—she decided not to rise to the bait. "What can I do for you?"

"We wondered if you were serious about coming for a ride with us," Isla said, "or just being a polite American."

"*Isla.*" Lynsey shook her head. "Don't mind her. We'll meet at the Stevenson statue in the morning. Rhona's coming along. You should come. Nothing strenuous."

"I'd love to. What time?"

"Will eight suit?" Lynsey asked.

"It gives the sun time to stick its lazy head over the horizon and us a short ride before work," Isla said.

"Cancelled if it's bucketing down," Lynsey said. "But no need to phone."

"Or no need to show up at all," said Isla.

Janet knew a dare when she heard one. "I'll see you at eight."

⁓

Christine woke up from her nap as Janet called goodbye to the last customer and Tallie locked the door. Christine looked askance at Ranger, who'd been snoring quite loudly. He woke up, too, shook himself, shook his tea towel, and took it with him to find Rab.

"Where's that book I was reading?" Christine asked. "Something about lighthouses with recipes for peppers. And why did you let me fall asleep? Actually—" She might have given herself a mental version of Ranger's wakeup shake. "Actually, *thank* you for letting me sleep. I needed it. I just hope I didn't snore like the dog. But where is that book?"

"Which do you want, the lighthouse or the peppers?" Janet asked. "They're different books."

"Peppers," Christine said. "More practical."

"It's *The Complete Herbal* by a Dr. Culpeper, so not really a cookery book," Janet said. "It's fascinating, though, with notes in the margins from people who used it. Culpeper published it in the 1600s. This one's from 1850 and feeling its age."

"Like so many of us."

"It isn't a goner, though. Treat it with the same care you do your mum. In fact, why don't you take it home and bring it back in the morning. She might like to see it. Perk her up a bit."

Christine's mother was a former district nurse and avid gardener. "It might, at that," she said. "Now, I should let you get on with your closing up and go help Summer with ours."

"All done," Summer said, entering from the tearoom. "Rab helped and then shimmered away."

"And . . . done here, too," Tallie said.

"Good. Then if you have time, I want to talk something through. I want some perspective," Christine said.

Janet and Tallie each shrugged a shoulder. "Sure."

"If your perspective won't take long," Summer said. "Date with the darts."

"Good," Christine said again. "First, have you heard much talk about Malcolm's death in Yon Bonnie?"

"Aside from Ian yesterday and Norman this morning, no," Janet said. She looked at Tallie.

"Accurate," Tallie said.

"It's been different in Cakes and Tales," Summer said. "Tea and shortbread make people chatty."

"Accurate," Christine said, "to borrow Tallie's excellent summary. The words I kept hearing over these two days were 'shock' and 'blow.' It's a terrible shock. It's a terrible blow."

"So 'terrible' is another word you kept hearing," Tallie said.

Christine shot a finger at her. "Accurate. But we didn't hear anything else."

"What else do you want to hear?" Tallie asked.

"I asked you that last night at Nev's," Janet reminded her.

"But now I have a better answer," Christine said. "Florrie says she won't mourn Malcolm. We don't hear anything like that from anyone else. I want to know why. Something must have happened. You felt that, didn't you, Janet?"

"I felt it between my shoulder blades when we stood at the door. She looked right through me at something else. Not something behind me, something way far off. I don't think it was anything I could see. Maybe nothing I'd *want* to see. Did I tell you I went past the house on my bike ride this morning?"

"Did you? I drove past."

"What did you think?" Janet asked.

"It was quiet. But not tranquil quiet. Watched or watching quiet. A quiet that implies something. Am I making any sense?"

"You are, but for the life of me, I can't explain what it means."

"Neither can I. And I might be obsessing," Christine said, "but I want to help the girl I used to know."

"How do you see that as obsessing?" Summer asked.

"Obsessing might not be the right word. It could be that I'm atoning. Atoning for separating myself so completely from friends for thirty years. Turning my back."

"You and Tony came back here most summers," Janet said. "Don't be so hard on yourself."

"I want to know why this woman is behaving the way she is, and to do that, I want to get inside her head."

"Did getting inside her house help?" Tallie asked.

"It helped to put it into *my* head."

They'd been standing in a close group in front of the bookshop's sales counter, in full view of the front door. They all startled when someone rapped on the door.

"Norman," Janet said. "I think he's heard something."

10

Constable Hobbs thanked Tallie for letting him in and then he greeted the other women. "But you look as though you were having a meeting. I don't mean to interrupt."

"What is it, Norman?" Christine asked.

"I just wondered if you've learned any more about the books you found this morning."

Christine said, "Oh, for—" but got no further before Summer put a hand on her shoulder and whispered something. Christine subsided.

Janet was more interested in the whisper and subsidence than Hobbs's question, so Tallie answered. "Nothing yet," she said.

"But I did tell you that I'd let you know," Janet said, playing catch-up.

"And I know you will. I might have a lead on them for you. I took the liberty of asking at Young's if they knew of anyone buying Dalwhinnie by the case. It's a Dalwhinnie box the books arrived in."

Janet thought Christine looked ready to shake off Summer's quelling hand. She jumped in before Christine got loose. "What did you find out, Norman?"

"Dr. Murray found it more cost-effective to order whisky a case at a time."

"Interesting," Tallie said. "But you haven't asked Florence about the books?"

"She might have seen enough of the police in the past few days."

"That's very thoughtful of you," Janet said. "Speaking of police, do you know what the Road Policing Unit is looking for? Something small enough that I could have picked it up or moved it."

"That's news to me," Christine said.

"Two officers stopped by while you were *busy* this afternoon," Janet said. "Do you know Sandra Carmichael and Fergus Macleod, Norman?"

"Part of the Fort William unit that responded to accident. I've not heard this about looking for something." His purple notebook and pen came out and he made a note. "Anything else you've learned?"

Janet felt the duo's secret relationship bubbling up inside her. She shot a panicked look at Tallie.

"They weren't forthcoming," Tallie said. "And Mom did her best to get them to cough up more information."

"I wish I'd been there," Christine said.

"Tough nuts to crack, members of the Road Policing Unit," Hobbs said. "But I'm sure if anyone could do it, it would be you, Mrs. Robertson. About the books, then. I'll leave it up to you what to do with the information about the whisky box. I'll be on my way, and you can get back to your meeting."

"Thank you, Norman," Christine said, and then to Tallie, who'd started for the door, "That's all right. I'll see him out."

While Christine went with Hobbs, Janet nudged Summer. "Quick, what did you whisper to soothe the cranky Christine?"

"Boudicca bids you to back down."

"Worked like a charm," Tallie said. "What do you think *cozy* Christine is saying to Norman out there now?"

Christine had stepped outside with Hobbs. They saw her smiling and Hobbs nodding and then he touched the brim of his peaked cap and was gone. When she came back in, she clapped her hands.

"This all sounds promising, don't you think?"

"What all?" Tallie asked.

"Oh, you know, the books. Malcolm's penchant for Dalwhinnie."

"As a doctor, he might have found *The Complete Herbal* a curiosity," Janet said. "I wonder if we should contact Florence. To clarify the situation. Find out what she expects us to do with the books."

"And let her know we aren't into dump and run deliveries," Tallie said.

"You two will be good at that, then," Christine said. "You're clear and well-spoken. And you're the senior book expert and junior book expert, respectively. Take notes, Tallie. Use your astute observational skills. I'm not at my best when I'm this knackered."

"What—you mean go this evening?" Janet asked. "And what do you mean, knackered? You slept most of the afternoon away."

"Tip of the iceberg, as far as my sleep deprivation is concerned," Christine said. "I can't do it, anyway. I need to get home and give Dad respite in case Mum's been fretful. And Boudicca has her darts practice. But this evening, yes. I think it's a good idea."

"I suppose you're right. Better to nip this in the bud in case Florence has taken up the art of Swedish Death Decluttering or suddenly finds no spark of joy in old books." Janet paused. "Oh dear. That sounded snarkier than I meant it to."

"I wouldn't worry about it," Christine said. "To hear Florrie—"

"It's *Florence*."

"To hear *her*, she's more into good-riddance decluttering."

∽

"I should have told Christine and Summer about the *i*s and *t*s," Janet said as she and Tallie drove over to the Murray house that evening after soup and sandwiches at their kitchen table.

"You went with the facts—Carmichael and Macleod are looking for something. Although, even that isn't a fact. You *think* they're looking for something. They might have asked if you picked something up, not because they're missing something, but to be sure they *aren't* missing something."

"That would make them very good and thorough investigators," Janet said. "Sticking with the facts. Good old safe facts and concrete evidence."

"You don't sound convinced."

"I can't help thinking they weren't satisfied with the facts I gave them. And then, of course, I can't help wondering why."

"*I* can't help thinking we should be even more careful about throwing around the word 'intentional' than we are about spilling the beans on Carmichael and Macleod," Tallie said. "Also that Christine orchestrated our trip to see Florence. What happened to her wanting to get inside Florence's head? Wouldn't this be a great opportunity to do that?"

"It might, but do you really want Christine along this evening?" Janet asked. "You *do* know how she gets."

"You don't think we could've done this with a phone call, though?"

"It's awkward, I know, but I think it's better to see her face-to-face," Janet said. "This might be a bit of a welfare check, too. Christine really is worried about Florence, but she's worried about her mum, too. Sometimes there's only so much room for those kinds of worries."

"In my experience, *you* have a bottomless pit for all kinds of worries. And I mean that as a compliment, but in my own worrying way."

"You might be surprised by my limits, dear. You'll like the Murrays' library, at least. It's warm and snug with a fireplace. I hope it's giving Florence some comfort. Though the rest of the house feels—"

"Christine said watched or watching."

"Mm. Let me know if you get that feeling, too."

Janet pulled into the Murray driveway. Unlike the night before, only a few lights shone. One of them lit a welcome glow over the front door.

"No heebie-jeebies yet." Tallie said as they followed the flagged path to that door.

"Maybe things have settled a bit. She couldn't have been at her best last night."

"Florence or Christine?" Tallie asked.

"Good point." Janet pressed the bell. "We'll be kind and hope for the best."

Florence opened the door, wearing jeans again, pushing hair off her forehead with the back of her hand. "Yes? Oh, I see. You were here last night," she said to Janet, then she stared at Tallie.

"Yes, Janet Marsh, and this is my daughter, Tallie—"

"Is Christine out there somewhere?" Florence tried to see around them.

"She's home with her mum and dad," Janet said.

"They're still alive, are they? And I suppose you want to come in again?"

"We wanted to ask you about some books," Janet said.

"Mind he doesn't get out before you close the door," Florence said and left Janet and Tallie looking at each other.

"He who?" Tallie whispered.

"Must be the dog. Last night he barked when we rang the bell. Come on."

They stepped inside and Tallie closed the door. Firmly. Florence was already disappearing through a doorway across from the library at the far end of the hall. They hurried after her, but before following her through that door, Janet waved Tallie over for a quick look into the library.

"Not at all snug," Tallie said quietly. "Not tonight."

No crackling fire. No cozy lamplight. And how did the library suddenly seem disused and dusty? And in disarray.

Death and its aftermath, Janet thought. *The great upheaval.*

"Florence must be going through Malcolm's things and started with the books," she said. "Although between you and me it looks more like a drunk's been reorganizing and re-shelving."

Tallie nudged her mother. "I think she's looking for us."

They found Florence across the hall in a room with almost the same footprint as the library, though it wasn't a twin or mirror image. It was somewhat smaller than the library and a bright overhead fixture lit the room to its corners. There were no windows. One wall consisted of built-in double-doored cupboards, all painted white. The other walls were plaster, also white. The floor was bare. One cupboard stood open, its multiple shelves holding stacks of dingy linens.

"Was this part of your brother's surgery?" Janet asked.

Florence, rummaging around the floor of a closet, looked over her shoulder. "There you are again," she said, "but where is *he*?"

"Would you like help finding him?" Janet asked. "What's his name?"

"I don't know when he left or where he's gone."

"When did you see him last?" Tallie asked.

"I've not searched the attic." Florence looked up at the ceiling, head cocked as though detecting footsteps or other movements two floors above. "He never liked the attic." She stood and pushed between Janet and Tallie. At the door, she turned to ask, "Are you going to help or not?" She left the room without waiting for an answer.

"We're right behind you," Janet called.

"Not so anyone would notice," came Florence's retort from farther down the hall.

Tallie grabbed Janet's arm. "What are we doing?"

"Helping. I think."

"And who are we looking for?" Tallie asked. "The dog or Malcolm?"

"Oh dear. I think we'd better go after her."

"I think we're going down a rabbit hole."

"*Up* a rabbit hole," Janet said. "She's heading for the attic. Let's try the main stairs."

"I have a better idea," Tallie said. "Let's split up. You look for her. I'll look for the dog."

Janet gave her a thumbs-up and went after Florence. She wondered about phoning Christine, too. Christine, with her inner Queen Elizabeth, would know how to handle whatever it was that this situation was turning into.

Janet didn't see Florence, but she heard her ahead, around a turn in the stairs, trudging upward and puffing as she climbed. *Good for me,*

Janet thought. *I'm not puffing at all. Florence should take up bike riding.* She regretted the thought almost immediately. Bike riding hadn't helped Malcolm.

In case Florence had balance issues on stairs, in addition to short breath, Janet didn't want to startle her by coming up behind her too quickly or quietly. She made her own tread heavier than it needed to be and was about to say something calm and unalarming, when Florence grabbed the railing and swung around to look down the staircase.

"*Why?*" Florence demanded.

Janet made a grab for the railing, too, glad she hadn't taken an unfortunate step backward at the outburst. "Why what?"

"Stomping up behind me like that. Why are you trying to scare me?"

"I was trying *not* to scare you." Janet wished Florence had had the same consideration for her. "I didn't do it very well, though, did I? I'm sorry. I didn't want to cause an accident."

"Why are you talking about accidents?" Florence took her hand off the railing and hugged herself, rubbing her upper arms as if she had a sudden chill. "What accidents?"

"Accidents on the stairs. We don't want them, do we?"

"Malcolm thought I didn't hear *him*. There's nothing wrong with my hearing."

"Have you heard the dog in the attic?" Janet asked. "Can he get in there on his own?"

But Florence had turned and started climbing again. When she reached the landing and stopped for breath, Janet saw her chance. She might not have an inner queen to call upon, but she had the next best thing. She climbed quickly, and crowded Florence away from the top of the stairs, and then Janet called on her inner Christine.

Fists on her hips, she stretched her spine as tall as her five-foot-three frame allowed, looked Florence in the eyes, and said in a firm, level voice, "Florrie."

"It's Floren—"

"Florrie or Florence or Ms. Murray, we need to talk. Then I will try to help you in whatever way I can, if you want me to. If I can't, I'll find someone who can. Do you understand?"

Florence looked . . . relieved? Janet wasn't sure, but she decided to take Florence's nod as progress.

"Shall we go back downstairs?" Janet suggested.

"There's a room I prefer along the corridor here, if you don't mind."

Janet wondered where Tallie was, but assumed she'd either found the dog or was making a meticulous and conscientious search. Florence led her down the corridor, slowing to look in the doorway to a bedroom. Malcolm's? The light from the corridor showed stolid, heavy wood furnishings. The room also looked as though he'd left in a hurry the morning of his accident—bed unmade, clothes on the floor, armoire door hanging open.

"I cannot deal with that today. I honestly cannot," Florence muttered and continued past. They went almost to the end of the corridor, where she entered another bedroom—lighter and airier Janet saw, when Florence turned on a bedside lamp. She also saw plenty of dust she knew she *wasn't* imagining. But Florence was crossing the room to another door and they ended up in a smaller corner room.

"This is a lovely room, Florence."

"My mother's sewing room. Sadly neglected."

It was actually the tidiest and most inviting room Janet had seen in the house that evening. Pale yellow walls, generous windows on two sides, a floral chenille rug, a hassock with a basket of knitting in easy reach of a settee, and two wingback chairs covered in chintz with lace-edged antimacassars. She got the feeling the dog would not be welcome here.

"When *was* the last time you saw the dog?" Janet asked.

"He's a lazy old git. Your daughter, was it, who came with you? She looked capable. I'm sure she'll find him." Florence sat on the settee and folded her hands in her lap. "I'm not aware of any business you have with me. You're an American."

"I am. But I live here now. My family and I spent many summers in Inversgail. Christine and I have been friends for about thirty years—she and Tony. We lived in the same town in the States. Did you know Christine's husband?"

"How am to know if I did or not? I never met him."

"Well that's—well." It seemed best to let that drop. "Christine and I, along with my daughter and another young woman, bought Yon Bonnie Books on the High Street. We've been there about six months now."

Florence studied her fingernails.

"We wondered if you left a box of books at the shop this morning," Janet said. "They might have belonged to your brother."

"A description might help."

"A Dalwhinnie Whisky box."

"I meant the books."

"Surely you'd remember if you left a box of books on our doorstep or not." Janet checked herself. She didn't need to start an argument, and she was sounding like Carmichael and Macleod. "The point is, we don't trade in used books, except in rare circumstances. If you're planning to downsize Dr. Murray's library, we'd ask that you take that into consideration."

"If I'm not in the habit of leaving boxes of books on stray doorsteps, then your point has nothing to do with me."

"So then you didn't leave the box."

"I didn't say that. A description might help."

Tallie was right, Janet thought. *Down a rabbit hole. A bloody big one and getting bigger by the minute.* She tried to smile without grinding her teeth.

"For instance, how many books are we talking about?" Florence asked.

"Thirty-seven," Janet said after a deep breath that did less good than she'd hoped. "The more interesting ones were published before 1950. One is an edition of *The Complete Herbal* published in 1850."

"Fancy that. Dull and dusty, no doubt. What else?"

"*Swallows and Amazons? The Sword in the Stone? The Bell Rock Lighthouse?* There's also a small leather-bound copy of *Kidnapped.*"

"Who *doesn't* own one of those? What else?"

"Florence, you either left the books on the shop's doorstep or you didn't." And if she didn't, there was no point in listing any more of them. Janet had trouble keeping the growing irritation out of her voice.

Florence *didn't* keep the irritation out of hers. "I'm sorry, but you might have phoned me with your questions and saved me the trouble of your visit." She got up and went to the door. "I don't recognize any of your dusty books and I don't know anything about a *box* of books."

Janet's phone buzzed with a text. She took it out and looked at it, which further irritated Florence. "My daughter found your dog," Janet said.

"Not my dog."

"Not your—" Janet snapped her mouth shut and looked back at Tallie's text. "She found him in front of the fireplace in the library. That's where he was last night. Didn't you look there?"

But Florence was gone.

Janet took advantage of her solitary moment. She bared her teeth, shook her fist, counted to ten, and then went on up to fifty. *The exasperated half-hundred*, she thought, and felt calmer.

She went downstairs and found Florence standing in the library doorway. Florence tried hard not to meet her eye, but Janet called on her inner Christine again and Florence shrank back against the doorjamb as Janet brushed past her into the room. Tallie had turned on all the lights and stood with her arms crossed tightly over her chest. The dog lay in front of the fireplace, his back to them.

"When we glanced in from the door earlier, it was too dark to see much," Tallie said. "We didn't see *him*. I found him here by the fireplace. He was shivering. I got him to go outside with me and took care of that business and then he whined to come back in. He drank some water. I rummaged for dog food, but by the time I found it, he'd slunk back in here."

"He's Malcolm's dog?" Janet asked. "Florence?"

Florence stayed at the door. "I don't go in there. I've never liked this room."

"What do you mean you don't come in here? You brought me and Christine in here last night."

"Because I remember Christine and how she is. She wasn't going to give up until she had her chance to blether at me. She was aye stubborn. Sometimes the quickest way is through."

Whatever that means. Janet looked around. Her earlier impression of the library in disarray was only slightly exaggerated. "Have you been reorganizing?"

"I told you, I've never liked this room."

Her way of giving answers and information was as disorganized as the room. But Janet realized that Florence's whole life had suddenly been turned upside down. *I'd be a mess, too.*

"We really would like to help, if you'd like it," Janet said gently. "What's happened? You had a fire going in here last night. It was lovely and cozy."

"I needed the fire. It kept the cold from creeping in. Kept it from seeping into the rest of the house." Florence rubbed her hands, perhaps at the memory of that cold, then tucked them in her armpits. She looked like an odd mirror image of Tallie.

"Cold creeping from where?" Tallie asked.

"The window." Florence took a hand from her armpit and pointed, and then tucked the hand back. "Malcolm opened it. Opened it and left it open. That's how I know he came back, because I'd shut it when he left the first time. Then he came back, after riding all over who knows where, and he opened it again.

"I told you all this yesterday. You and Christine. I heard him come in. I called hello, and he did just the way he always did—said nothing. He rarely said anything when I spoke to him. He wasn't sociable that way. If you ask me, his mind was beginning to go. I'm not surprised he went off the road like that. I told him he wasn't safe." A tear rolled down her cheek.

"Florence—"

"I was not my brother's keeper. He didn't listen. He never listened to me. He opened the window again and left it open and went out. Again.

And I didn't know until after Norman Hobbs came and told me he was gone, and I didn't believe him." She wiped angrily at more tears with the back of her hand. "Left with the window still open so it stayed open all night and let the cold in. He'd no thought for anyone but himself and the dog and not as much for the dog as most would think."

"Will you keep the dog?" Tallie asked.

"I've no immediate plans. No plans for distributing dogs or books about the town. I've been keeping house for Malcolm, and that's all. Not his books. You've wasted your time coming here to ask about boxes and books that I know nothing about and care about even less. Do you know what I'd like to do with his books? Throw them out his bloody window."

Anger seemed to be doing Florence some good. Or maybe it was the tears.

"We don't feel it was a waste of our time coming here this evening. Do we, Tallie?"

"Not at all. We helped you find the dog, if nothing else."

"And you're right, Florence," Janet said. "I could have called you to ask you about the books, but I was glad to see you again."

"I can't imagine why." Florence dabbed at her nose with her sleeve.

"We've bothered you enough," Janet said. "I feel like we've been nosy, and I don't want to intrude even more, but I do want to ask if anyone is helping you with the funeral arrangements."

"No."

"Is there anyone who can? What about Gerald?"

"*Gerald?* He was worse than Malcolm. Malcolm was just antisocial. Gerald was obsessed. I've not seen or spoken to him in years."

"Not even now? Since Malcolm's death?"

"Why would that make any difference to him? Bloody great gi—" Florence bit the last word in two. "That's enough about him. No doubt you've other places you'd rather be. Don't let me keep you."

She turned and left, and Janet half expected to let themselves out, but Florence walked ahead of them to the door.

"We left the lights on in the library," Tallie said. "I can run back and turn them off, if you'd like."

"Don't bother. I'll get them. Or not. It wouldn't be the first time they're left on all night."

Janet decided to try one more offer of help, this time in the form of a suggestion. "Florence, do you know Maida Fairlie?" Maida and Janet were in-laws—Maida's daughter and Janet's son being married and living in Edinburgh with their two wee boys. "Maida's a great one to phone for sorting, cleaning, packing things away, anything like that. She organizes that kind of work for a cleaning firm. She's reliable, no-nonsense, and discreet. I can give you her number, if you'd like."

"Hurry, before he gets out." Florence opened the door and gave no sign she'd heard Janet. Nor did she acknowledge their good nights. As she closed the door, they heard her say, "He was aye strange."

"He who?" Janet asked. But Florence shut the door with a solid thud and turned the lock. Janet looked at Tallie. "She did it again. She left us hanging like that when Christine and I were here last night, and she just did it again. *Again*. I really don't like that word."

"Fair enough," Tallie said. "But let's get in the car and go on home."

Janet slammed her car door and started the engine. Then she shut it off. "Look at me, Tallie. Look at me and promise me this. If I ever open a metaphorical door like 'he's always been strange,' and then slam it shut in your face by not explaining myself, tell me to cut it out. And don't you ever do it, either. No one should be allowed to toss an indefinite pronoun like a grenade and run away."

"Okeydoke."

Janet looked up at the Murray house and howled, "He *who*?" Then, remembering the white-knuckle ride with Christine the night before, she took an immense breath and held it to the point of exploding. Then she relaxed her shoulders, let the air out slowly, started the car, and drove sedately home.

Smirr and Butter met them at the door and escorted Janet to the living room for a session of ear rubbing and chin stroking. Tallie poured two glasses of sherry and joined the others in their tidy, cozy, well-lit and warm living room.

"I've figured it out and I propose a toast," Janet said, raising her glass. "To the collective 'he'—Malcolm, Gerald, and the dog—all three are strange, and possibly always have been."

"Here's a variation," Tallie offered. "To the collective 'they'—*all* the Murrays—because you know we have to consider that Florence has always been strange, too. But we really shouldn't take it out on the poor dog."

11

A wind from the west arrived in the night, tossing itself around the harbor and shuffling discarded chocolate wrappers along the High Street. It left some of these at the feet of the Robert Louis Stevenson statue. He ignored them. Silent, stony, Stevenson forever kept his eyes on the Inversgail lighthouse and the seas beyond. Another wind blew in behind the first, bringing buckets of rain.

Janet woke to her alarm, rain on the roof, and two winking cats sitting on the extra pillow, staring at her. "You look optimistic about someone hopping out of bed immediately to give you breakfast," she said to them.

The cats didn't wait to see if she'd agreed to their request, so optimistic were they. Janet took her cue from them and, despite the rain, pulled on her yoga leggings and a navy blue jersey and went down to the kitchen. She fed the cats and then stood at the kitchen window with a cup of coffee. But after the buckets of rain, and after breakfast, lashing rain and then more buckets convinced her that no one in her right mind would be out riding a bike.

"Phooey," she said, and looked around for commiseration from Smirr and Butter. They'd already abandoned her for the living room and morning naps.

"Dithery," Janet said at Yon Bonnie Books that morning. "That's a better description of Florence than doddery."

The four women were having their meeting in the doorway between the bookshop and the tearoom. Summer had brought samples of the scone of the day—apricot and blue cheese—and she'd reported encouraging darts progress. Christine's mum had spent a better night and so had Christine. Janet and Tallie told them that Florence hadn't left the box of books on their doorstep, and then described their evening.

"She isn't feeble physically," Janet said. "I don't think she's feeble-minded, either, but she's scattered, and she's definitely stressed."

"As only makes sense under the circumstances," Christine said. "And stress can wreak untold havoc on a person's health, mental and physical."

"Her anger was interesting," Tallie said. "It seemed to focus her thoughts."

"It did," Janet said. "When she ranted, we weren't so much in danger of whiplash."

"No kidding." Tallie rubbed the back of her neck. "She reminded me of a student we had in the mock trial program. I worried, when he entered, because he stuttered. But he knew what he was doing, and when he presented cases the stutter almost disappeared. Florence was like that. When she really got going, her sentences were more coherent, less disjointed."

"But you're saying she was angry and possibly unbalanced?" Summer asked.

"Angry, yes. Unbalanced?" Janet tipped her hand back and forth.

"Okay, but not a good combination," Summer said. "You were going up and down stairs, along corridors to you knew not where, in an unfamiliar house, following this angry, unpredictable person. And *you*"—Summer gestured at Tallie with the scone plate—"you were off looking for a dog you didn't know who might have been just as unpredictable and angry."

Tallie helped herself to another scone from Summer's plate. "Point taken, but he turned out to be as sweet as these."

"The real point is that we have rules about getting into dangerous situations." Summer pointed the scone plate at Janet. "*You* came up with the rules."

"And you didn't like them at the beginning," Janet reminded her. "But I've given the wrong impression of the situation last night. We've used the rules for murder investigations. For dangerous situations *within* dangerous situations. This was nothing like that. It was just sad."

"You can call it sad, or say that she's dithery or doddery or suffering the untold havoc of stress, but how *angry* was she?" Summer asked.

And how angry are you? Janet wondered. *And for Heaven's sake, what's brought this on?* She took another scone, too, hoping that would soothe the agitated baker.

"You're right to bring up the rules, Summer, and I appreciate your concern. I don't think it was that kind of anger, though, where we were the target or in any kind of danger. There were a few tears, too. She didn't fall apart and boo-hoo, but there were tears running down her cheeks. I think they made her angry, too. Taken together, the anger and tears, I hope they were cathartic. I hope she went up to bed and had a really good cry after we left."

"That's a very Janet thing to hope," Christine said. "You tend to look on the bright side of people."

"Except when I'm accusing them of murder."

"That's why I said 'tend.' But the librarians of my experience are natural-born helpers. On the other hand, Boudicca and I see the damage in people and we keep our eyes on the more worrisome aspects."

"Don't be silly," Janet said. "You spent your entire professional life helping people."

"Yes, but a librarian is the golden retriever of helpers, all bounce and bonhomie. As social workers and newspaperwomen, we're the border collies—suspicious, alert." Christine demonstrated her impression of a border collie on the job.

Janet scoffed. "You can't be a border collie. You're afraid of sheep."

"The best border collies never trust the sheep in their fold," Christine said. "That describes me to a *T.*"

"Where does that leave me?" Tallie asked. "If you all get to be dogs, I want to be one."

Christine studied her. "A cairn terrier, like Ranger. A good lawyer is smart and full of surprises. So what's your assessment of the situation with Florence?"

"I agree with Mom. Florence wasn't angry at us. She's angry at her brothers—antisocial Malcolm and obsessive Gerald."

"She called them that?" Christine asked. "Another jarring description compared to 'the good doctor' of local lore and legend. I wonder what she thinks Gerald obsesses about. That's an interesting take on the boys and one I've not heard before."

"And that's why I wouldn't completely discount her actually being dithery or doddery," Janet said. "Her opinions of her brothers might all be in her head. Or they might come from grownup sibling rivalry. Though I did think of another possibility, given the whisky box and her general lack of focus."

"Drink? That truly would be sad," Christine said. "Drink can wreak untold havoc, too. *Had* she been drinking?"

"It's possible, but we should be careful about drawing that conclusion," Janet said. "I didn't smell anything on her breath, and alcohol might not have occurred to me, except that we have the whisky box."

"But now we know she didn't drop it off here," Tallie said. "And while I was looking for the dog, I didn't see anything that would lead me to believe that anyone in the house has or had a problem. Although, unless the signs were obvious, I might *not* see anything."

"I did an article on Al-Anon a few years back," Summer said. "According to the families I interviewed, some of their drinkers were so good at hiding their problems they could win Tony Awards for acting and set design."

"Then I think it's best if we go with dithery for now," Janet said, "and leave the other *D*—drinking—out for lack of evidence."

"*Evidence*," Christine said with a Tony-worthy shiver of her shoulders. "I love it when you talk *detective* to us. And now it's time, lassies. Open the doors and to our posts."

Rain continued in periodic blatters throughout the morning, chasing tourists back into the shops along the High Street every time they chanced to pop out, and giving Janet a workout after all. During a lull in blatters, and a corresponding lull in business, she and Tallie caught their breath together behind the sales counter.

"What did you think of our doorway meeting this morning?" she asked Tallie.

"Not that I have anything against Ranger, or cairn terriers in general, but I was kind of hoping for corgi."

"At least you weren't labeled 'bouncy.' But I want to know why Summer sounded angry."

"Especially after hitting a bull's-eye with those scones."

"She certainly did. But you agree that she sounded angry?"

"I agree that *you* think she sounded angry. *I* think she sounded like she was arguing a point as a concerned friend, and that our time with flustery Florence over-sensitized you to strong emotions."

"There now," Janet said. "I'm sure that's the kind of cogent thought that goes through Ranger's mind all the time. Can you imagine the royal corgis being even half so erudite? But if Summer was arguing a point, then I want to know why. Were *we* arguing with her?"

Tallie pulled her glasses halfway down her nose, looked at her mother, and said nothing.

"As you told Sandra and Fergus," Janet said, "I like to know the *why* of things."

Tallie nodded. "I'll talk to her later and see if anything's up."

"I could text Christine and ask her to follow up."

"Let's say no to that."

"Hmph." Janet put her phone away.

"But to make up for *not* getting Christine all worked up over something that's probably nothing, here are two other things for you to think about." Tallie pushed her glasses back up her nose. "First thing—what if, when Summer and Christine have enough recipes, we put them together in a sort of chapbook cookbook and sell them?"

"That's a fantastic idea! I wonder if they have enough already? Would it make it too expensive if we use color pictures throughout?"

"The reaction of a true golden retriever. Let's see what Summer and Christine think."

"They'll love it. Shall I bounce right in there and ask them, or do you want to tell me your second thing?"

"The second thing, before it rains again and customers come back. This one might be fantastic, too, but only in the fantastical sense of the word, because it might be *havers*."

"I won't laugh."

"It woke me up a few times last night. It came from something you said to Florence—you told her we didn't want to intrude even more."

"I think I said *I* didn't want to. I was speaking for myself, but I thought you would agree. *Did* you want to intrude more than we did?"

"No, no. You were right. But what if someone else intruded? I mean, literally intruded. What if someone got in and searched the library? You said it looked like a drunk tried to re-shelve."

"It reminded me of the quiet Saturday morning at the library when one of the staff, a secret tippler it turned out, reorganized the self-help section for us. He did it according to Dewar's instead of Dewey. I pictured Florence doing something like that—getting maudlin, having a few too many, and nostalgically careening through Malcolm's books. But an intruder—it's a stretch, don't you think? The stuff of waking in the wee hours?"

"I'm willing to believe that. And the flaw, if there's any sense at all in my worries, is that I'm suggesting someone got in between your visits Monday and Tuesday, not the night Florence says the window was open. Kind of a big flaw."

Janet sat down on the tall stool. She put her feet on the top rung, propped her elbows on her knees, rested her chin on knitted fingers, and studied her daughter's face. Tallie, the excellent lawyer and law professor, who hadn't just agreed to transplant her life to a West Highland bookshop on a romantic notion or whim. Who didn't immediately run with the idea that the Road Police must be looking at a finding *beyond* accidental death. Tallie gathered information, organized it precisely, digested it thoroughly, and drew conclusions carefully.

"After talking to Florence, we know she doesn't like the library," Janet said, "so she might not treat the books the way we would. That could account for the higgledy-piggledy state of things."

"True."

"But." Janet pictured the library on both evenings she'd seen it and considered the difference one day could make. "We don't know how Florence usually is and we don't know how the library usually looks. She and I passed a room last night that I assume was Malcolm's. If he left it in that state, he was a bit of a slob."

"Unless someone searched that room."

"It's so irritating that we don't know what Sandra and Fergus are looking for," Janet said. "Irritating enough that I'm going back to calling them Carmichael and Macleod. But we wouldn't be able to tell if someone searched Malcolm's room if he *was* a slob."

"He's as irritating as Carmichael and Macleod."

"Florence sure feels that way. Think about this, though, Tallie—I was surprised by the disarray, but Florence wasn't. It makes more sense that she spent time in the library doing whatever—deciding which books to throw out the window first, maybe."

"You're probably right, but can we trust her reactions?"

"Her brother died just two days ago. Whether or not he was antisocial, that fact alone can cover a multitude of behavioral tics. I'm sorry you lost sleep over this, dear, but it shows what a tender heart you have."

"Or how cynical cairn terriers are. I'm still gnawing on one thing."

"What is it?"

"If leaving the window open was Malcolm's habit, who knew that?"

The afternoon brought dreeps, dribbles, and drouks of rain and a steady stream of customers. Tallie said no more about her worries, but Janet turned them over and over as she rang up postcards, guidebooks, and rainy-day reading. By the end of the day, Janet knew what they should do.

"We should tell Norman," she said to Tallie as they counted down the cash register. "We don't know that something happened or that anything is going on, but that's what a constable is for."

"Makes sense," Tallie said.

"That's settled then. We'll tell Norman."

"I've the ears of a border collie," Christine said, coming through from Cakes and Tales. "You say there's something we need to tell Norman? What a coincidence. There's something I need to tell you."

"I told you she was cooking something up," Tallie said as she and Janet set up a card table in the living room that evening.

"You said she orchestrated our trip to see Florence."

"She did. It was concurrent cooking and orchestrating. She invited Norman over here, for tonight, when she stepped outside with him yesterday. Then she came back in and sent us on our merry way to see Florence."

"First one, and then the other, sounds consecutive, dear."

"But the idea for both probably zapped her between her conniving shoulder blades like a single bolt of lightning. I'm not complaining, though. Scrabble night will be fun."

"And she's bringing the snacks, so there you go. And now there's the door. I'll get that if you'll get the sherry. And bring the chairs from the kitchen."

As Janet welcomed Christine, Hobbs arrived. Janet took carrier bags from Christine and showed them both where to hang their rain gear. Christine then reclaimed the carrier bags, waved Janet to the living room with Hobbs, and went to the kitchen to lay out oatcakes, cheese, and red grapes.

Tallie was in the kitchen setting out wine glasses and Christine greeted her like a coconspirator.

"The plan is coming together nicely," Christine said quietly. "Where's your cheese board?"

Tallie found the cheese board and handed it to her. "Are we allowed in on the details?"

"Home turf advantage," Christine said. "Cheese knife?"

Tallie handed her the cheese knife. "How so?"

"Code word: Nana Bethia. We'll need to rinse the grapes."

"Will you ever let the poor guy live that down?" Tallie asked, running water over the grapes.

"Will your mother?"

"Nope."

Tallie handed Christine a bowl.

"Thank you. I was just going to ask you for something to put the grapes in. And I'm glad you agree about Norman. He softens up when he's here. Not because he relaxes, but because he knows we won't let him forget his egregious overstepping of bounds by housing his grandmother here without permission or paying rent while you and your mother were unaware and displaced."

"Shhh. We're on your side. But don't you think it's interesting that he ever comes here, knowing we'll take advantage of him?"

"That's either atonement or hubris—he still feels guilty or he thinks he can outsmart us. Come on."

Hobbs, sitting on the couch with Smirr on his lap, was trying to distract the kitten from wrestling a loose end of wool it had discovered at the lower edge of his sweater. He stood when Christine and Tallie came in, Smirr tucked in the crook of one arm. He flinched as Butter scaled the other to sit on his shoulder.

"Lovely jumper," Christine said. "Did your grandmother knit it?"

"She did. Is Summer not joining us?"

Tallie carefully disengaged the kitten from the constable. "Summer had other plans, plus early morning baking. How is Nana Bethia?"

"Getting on very well."

"Please tell her we asked after her," Janet said.

"I will."

"Excellent," Christine said. "Let the game begin."

Hobbs deposited the cat next to the kitten on the couch and joined the others at the card table. He won the draw to go first, then they all chose tiles for play and set them on their racks. Hobbs arranged and rearranged his, giving them the same serious consideration he gave any question before him.

"Are we playing in Scots, Gaelic, and English?" he asked.

"Scots, Gaelic, English, and American," Tallie said.

"Brilliant. Any news on the books?"

"Sorry, no," Janet said. "Florence didn't bring them, although it certainly looks like she's been doing some rearranging in the library. We'll keep you posted."

Hobbs laid his tiles on the board one by one. "DUILICH. That's seventeen for the word—with the *H* receiving double points—and the whole word doubled for the opening hand, plus the fifty-point bonus for using all seven tiles. Put me down for eighty-four points, please."

"Meaning?" Christine demanded.

"Sorry." Hobbs drew seven more tiles then, after arranging them on his rack, glanced up to see the three women looking at him, waiting. "Ah, I see the problem. *Duilich* is Gaelic for sorry."

Janet thought he looked unusually pleased with himself. *Ab-norman-ly* pleased. She chortled.

"What's so funny?" Christine asked.

"Nothing," Janet said. "Duilich. Hm. I don't see much I can do, and I can only use three tiles, but there." She arranged them using Hobbs's *D*. "DAZE. The *Z* gets triple points for a total of thirty-four. Not too shabby."

"You'll see, Norman," Tallie said. "We'll give you a run for your money." She put out four letters and spelled QUICK using the *C* in DUILICH, and then clinked her sherry glass against her mother's. "Triple letters for the *Q* and the *K*. Fifty total."

Christine's mouth grew small for her turn. "Lousy luck and a lousier draw," she muttered. As a mutter, she might have been talking to herself, but as mutters go it was less subtle than most. Her subsequent mutters weren't subtle either. "I haven't anything useful and I find games that hinge on this kind of luck irritating." She blew out a breath. "Simply awful." She tossed two tiles on the board and jabbed them into place to the left of the *E* in DAZE. "SEE for a whopping four points. The *S* is on a double letter square."

"You've shorted yourself," Hobbs said. "That's a double word square, not a double letter, so you have a whopping six points."

"You're wonderfully accurate," Janet said, bracing for steam to jet from Christine's ears or nostrils.

They were saved by a loud knocking on the back door.

"Three guesses," Tallie said as she went down the back hall to answer. "And if the answer is nosy neighbor, you get the fifty-point bonus."

Janet knew Tallie was almost certainly right. Ian only ever came to the back door. Janet had a theory about this backdoor preference that had nothing to do with Ian's combined nosiness and sneaking ways and everything to do with the *front* door. She liked to think the door knocker—a lovely antique brass wolf's head holding the knocking ring in its teeth—scared the bejeebers out of him.

They heard the door open and then the disingenuous voice of Ian Atkinson. "I say, Tallie. A *braw bricht moonlicht nicht the nicht*, what? Do you mind if I step in out of it? And I'd like to borrow a cup of sugar if you have such a thing. I'm making pudding. A lovely thing called spotted dick."

Janet braced herself again, this time for an explosion at the back door. There was only a minuscule pause, though, before she heard Tallie's curt, "Sure," and two sets of footsteps. The lighter set went into the kitchen. The heavier tread came to the living room door.

"Evening, all," Ian said, leaning artfully against the doorjamb. "Absolutely *oorlich* out there. Did I get that right, Constable? Damp and nippy?"

"Aye, brilliant."

"Grand. Glad to have friendly neighbors. A spot of Scrabble? Jolly good."

"Here you go, Ian." Tallie handed him a container. "You might want to check your recipe. Pretty sure spotted dick only calls for a third of a cup."

"Does it? Well, perhaps I'm making a triple batch. Cheerio the noo."

After they heard the back door close behind him, Tallie went to lock it.

"Cheers," she said when she sat back down. She held up her sherry glass and drained it. "There. I believe I've earned a hundred bonus points for not jabbing Ian in the nose in front of a constable."

"The constable might deserve the bonus points for keeping the peace just by being here," Janet said. "Or you can split it."

"The constable has earned his own bonus," Hobbs said. "It is my turn, is it not? In that case . . ." He laid out his tiles, working down from the first *I* in DUILICH. "IARRAIDH. That's thirteen points for the word—the second *A* earning double points—and the word tripled to make thirty-nine points, plus the fifty-point bonus for using all seven of the tiles. Add on four for building off of Christine's SEE to make SEER.

Put me down for ninety-three points, please. Oh, and *iarraidh* means asking for, seeking, searching. Enquiry."

"You know more Gaelic than you let on," Christine said.

"A word or phrase here and there and nothing really practical. It's not the same as knowing the language. Only enough to be dangerous." Hobbs took out his phone and snapped a photo of the board.

"What are you doing?" Christine asked.

"I'll send it to my sister. She'll be chuffed." He definitely looked chuffed.

Christine, meanwhile, had cut a few slices of the cheese she'd brought. She put some on an oatcake for herself and then passed the board. "Cheese, Norman? It's Janet's favorite—Isle of Mull Cheddar."

While Janet waited for the cheese board to come to her, she saw Christine glance at the cats on the couch. And then, ever so slyly, Christine broke off a corner of her cheddar and dropped her left hand below the edge of the table. Her upper arm remained almost stationary but not quite. Janet watched that upper arm as it moved ever so slightly left and right and left again, and she had a hunch that if she looked under the table, she would see Christine trailing her hand back and forth. Janet heard the telltale thump of Smirr jumping down from the couch and, sure enough, there he, and then Butter, came, sniffing toward Christine.

Christine moved the tiles on her rack and seemed wholly unaware she'd lured two interested parties to her cheese hand. Tallie and Hobbs, enjoying their cheese and oatcakes, were more believably unaware. Janet saw Christine's verifying sidelong glances.

Tallie passed the cheese board to Janet. Janet—seeing Christine casually bring her left hand, still with cheese, up onto the table—guessed it would be prudent to hold the cheese board up off the table. Her prudence was immediately rewarded. Smirr leaped nimbly into the middle of the table. Butter scrambled after, upsetting Hobbs's tile rack. (Or was that a flick of Christine's hand?)

"Oh, for Heaven's—here, you two," Janet said. "Get down, darlings."

"Is the smaller one playing football with the tiles?" Hobbs asked. "Or maybe they've taken up curling and the older one is brushing the ice with his tail."

"Either way, it looks like the game is over," Christine said. "And just when it was going so well. What a shame. Have you got a nice treat for the *moggies*, Tallie?"

"Mingin' Mackerel Morsels," Tallie said. "They're crunchy, fishy, and extremely smelly, so they must be good. Come along, laddies," she called and went to the kitchen.

Christine scooped up Butter and followed Tallie, leaving clean-up of the Scrabble tiles to Janet and Hobbs.

"Did you see that?" she asked Tallie when they were in the kitchen.

"What? You teaching the cats to jump up on tables after food?"

"Havers. I could never teach such a good kitten bad manners." Christine kissed Butter on the head and set him down next to Smirr at their food dishes. "Did you see the way our plan is going? Norman is completely lulled now that we've let him have a taste of winning. But it's payback time."

"Please remember," Tallie said, pointing at herself. "Still a licensed attorney. You aren't planning to bend a law and compromise a constable, are you?"

"We'll be fine. Just follow my lead." Christine patted Tallie's cheek and turned to go.

"Hold on. What about *him*?"

"I'll merely offer suggestions. He's bright enough. He'll pick up on them. I'm not sure it's humanly possible for him to live long enough to ever live down the Incident of the Undisclosed Nana, but don't worry, he'll be fine, too."

12

Hobbs had replaced the tiles on the game board.

"It was easy enough to re-create," Janet said when Tallie and Christine returned to the living room. "We weren't that far into the game and Norman has the picture he snapped."

Hobbs held up his phone. "No doubt there's mention of such catastrophes in the official rules and how to deal with them," he said.

"No doubt," Christine echoed.

"We thought it would be fair if we all draw tiles again," he continued. "And may I wish better luck in your draw this time, Mrs. Robertson."

"Always nice to have a bit of excitement, though," Tallie said.

"The Case of the Mysterious Moggie Mayhem," Janet murmured as she chose her tiles.

Christine pushed her rack away and sat back. "But my heart's not in it. I'm that worried about Florence."

"She's right, Norman," Janet said. "We're all worried about her. And *you're* right not to spread gossip, but—"

"But we're not asking you to spread gossip," Christine said. "We're asking you to listen to our impressions of her situation and her state of mind."

"What you call her state of mind might be the way she processes death," Hobbs said. He looked with some regret at the tiles he'd chosen and then pushed his rack aside, too.

"We realize that," Christine said. "And we appreciate you taking us seriously. Did you follow up on her claim that Malcolm came home after the ride and then went out again?"

"It's the determination of the Road Policing Unit that he died earlier in the day and that he could not have returned home as his sister says. In her distress over his death, she might have fabricated his return."

"Is their determination based on autopsy results?" Tallie asked. She watched his face. "Or autopsy results among other things?"

Janet saw the least bit of a nod at Tallie's second question. She asked Hobbs, "Have you heard anything more about what they thought I might have picked up or moved?"

"My experience was similar to yours—they were not forthcoming."

"Do you think it's something they expected to find but didn't?" she asked.

"If they knew how conscientious you are about trying to do your public duty, I'm sure they would appreciate it," Hobbs said. "But if you didn't pick up or move anything, then there's no further need for you to worry about it. Is there perhaps a wee bit more sherry?"

Which obviously means we've reached the end of that *conversational thread,* Janet thought. She was glad when Tallie picked up the sherry bottle and picked at another thread.

"Did we tell you that Florence says she won't mourn Malcolm?" Tallie asked as she refilled their glasses. "She said 'good riddance.' That seems to contradict the idea that in her distress she imagined him coming home."

"She might just be putting up a good front," Hobbs said. "Trying to be tougher than she is. Another thought—fabrications aren't always the result of happy memories."

"That's part of what worries us," Christine said.

Hobbs's phone buzzed with a text. They watched as he read it, made a barely audible "tsk," and slid the phone back in his pocket.

"Nothing urgent?" Tallie asked.

"Lachlann Mòr overdid it. *Mòr* meaning big," Hobbs said to Janet and Tallie. "It isn't his name, but it's what he's called—Big Lachlann—and it's how he does things."

"Like drinking too much?" Christine asked. "Is he *blootered*?"

"I shouldn't think so. *That* would not be like him."

"Aren't you curious?" Janet asked. "You can step into the kitchen for privacy if want to phone."

"It'll keep. His wife gets in a state from time to time. Premonitions, as she calls them. Best to ignore."

"Is this gossip, Norman?" Christine asked. "Shall I be aghast?"

"If you like. But no, Lynsey will be the first to tell you."

"Lynsey—is she a whippet-thin young woman?" Janet asked.

"Describes her well enough."

"She rode in the half-hundred."

"Did she now? I did not know that."

"She said something a little woo-woo at Nev's Monday night," Christine said. "What was it, Janet?"

"You asked them if they had any idea what happened to Malcolm, and I thought I heard her say, 'I said it would happen.' She said it so softly, though, and the others didn't bat an eye. But if she goes in for premonitions, then that might explain it."

"It explains the others ignoring her, too," Christine said. "Like Norman, here. Havers, pure and simple."

"Who were these others?" Hobbs brought out his pen and notebook.

"Rhona McNeish," Janet said, "and Isla, who's a district nurse."

"Lachlann Mòr is a district nurse as well," Hobbs said.

"Where did you pick up that tidbit about Isla?" Christine asked Janet.

"She and Lynsey came in the shop and invited me to ride with them. She was wearing her uniform. Don't you have a list of the riders, Norman?"

"I'm sure the Road Policing Unit does. I'll give Rhona a call. Now, what are your other worries?"

"There were a few tears last night," Tallie said, "so what you said about fabrications not always being the result of happy memories could be right. And Ian seems to have met her, or he might have been parroting Malcolm. He called her a doddery old duck."

Hobbs made a derisive noise, then apologized. "That was a personal comment and I hope you won't repeat it." An uneasy furrow appeared between his eyebrows.

"That's all right, Norman," Christine said. "You can trust us."

Another furrow joined the first between Hobbs's eyebrows. He took a rather large sip of sherry.

"And what he said is wrong in so many ways," Janet said. "One, Florence is no older than Christine or I. Two, if doddery implies wobbly on her feet, she isn't. And three, if 'old duck' is meant to be endearing, it most *certainly* isn't."

Janet hoped her vehemence at Ian's opinion would help ease Hobbs's anxiety furrows. So far, she didn't see that happening.

"Ian's remark meshes better with the distress and fabrication theory," Tallie said, "but what if it wasn't a fabrication? Do you know about the open window?"

Hobbs turned his furrows toward Tallie. "Tell me about it."

"According to Florence, Malcolm had a habit of opening the window in the library and leaving it open," Tallie said. "It sounded like a regular argument between them, or a regular conversation with her becoming regularly frustrated."

"Because nothing changed," Janet said. "He still left it open."

"Passive-aggressive foolishness," Christine said. "I'm glad Tony and I never went in for that."

"Your Tony was a good man. You were aye a bonny couple," Hobbs said.

Christine's eyes grew suddenly bright. She scooped up the kitten and went to the kitchen.

"She'll be fine," Janet said to a now flustered Hobbs. "But that's a good example of why we can't know for certain what's up with Florence. Grief comes and goes, and manifests in so many different ways."

Hobbs nodded then looked at Tallie. "The window?"

"Florence said that, apart from hearing Malcolm come in and calling out to him—"

"And getting no answer," Janet put in. "That sounded like another source of regular irritation between them."

"But she didn't see him," Tallie said. "There's no proof it was Malcolm."

"You reckon someone else was there?" Hobbs asked. "Opened the window?"

"I think it's possible," Tallie said.

"Aye. It is," Hobbs said. "Though all that window opening and complaining could have happened much earlier in the day as well, mind."

Tallie thought about that, adopting her mother's thinking pose, her chin resting on knitted fingers. "Not to belabor the point, but Florence said she closed the window when Malcolm left for the ride, but then it was open all night. It let in so much cold air she lit a fire in the fireplace, something else that irritated her, because she says she doesn't like going in the library."

"That's certainly a very specific set of details to fabricate. What else?"

"What else worries us?" Janet asked.

"What other specific details do you remember from your visit? Tell me what you saw and heard."

"Two visits," Tallie said. "Mom, you were there for both. You go ahead."

"Just the facts?" Janet asked.

"Impressions, as well," Hobbs said. "Describe the visits for me."

So, while Hobbs listened, Janet walked him up the flagged front path to the Murray house and through the door on Monday and Tuesday evenings. While he made an occasional note—or he might have been doodling—she demonstrated Florence's distracted, disjointed conversation, startled him on the stairs as they went looking for the dog, wondered about the state of the bedroom they assumed was Malcolm's, showed him the difference in the library one night to the next, and gave him a dose of Florence's anger at her two brothers.

"A problem, though," she said, "is that we don't know if Florence has always been this way—"

"She wasn't as a girl," Christine said from the doorway. The kitten had fallen asleep with its head nestled under her chin.

"We don't know if she's been like this in recent years, then," Janet said, "or if it's our visits that upset her, on top of talking to the police for who knows how long or how often."

"It might be all of that, plus falling apart under the stress," Tallie said.

"I didn't feel easy about leaving her Monday night," Christine said. She came and sat down at the table again, still cradling the kitten.

"I didn't feel easy about leaving the dog," said Tallie.

"I'm never quite sure who Florence is talking about," Janet said. "She says something about 'he' and then closes the door. Metaphorically and literally."

"Presumably Malcolm or Gerald?" Hobbs said. "I didn't or don't know either of them well, but apart from looks, they never struck me as much alike. Except now it sounds she's not happy with either of them, so there's that similarity, as well."

"She's not happy with either of them or the dog," Janet said. "I still don't know what *his* name is."

"*Tapsalteerie*," Tallie said.

"Aye." Hobbs nodded. "It does sound as though things are going that way since Dr. Murray's death."

"Going what way, Norman?" Janet asked. "And what gibberish are you spouting, Tallie? Don't you two start talking like Florence, please. We don't need any more jigs and jogs. Not tonight."

"There was no jog," Christine said.

"Tallie described what you've been talking about exactly," Hobbs said. "With everything that's happened, it's no wonder Florence and the house are turned upside down—*tapsalteerie*."

"I meant the dog," Tallie said. "That's the name on his collar."

"Of course. Why not?" Janet squeezed her eyes shut and massaged her forehead. "A perfect name for a dog in that family."

"Is the library at the back of the house?" Hobbs asked.

"It is," Tallie said. "I hadn't thought about that—about neighbors having a clear view of someone coming or going through the window."

"It's not out of the question, but unlikely anyone would notice," Hobbs said. "The houses along there have large back gardens. Quite private."

"When you called on Florence on Monday, to tell her about the accident, did the dog bark?" Janet asked. "We heard him Monday evening but not Tuesday."

"I don't remember hearing him," Hobbs said. "So not a reliable watchdog, then."

"With a name like Tapsalteerie, why would he be?" Janet said.

"How did Florence take the news when you told her about Malcolm?" Christine asked.

"Sudden death is rarely easy to believe. We started at a disadvantage, mind. She did not believe I'm a policeman. She possibly still does not."

"She might not, at that. But if she's this confused, and if she's fabricating to the extent that *we* don't know what's real and what isn't, then she seems to be living on the edge of something and she needs help," Christine said. "What kind of services are there for someone in her situation, Norman?"

"I'll stop round to see her again. Make some calls. I'll speak with Carmichael and Macleod, again, too."

No one spoke for a time after that. Hobbs rearranged three tiles on his rack and then he broke the silence.

"I'm not saying it didn't happen, that someone did not get into the house. There are people who target houses of the recently deceased. I'm not convinced it happened in this case, though I do appreciate the thought you've given this, Tallie. What do you reckon this person wanted?"

"The same thing Carmichael and Macleod are looking for."

"That's a jump."

"I know."

"But if it's something your mother might have picked up at the scene, then Dr. Murray had it with him. So why would someone then come looking for it in his house?"

"I don't think even Carmichael and Macleod are sure he had it with him," Tallie said. "It might be something valuable. And, yes, I absolutely do know that I'm fabricating."

Hobbs gave a quick smile.

"There's another possibility," Janet said. "Something I wasn't going to suggest for lack of evidence, but as long as we're going full tapsalteerie this evening, including the Scrabble game, then I'll go ahead."

"Nothing to lose but Constable Hobbs's good opinion of us," Tallie said.

"I'm often called out by my superiors for seeing the world through spectacles far rosier than allowed at my rank," Hobbs said. "Please, carry on."

"This is a far from rosy view," Janet said. "What if this thing Carmichael, Macleod, and person X are looking for is something that either the presence or absence of can prove intent? If Malcolm's death wasn't an accident."

"That's—" Hobbs started to say.

But Janet's phone trilled like an overamplified songbird. "Sorry, sorry. Forgot to turn it down," she said. "My new ringtone. I was testing it on the birds in the garden. It's like having a robin in my pocket."

"Answer it," Tallie said. "Before the cats attack."

"Janet Marsh speaking."

Janet listened and tried to interrupt politely. She finally stood up and broke into the flow with her no-nonsense librarian's *shush* voice.

"Hold on one moment, will you? I'm going into another room where I can hear you better." Janet held the phone to her chest and whispered to the three at the table, "I'll take this in the kitchen. Shouldn't be too long."

When Janet came back into the room, she pulled her glasses down her nose to look at Hobbs. "That was Lynsey on the phone. Her husband didn't overdo anything. He's over*due*, as in late getting home. He's missing."

"How can he be missing?" Christine asked. "If he's called Lachlann Mòr, isn't he too big to be missing?"

"Not a time for jokes, Christine," Janet said. "Lynsey's beside herself."

"Why did she call *you*?" Hobbs asked.

"More likely she called *us*," Christine said. "And the reason is obvious. We're vocabularily more reliable."

"We know the best words, too," Tallie said.

Hobbs looked at his phone again. "She spelt 'overdue' incorrectly, and she a teacher. *Tcha*. Look at that." He held the phone for Christine to see.

Christine ignored it. "What would Lynsey like us to do, Janet? Would she like us to come round?"

Christine and Hobbs both stood. Janet waved Christine back down.

"I'll call round there now and clear this up," Hobbs said. "If she'd been plainer from the beginning, I'd no doubt have it sorted by now." He started to take his plate and cup to the kitchen, but Janet stopped him. He looked sadly at the game board and his rack of tiles. Then he looked at the board again, and deftly added his seven tiles to the grid. With a sigh, he started for the front door, and with another sigh called back to them, "No need to see me out."

"Tell Lynsey we hope Lachy's home soon and that it's nothing more than a misunderstanding," Janet said. "If you see her."

The front door closed behind him.

"*If* he sees her?" Christine said.

"Did I say if? I must have meant *when* he sees her. What are you doing, dear?"

"Taking a picture of the board for Norman," Tallie said. "I don't know what HIRPLING means, but he just scored another triple word score and another fifty-point bonus. Ninety-two total."

"Limping," Christine said. "It means limping, and it's what he'll be doing if we ever play this game with him again. He must spend all his off hours memorizing dictionaries."

Tallie gathered Hobbs's cup and plate and her own and started for the kitchen. "Can I get anything for anyone else while I'm up?"

"Put the kettle on, will you, dear? And set out another cup and saucer," Janet said. Tallie and Christine looked at her. "Lynsey's on her way here."

13

"Why did you send Norman to Lynsey's house if she's coming here?" Tallie asked.

"He decided that on his own," said Christine. "Not your mother's fault, just her tapsalteerie circus. Help me put the game away and fold this table. Extra chairs back in the kitchen, too, so we look more professional. And you, Janet, tell us what's going on."

"Professional what?" Tallie asked.

"Are you forgetting?" Christine asked. "We are the Shadow Constabulary of Nosy Eavesdropping Snoops—S.C.O.N.E.S."

"The name wasn't a compliment when Daphne made it up, and it still isn't," Tallie said.

"But we showed her," Janet said. "We solved *her* murder. Oh, that didn't sound very nice, did it?"

"Not really." Tallie dumped tiles from the racks onto the game board and then swiped tiles and racks into the box with one sweep of her arm. "And if this is a matter for the police, then we should get Norman back here."

Janet recognized the signs of a lawyer daughter blowing off steam. It was venting rather than an eruption, though. Tallie hadn't reached for her phone to contact Hobbs.

"She's coming to see *us*," Janet said. "Lynsey didn't know Norman was here and she might not have come if she *had* known. I must say, I'm surprised he was so blasé about her text."

"That might've been the sherry," Christine said. "Something to remember if we ever need a malleable constable in future. Och—what are you doing?"

Tallie had marched over and was removing the kitten from Christine's arms. "I need him. If I have to listen to you two plotting and planning, then he will keep me sane. Do you hear that Butter?" She held the kitten in front of her face. "That's a lot on your shoulders. These two are relentless. Can you handle it?"

The kitten reached out a paw and patted Tallie's nose.

"Mental health through moggies. It's aye the best," Christine said, adding her own pats to Tallie's back. "And there's the door. I'll go."

As they heard Christine greet Lynsey and offer to take her coat, Janet leaned close and reassured Tallie. "If we hear anything that Norman needs to know, we'll call him."

"Two words, Butter," Tallie said to the kitten. "Witness tampering."

"Come ben, come ben," Christine said, ushering Lynsey into the living room. "Have you met Janet's daughter? Lynsey Maclennan, Tallie Marsh and friend Butter. You're not allergic, are you?"

Lynsey touched the kitten's head and shook her own. "I wish I could have one of my own. Lachy's never liked them."

Tallie passed the kitten to Lynsey. "I'll bring the tea."

"Come sit down," Christine said. She sat on the couch next to Smirr, and Lynsey sat at the opposite end.

Tallie came in with a tea tray and set it on a small table. She poured a cup and offered it to Lynsey. Lynsey shook her head. Christine took it and helped herself to cream and sugar.

"Mom?" Tallie held up a cup.

Janet shook her head, too. She sat in her favorite comfy chair. It swiveled so she could look out into the back garden when she liked.

She turned now to face their visitor on the couch. Tallie sat in the matching chair.

"Tell us what's going on, Lynsey," Janet said. "Why did you call us?"

"I didn't mean to interrupt your evening." Lynsey looked less the sleek whippet ready to race than a miserable, stray ready to cower. Her accent sounded thicker in her misery, and Janet, though she thought of her ear as well-tuned, hoped the sense of Lynsey's words didn't disappear into the brogue. "It's what Rhona said at Nev's. *Did* you help solve those murders?"

"We did," Janet said, "but—"

"Then can you help find Lachy? He's never this late. Never without phoning or texting."

"You don't think he met up with friends and forgot the time?" Christine asked.

"*Never* without a call or text. He knows what it's like for me. The charge nurse was the first to miss him."

"He's a visiting nurse?"

"District nurse, aye. Drives tremendous distances."

"My mum was a district nurse," Christine said. "It gave her great pleasure."

"Lachy loves getting out to folk who can't. Loves the driving, too. And he's a good driver."

But of course, after Malcolm, she's thinking about people veering off roads, Janet thought. "You've checked with the Road Police?"

"No accidents reported."

Neither was Malcolm's. Janet couldn't bring herself to voice that thought. Instead she asked, "What have the other nurses said?"

"You can read." Lynsey brought out her phone and jabbed it on with a finger. "When he wasn't home for tea, I texted the charge nurse and another district nurse, Isla. You've met her. There." She handed the phone to Christine. "Tracey's the charge nurse."

"The first question is yours?" Christine asked.

"Aye."

Christine looked at Janet and Tallie. "I'll read them out, shall I?"

Lynsey: seen lachy?

Tracey: saw before he left for ardtoe. out of range? lo batt?

Isla: that appt phoned. he was no show

Tracey: news to me

Lynsey: that's not like him. what about other appts?

Tracey: checking schedule. made his a.m. appts. other p.m. appts cancelled.

Lynsey: then where is he?

Tracey: lucky lachy free afternoon. whoop whoop?

Isla: dinnae fash. he's lachlann mòr. too big to go missing. he'll show up

Tracey: dinnae fash

"And that's the last I heard from anyone," Lynsey said. "And that's what they all say. As if *dinnae fash* ever did anyone any good."

"Does Lachy ever 'whoop whoop'? I'm not even sure what I'm asking," Janet said.

"I'm not sure Lachy would know, either. An evening at Nev's is about as far whoop as he goes, and that not often. He takes his job seriously, and with all the driving, it wouldn't do."

"How long since you heard from him?" Janet asked.

"When he went out the door this morning. I expected him home three hours ago. And really, this isn't like him. So I waited and I tried not to worry. But then I couldn't wait any longer."

"What did you do?" Tallie asked.

"I contacted Lachy's da and his mate Brian to see did they know anything. Brian said he'd go out along the route Lachy would take to Ardtoe, see if he'd car trouble. It's a long way to go, but he's a good mate. He found nothing. And Lachy's da only asked did I know what was bothering

Lachy. Thinks he's a great psychiatrist. Then I sent a text to Constable Hobbs. Lot of good that did. 'Sorry to hear that,' he said. Great eejit."

"No doubt Constable Hobbs was involved in something that took his full attention and he missed the urgency of the situation," Christine said.

"Is Lachy's dad a psychiatrist?" Tallie asked.

"He's a plumber."

"Sometimes the same thing," Christine said.

"Why have you come to us?" Janet asked. "Apart from what Rhona said at Nev's. What do you hope we can do?"

Lynsey shrank into herself and shook her head. The kitten had abandoned her and gone to curl up with Smirr. Tallie took a knitted throw from the back of her chair and tucked it around Lynsey.

"Would you like a cuppa now?" Tallie asked. "Or a glass of sherry?"

Lynsey shook her head again.

"*You* said something at Nev's, too," Janet said. "Do you remember? We were talking about Malcolm Murray, and you said, 'I said it would happen.' What did you mean?"

"I told Lachy."

"Told him what?" Janet pressed.

"Just that. I said it would happen. He believed me. He always does. He didn't want me to go on the ride. But it wasn't me who had to worry. I told Lachy that, too, and I stayed well away from Malcolm."

Janet felt the hair stand up on her arms.

"Did you know *how* it would happen?" Tallie asked.

"No, thank heaven. Can you imagine knowing a thing like that?"

"Do you always know when something like that is going to happen?" Christine asked.

"Again, thank heaven, no."

"Well," Janet said, stirring herself. "Let's be practical now, and we'll try to work through this puzzle. To be completely practical, we probably can't do much outside in the dark tonight. Not immediately anyway, but we can start with more questions. Is that all right?"

"Aye."

"Not to worry you unduly," Christine said, "but have you called hospitals?"

"No. People at area hospitals know him. I'd have heard."

"We should phone anyway," Janet said. "But the questions first, and with very good luck, before we're finished, you'll have heard from him. A list would be good so we can keep track of everything we cover. Tallie?"

"Pen and paper coming up." Tallie went into the kitchen and came back with a notebook and pen. "Is a list okay, Lynsey? It might be upsetting."

"Can you imagine what's already been running through my head? Here's part of it. You can start the list with these: phone died, car died, he died."

"From benign to horrifying in six words," Tallie said.

"Aye. So whatever else you put on it, this list can't be much worse than that. You can add he ran off on his own or with someone, but I don't believe that one at all."

Tallie added "ran off" to the list anyway. With suggestions from each of them, the list grew:

Phone died
Car died
He died
Ran off
Still with a patient, unable to phone
Car trouble on side road or farm track, unable to phone
Went off road, can't be seen, unable to phone
Health crisis, unable to phone
In hospital, unrecognized, no ID, unable to phone
Met up with friends, unable to phone
Fell asleep at a movie

Took a hike, fell, unable to phone
Kidnapped
Held captive by patient

"Let me see it," Lynsey said. Tallie handed it to her and they watched her read it over. She flicked it with a finger when she'd finished. "These two—movies or a hike—they don't sound like my Lachy. Still with a patient is more like him."

"Could that be what's happened?" Janet asked.

"Of all of these, that's what I want it to be. He's that committed to the job. But after all this time? All afternoon and evening? I reckon it's possible, and I still like that better than the other. These last two make me laugh, but."

"That was partly my intention in adding them," Christine said. "Mind, truth is sometimes stranger than fiction."

"You've not met him, have you?" Lynsey's eyes lit up in a way they hadn't since she'd arrived. "He's Lachlann Mòr. Have you ever been to the games? He's champion at all the heavy events—caber, stone, sheaf. Kidnap Lachlann Mòr? I'd like to see the numpty who'd try." She thought for a moment and then asked Tallie to add something else to the list. "Attacked by gang."

"Does he know gangs?" Christine asked.

"He's a nurse. He carries medications. They might know *him*."

"When was the last time you tried texting or calling him?" Tallie asked.

"Just before I knocked on your door. In case I could turn my bike round and ride back home and find him there. I left another message, too. He'll think I've gone mental if he gets them all."

"He'll thank you for your worries," Janet said. "But you rode here in the dark?"

"We've only the one car." Lynsey picked up her phone from where it lay next to her on the couch. She swiped and tapped the screen, held it to her ear. "Ringing, ringing, ringing." She let the phone drop to her lap and hugged herself.

"Where was he last seen?" Tallie asked. "Where was his last appointment?"

"I *dinnae ken*. Before he left this morning, he said something about a visit on Achnamuck."

"We've heard that name recently." Christine looked at Janet.

"When you were asking about the Mull Eigg Road the other morning," Janet said. She felt funny being secretive about the circumstances of that discussion with Hobbs, but also didn't want to get sidetracked.

"I remember," Christine said. "I can't say I'm familiar with the place, though. Where is Achnamuck?"

"Not a place," Lynsey said. "A road. Out of the way for traveling on to Ardtoe, if that's where he was going next. That's the way the job is, though. Lachy didn't mind."

Janet wondered if Lynsey realized she'd just said *didn't* instead of *doesn't*. And what did that mean? Christine was looking at Janet. She'd noticed the slip, too.

A knock came at the back door, and Janet nearly shot straight up to the ceiling.

"What's Ian Atkinson doing here?" Lynsey asked.

The others stared at her, and Janet felt the hair on her arms rise for the second time that night. "How do you know it's Ian?" she asked.

Lynsey pointed. "There's a gap in your curtains there. He's looking in. He just waved." She waved back. "He knows Lachy. He was kind when he came and interviewed him for one of his books."

"Ian?" Christine said.

"Aye. About veterans and the problems of suicide. Some of Lachy's patients are vets."

"I keep forgetting Ian's only an ass in real life," Christine said. "Get him behind a pen or a typewriter and the man has a brain in his head."

"Maybe he's heard something," Lynsey said. "Shall I let him in?"

Tallie got up. "I'll go. I'll bring him up to speed so you don't have to go through it all again." As she passed Janet—with her back to Lynsey—she growled a whisper through clenched teeth, "I'll warn him not to spill about Norman being here."

They heard Tallie open the back door and Ian's greeting, but over the top of him they heard Tallie. "Oh my gosh, the stars! Ian, come on, you have to see. They're astounding!"

They heard confused noises from Ian and the back door close. Janet pictured how Tallie must have grabbed his arm to drag him back outside for a rundown on the situation with Lachy and a fierce warning not to mention Hobbs's visit. She also thought Tallie had leaned on the first syllable of *astounding* with more force than strictly necessary, but with obvious satisfaction.

The back door opened again and a slightly wary Ian followed Tallie into the living room. But he rallied at the sight of Lynsey, and the best-selling novelist, who yet saw himself as a leading man, went to her with his hands out to take both of hers, and with a catch in his voice, said:

"Linda, my dear, I saw you arrive on your bicycle, and I would have been over sooner, but I had something in the oven. How are you holding up? We'll hope for the best rather than the worst, shall we?"

The cats, either reacting to the approach of Ian's hands, the catch in his voice, or the cologne he'd used rather liberally, left the couch and slunk from the room. Lynsey reacted the way a young woman under a great deal of stress and faced with sudden, smarmy, tone-deaf solicitude might be expected to. She fell apart. Ian froze, alarm on his face, then shrank back, and Janet found herself feeling sorrier for him than Lynsey. The tears would do Lynsey good, but Ian's leading man visions must not have factored in being faced with the raw emotions of real life.

"Sit here, Ian. Take my chair." Janet got up and shooed him toward it.

"But what did I *do*?" he whined. "Was it something I said?"

"For starters, her name is Lynsey, not Linda."

"Is it?"

"Yes, Ian. And she thought, *hoped*, you might have heard something helpful about her husband. If you hadn't mentioned 'the worst,' you *might* have helped. She'll be all right, though. She'll settle down. She's strong and Christine knows what she's doing."

Christine had scooted across the couch. Lynsey now sat with her head on Christine's shoulder. Tallie had brought her a box of tissues.

Janet's sympathy for Ian trickled away with his continued clueless gaping. With the last of her goodwill, she finally got him to sit. "It's the most comfortable chair in the house. And it'll be best if you don't say anything more, don't you think? You can observe and Lynsey will appreciate the support of your continued presence." Having run her reservoir of sympathy dry, Janet leaned close and cowed him further with a reminder. "Not a word about seeing Constable Hobbs here earlier or you're out the door. Got it?"

Ian mimed zipping his lips. He resettled the shoulders of his camel jacket with a couple of shrugs, tugged his sleeves and cuffs into place, flipped lank hair from his forehead, and crossed his legs—and he'd made a complete return to authorial elegance. Janet would have laughed but for the circumstances.

Tallie gave Janet her chair and sat on an ottoman. Christine had made good progress calming Lynsey—speaking quietly, letting the tears finish, and then letting her pull herself together. When Lynsey was ready to talk, Christine scooted back to her place again to give Lynsey space.

"What now?" Lynsey asked after wiping her nose one last time.

"Have you tried contacting Isla or the charge nurse again?" Janet asked.

"I told you. The texts were the last I heard from them."

"You did tell us that, but have *you* tried contacting *them* again?" Janet asked.

"Or are there other nurses who might know something?" Tallie asked.

"Not Isla. I left a message for Tracey."

"You haven't tried Isla or you don't think she'll be able to help beyond 'dinnae fash'?" Christine asked.

"Aye, that's about right."

"Which one?"

"Both." Lynsey looked at her phone again, put it down, and clutched the top of her head.

"Is Lachy's dad right about something bothering him?" Tallie asked.

Lynsey's hands moved from the top of her head to her cheeks. She spoke to her lap. "Lachy's conscientious. He cares for his patients. Above and beyond. He's the best thing that's happened to some of them in years."

Which either is or isn't an answer, Janet thought.

"You said some of his patients are veterans," Tallie said. "Is one of them Gerald Murray?"

"He takes their privacy seriously," Lynsey said. "I know a few. It can't be helped. But I'm not sure I should tell you who they are."

"At a time like this, it might make a difference. Gerald is a vet. He just lost his brother. If he were having a bad time, would Lachy stay with him, help him through?"

"But why wouldn't he let me know? Or answer a text or call? Or let Tracey know there's some kind of emergency?"

"You know him better that we do," Christine said. "Better than anyone. Maybe he's there and hoping you'll understand. Is that a possibility? If not with Gerald, maybe another patient?"

"What's Gerald like?" Lynsey asked. "I saw him come into Nev's, but I don't know him."

"If I may?" Ian asked quietly. "Gerald Murray is a fine man. I'm glad to know him. If he needs help, and if that's where Lachlann is, then they're both in good hands."

"Thank you for that," Lynsey said.

"I think," Janet said, "that we've come to a point where there's not much more we can do this evening—except call Constable Hobbs again."

Lynsey nodded.

"There is one thing, though," Janet said. "This might sound rather odd, but did Malcolm Murray carry anything with him during the ride on Sunday, or at any other time, that someone else would want? That someone would take or look for?"

"I told you. I stayed away from him during the ride."

Bagpipes started playing "Flower of Scotland" on the phone in her lap. Everyone but Lynsey jumped. She stared at it.

"It's not Lachy. Not his ringtone."

"Go on and answer it," Christine said. "Or shall I?"

Lynsey picked it up and answered and then put a hand over it and whispered, "It's Constable Hobbs." She put the phone back to her ear. "Sorry, aye. Can you not wait there? I can be home in ten minutes." She listened and then disconnected, looking confused. "He said not to bother. Then he rang off."

Immediately after, someone gave the wolf's head at the front door three banging knocks. Before anyone could get up to answer, they heard the door open and a familiar constabularial tread. At the sound of a second set of feet, Janet felt a flood of relief—Lachlann Mòr. But wouldn't he have phoned himself?

She looked at Lynsey, expecting to see hope there, too, maybe spilling over into relieved tears, but then Norman Hobbs stepped into the room. Janet had only a moment to register his somber face before he moved aside and she saw the man with parade ground posture behind him—Inspector Reddick.

Janet, Tallie, and Christine knew Reddick and liked him. He was quiet, personable, and the dark circles under his eyes were a testament to his professional dedication. He was also a member of a Major Investigation Team from the Specialist Crime Division of Police Scotland. Whether Lynsey knew it or not, Reddick's presence shut down most avenues of hope for a happy reunion with her husband.

"Good evening. We're sorry to intrude," Reddick said. He held up a leather wallet with his warrant card. "Are you Mrs. Maclennan?" he asked Lynsey. "I'm Inspector Reddick. I believe you know Constable Hobbs. We'd like a word in private. Would you like to come with us?"

"No." Lynsey's anguished syllable clearly wasn't directed at either Reddick or Hobbs. She turned her face away from them, drew her legs up, pulled her knees to her chest and started rocking. "No, no, no, no, no, no, no."

"Whatever news you've brought, she needs someone to lean on." Christine moved over again and put her arm around Lynsey.

"Mrs. Maclennan, can we call anyone for you?" Reddick asked.

Lynsey burrowed into Christine. Christine wrapped the throw around Lynsey's shoulders and stroked her back. "You'll get through this, hen. We dinnae ken what it is, though, do we?" To Reddick, she said, "You need to tell her."

Hobbs went through to the kitchen and brought back a chair. Perhaps he and Reddick had made a plan before arriving. They exchanged slight nods and then Reddick stepped back. Hobbs placed the chair in front of Lynsey and sat so that if she let her knees go, they might have touched his. He leaned forward with his elbows on his knees and his chin resting on his fists, and waited for a moment before speaking.

"It pains me to bring you this news, but your husband has been found, Mrs. Maclennan. *Tha mi duilich*. I am sorry."

"How?" Lynsey asked.

"We came to you first," Hobbs said to Lynsey. "Is there anyone else we should talk to? Is there anyone we can phone for you?"

She sat up, put her feet on the floor, and pulled the throw tightly around her. Hobbs hadn't moved so they sat knees to knees, and now her eyes didn't leave his face. To Janet, Lynsey's eyes looked fevered, devoid of hope. Janet couldn't see Hobbs's eyes, but his back, the slight tilt of his head, his even breathing, were calm and solid.

"I want to know how," Lynsey said.

Hobbs and everyone else looked at Reddick. Janet glanced at Ian. It was interesting to see him serious and still, possibly thinking of someone other than himself.

"The investigation is ongoing," Reddick said.

"Rubbish." Lynsey looked back at Hobbs. "Have you seen him? May I go to him?"

"It's best you come with us now," Hobbs said. He stood and held out a hand.

"Tell them it's all rubbish," Lynsey said, turning to Christine.

"They're right, though," Christine said. "Would you like any of us to come with you, Lynsey?"

"No." Lynsey unwound herself from the throw. Then, ignoring Hobbs's hand and muttering something that sounded like "great eejit," she walked ahead of the two policemen to the front door.

Janet and Christine followed.

Hobbs turned and saw them. "Mrs. Marsh, Mrs. Robertson, you'll not be coming with us."

"No, Norman, we'll be closing and locking the door behind you," Janet said.

"Very wise, Mrs. Marsh." Reddick opened the door. "You never know who might be wandering your neighborhood breaking and entering."

"Or knocking and entering," Christine said.

"We can leave your car here, Mrs. Maclennan," Reddick said. "I'll send someone round to fetch it for you." The flash of humor Janet had seen in his eyes at Christine's remark was there and gone.

"I've my bike," Lynsey asked. "How are we going? Can we take it with us? And where's Lachy's car? Will someone bring it round? Or take me to it?"

"Can we fit the bike, Constable?" Reddick asked.

"I'm sorry, no."

"I'll put it in back with mine," Janet said. "Is the bike locked, Lynsey?"

Lynsey didn't answer.

The bike stood beside the front path. Hobbs went to look it over. "It's not."

"We'll bring it round tomorrow," Christine said.

"Kind of you," said Reddick.

Hobbs gave them a considering look but said nothing more, and then he went to the car parked in front of the house. Reddick put a hand on Lynsey's elbow and walked with her to the car. He opened the rear door for her and then got in the front passenger seat.

14

R eddick didn't answer Lynsey's question about Lachlann Mòr's car," Christine said as she and Janet watched Hobbs drive away.

"It puts terrible images in your mind, doesn't it? And it's so frustrating. They're very good at keeping back key pieces of information."

"Norman less so, if you know what you're doing," Christine said. "We'll have to remember the trick of plying him with sherry if we're ever in a pinch. I wonder what else and who else that works with? You put the bike away. We left Ian alone with Tallie. I'll see if he needs protecting."

High-flying clouds moved in to cover the stars as Janet wheeled Lynsey's bike down her front path and along the pavement to her driveway. She thought she might smell rain coming. Or maybe it was the rain they'd already had. It often smelled of rain. A dog barked somewhere. A car in front of the house beyond Ian's started up and drove away. Janet went down the drive and through the garden gate and parked Lynsey's bike next to her own, on the deck beside the back door. She locked the two together and wondered if Lynsey's parents were in the picture and could come to her.

When Janet went back into the living room, she found Tallie, Christine, and Ian each lost in thought—although Ian had gotten lost in his while still in her chair. She dropped onto the couch with a purposefully loud and irritated sigh.

Tallie stirred herself. "You didn't hear anything more about what happened?" She waved a hand at Christine. "*She* only came in, stared at each of us, and then sat and stared at nothing."

"Norman and Reddick were careful," Janet said. "The only thing we might have learned is from something they *didn't* say. Lynsey asked about Lachy's car and would someone bring it or take her to it. Reddick's very smooth. He didn't answer and didn't call attention to that fact or the question."

Smirr strolled back into the room, testing the air with the nose of a connoisseur. He sat down a wary distance from Ian, looked at him, and meowed loudly.

"Hullo, old chap," Ian said. "What do want? Are you looking for a friendly lap?"

Smirr got back to his feet, turned his back on Ian, and did a full front-leg-extended, tail-and-rear-end-held-high stretch. Refreshed, he walked to the couch, jumped into Janet's lap and licked her hand. Ian might have pouted. He picked up a pen and notebook from the arm of the chair.

"When Norman asked if there was anyone else they should talk to, that was carefully phrased, too," Tallie said. "It was pretty obvious what they were getting at, but they never once said Lachy is dead."

"What are you doing there, Ian?" Christine got up and stood in front of him more aggressively than Smirr had. "What are you writing?"

With the speed of a cat swiping a bite of cheese she grabbed the notebook from his hand. She turned her back on him and looked through the last several pages of the book. "You've been taking notes. He took notes from the time he got here."

"Back-filled, actually," Ian said. "While thoughts were still fresh."

"I'm speechless," Christine said without taking her eyes from the notebook.

"It's how I process things. How I work. An occupational hazard, if you will."

"It's in extremely poor taste." Christine continued turning pages, eyebrows rising and falling as she went. "But there aren't any names." She sounded more disappointed than speechless.

Ian smirked.

"How do you keep things straight without names?" she asked.

"Code. Keeps things from getting nasty in case of losing one."

"Did you learn that the hard way?" Tallie asked.

"Not I, thank God," Ian said. "A bestselling author who shall remain nameless had that misfortune, and I learned from that mistake."

Janet heard a faint buzz and saw Ian's phone on the arm of the chair. He looked at it and tapped the screen.

"Texting, too?" Janet asked. "What is this? Mystery writer multitasking?"

"Again, an occupational hazard. Texts from a colleague with interesting connections."

"I'm appalled," Janet said.

"And I apologize. Although, I rather doubt you're as appalled as all that. In fact, you might like to know what I learned from my colleague—confirming what you already surmised. Lachlann Maclennan was found dead in his car this evening."

"Lynsey, you poor dear," Janet murmured.

"Where and how did it happen?" Tallie asked. "Was anyone else involved or hurt?"

Ian's answer came as a single word, but it was indistinct, and he held up a hand. Then he put the hand to his chest—possibly to his heart—and cleared his throat. "Shot. He was shot. I have no further details."

The enormity of the single word—*shot*—shook Janet and silenced them all. Janet swallowed and made herself breathe deeply before charging into Ian.

"What do you mean you have no further details?"

"There's no more than that in his notebook, unless he hasn't written it down yet," Christine said. "Or unless I grabbed it before he could."

"But for your colleague to know that much, he or she must know more." Janet stared at Ian until he looked away. She kept staring, trying to—*what am I trying to do? Pry open his skull to find the information myself?* She shook herself to get rid of the horrible thought. Another took its place. "Will Lynsey have to identify him?"

"It shouldn't be necessary," Ian said. "Depending on the circumstances, one or two people will be required, but neither of them need to be next of kin."

"You know a ghastly thing like that off the top of your head?" Christine asked.

"I know a number of ghastly things. I'm a crime writer."

"You must be wonderful entertainment at dinner parties," Christine said.

"That's not the type of dinner party I'd like to attend," he said. "I interviewed Lachlann for the WIP a few months back. I liked him immediately."

"For the *Whip*," Christine said. "What is that? Do you also write for a smut rag?"

"Work in progress. W. I. P. The book I'm currently writing."

"Is it? How fascinating." Christine surprised Janet by sounding as though she meant it. Then again, her smile looked as though she was filing the information away for future use—possibly in a way to irritate Ian.

"What sort of information were you looking for from Lachlann?" Tallie asked. "Does your WIP involve heavy event athletes?"

"Tangentially." He trailed off, picked up his pen. Christine still had his notebook. He put the pen away in the inside breast pocket of his coat. "The book involves the problems of returning military veterans. I don't want to say too much about it and jinx it."

"Say enough so we have a better idea of Lachlann," Tallie said.

"Sleuthing?" A bit of arch-Ian came through in the question, but Janet didn't think his heart was in it.

"Trying to understand a tragedy," Tallie said.

"One of the reasons I write. Well. As I said, I liked him. He was a dream interviewee. Thoughtful. Listened carefully to questions. Spoke sparingly but with intelligence and passion. If he was the same with his patients, then I have no doubt he provided excellent care. And I believe he provided an overlooked and undervalued service to his patients who are veterans. I asked him if that came from being a vet himself. That was a question he did not answer. But he spoke with passion about the problem of veteran suicides. I hope this was not a suicide. Lachlann Mòr was big in more ways than physical size."

Ian looked at his phone, slipped it into his inside pocket, and stood up. Christine handed him his notebook. He patted other pockets as though checking possessions he might have shared around.

"Good night—oh." He looked at Tallie. "You were right about the pudding—the amount of sugar. It's my mother's recipe. On closer reading, I saw she'd increased it for a church fete. It also takes longer than I'd remembered, so I'll leave it for another day. No need to see me out."

They watched Ian, minus his usual bluster or fanfare, step carefully over the kitten. Before turning down the back hall, he stopped and looked over his shoulder at them. "I wonder who identified Malcolm?"

The three women listened to his footsteps recede toward the back door, and to the door open and close. Then Tallie went to lock it. "Was that Ian who just left?" she asked when she came back to the living room. "Where was the buffoon who usually wears that jacket?"

"I caught glimpses of him," Christine said. "But did you ever picture him cooking?"

"I think this evening deserves another small sherry each," Janet said. Tallie started to get up. Janet waved her back. "I'll get them. I need to do something normal."

When they had their glasses, Tallie held hers to the light, turning it. "I have a confession to make. Something I did when I took Ian outside, when he showed up after Lynsey came, and I warned him not to say anything about seeing Norman here earlier." She took a sip of the sherry, then a larger one. "Ian called Lynsey Linda, and I didn't correct him. And then he came in here and I don't know if that made her cry, or cry harder, or—"

"*Pffft,*" Christine said. "That's a complete nonstarter. The buffoon we know would have found some other way to put his foot in it and make her cry. Not your fault."

"It was mean, though," Tallie said. "I did it on purpose, and considering the changeling Ian who just left, I feel kind of bad."

Janet raised her glass. "I propose—well, it's not a toast. It's a question, maybe a speculation. Is *anyone* who we think they are?"

∽

Christine came by in her parents' Vauxhall just before dawn the next morning. She knocked softly on the front door with the wolf's head. Janet had found the knocker in a shop in Tobermory decades before, when she and her husband bought the house and they and their young children spent summers in Inversgail. Christine took pleasure in reminding Janet that the handsome wolf was on track to be in her life longer than Curtis, Janet's handsome rat of an ex-husband.

Tallie opened the door and let Christine in. "Mom's upstairs. Coffee's in the pot." She led Christine to the kitchen, poured two cups, and yawned as she handed one to Christine. "Why the clandestine knock? I barely heard. And why so early?"

"It only seems early. You haven't lived here through a winter, have you? Believe me, when you do, you'll know you aren't in central Illinois any longer. You think sunrise at half seven is dismal, wait until late December. If you see the sun even thinking about showing its face much before nine, you'll think it's a miracle."

"You're saying the Scottish winter sun is a sullen teenager?"

"Sullen, and depending on the weather, snarling."

"But what I meant is why are you taking the bike back so early? Lynsey probably had a horrible night's sleep. She might still be in bed."

"I doubt she slept at all," Christine said.

"But we might be lucky enough to arrive before the police." Janet came into the kitchen wearing her jersey and leggings. "If they plan to call on her this morning, we're counting on them having better manners than we do."

"And what sort of manners do you have, going dressed like that?" Christine asked.

"I'm with it," Janet said. "My leggings speak Lynsey's language. Ready?" She and Christine headed for the back door and Janet called back to Tallie, "We'll see you at Yon Bonnie in time to open."

Christine had parked in the driveway behind Janet's car. She opened the boot while Janet unlocked Lynsey's bike and brought it through the garden gate. "Right then," Christine said. "Help me lift it. Upsy-daisy and in it goes—*oof*—twist it the other way—not quite like that—there— and—almost—and—no, it bloody well is not going in."

Puffing, they set the bike back on the ground.

"You knew that, didn't you?" Christine asked.

"I'll go get my helmet and meet you there."

Janet coasted down toward the harbor and along the High Street. She passed Yon Bonnie Books and Cakes and Tales and then pedaled out the coastal road going south. The ride wouldn't be as pleasant in a stiff breeze or if the road became packed with tourists and coaches. This morning, though, she heard shore birds crying over the sound of waves. Several miles along, she made a turn into one of the housing estates that had sprouted up on the southern edge of Inversgail.

Tallie had found the Maclennans' address for her, and she spotted Christine's car in front of a pebble-dashed semi-detached. The Maclennans lived not quite on the opposite end of the social scale from the Murrays, but certainly a much plainer life.

"I've been getting looks," Christine said as she got out. "Neighbors heading for work and school. I'm surprised no one knocked on my window and asked my business."

"You look respectable," Janet said. "Like a social worker."

"You look like a friend." Christine reached into the car on the passenger side and took a bouquet of flowers and a casserole dish from the dashboard. "I'm a canny social worker, as well. I brought props to soothe the nosy neighbors."

"The flowers are beautiful," Janet said.

"No point in going halfway."

Smoke rose from a few chimneys. Cars along the street started and puttered away. The Maclennan house appeared sound asleep. Janet wheeled the bike up the front path beside Christine, wondering when they'd gotten into the business of calling on the newly bereaved. *Not a business, though*, she thought, *and not a bad habit to cultivate.*

Christine pressed the doorbell and they heard it ring inside. They waited, hearing nothing else. Christine pressed the bell again. No one answered. Janet took an envelope from inside her jacket and slipped it through the mail slot.

"I came prepared, too. A sympathy card. I asked her to phone or come by. I gave her your number, too. I'll take the bike back to my place."

A young woman opened the front door of the other semi and called to them as they left. "Do you ken what's happened? She's not home. Police brought her home last night. After they left, someone else came round and she left with them. Lachy's not been home at all."

"There's been a death in the family," Christine said.

"Not Lachy's da?"

"No," Christine said.

"That's good then. After their *rammy*, Sunday last, it would have been too bad."

"Lachy and his da?" Janet asked. "Never! Do you know what it was about?"

"The language! I made the weans come inside so I missed most of it."

They heard squeals and an eruption of tears from somewhere in the house.

"Something stolen, that's what I'd guess," the woman said. "But I'd best get back inside before the wee *scunners* do each other permanent damage. If I see Lynsey, I'll tell her you called round."

"Tell her Christine and Janet," Christine said. "Ta, hen."

The woman returned Janet's wave and shut her door.

"You sounded like a native gossip, there, Janet. Now, shall we try wrestling that wee scunner into the boot one more time?"

"The ride will do me good."

"I wonder if Lynsey appreciates having such a chatty neighbor?"

"I wonder what was stolen and from whom. And if Lachy owned a gun."

"Or his da."

15

The four women stood in the doorway between the bookshop and tearoom for their meeting before opening that morning. Tallie, Janet, and Christine had given Summer a quick, subdued recap of their game night.

"How?" Tallie said. "That was the first thing Lynsey asked when Norman said he was sorry. Is it just me, or did that strike you, too?"

"Wait, have I met Lynsey?" Summer asked.

"She came into the bookshop a few days ago," Janet said. "She's one of the cyclists who rode in the Haggis Half-Hundred."

"Thirty, give or take a few years. Slim, athletic, dark hair—" Christine broke off with an irritated noise. "I have no idea if you've met her or not. Does it matter?"

"It doesn't, but I want to picture her," Summer said. "You spent quite a bit of time with her last night and you're worried about her this morning. And you like her, right? This has been a hard week for people you like."

"Please keep that in mind, all of you," Christine said. "Not so much for my benefit as yours. I don't want it happening again."

"We'll do our best." Janet moved so she could put her arm through Christine's. Queen Elizabeth was present and imperious, but she was a monarch in mourning. "What was it that struck you about the 'how,' Tallie?"

"She did say 'no, no, no,' when Hobbs and Reddick came in, but I didn't see disbelief in her face or hear it in that 'how.' It seemed like she already knew he was dead. Or maybe it only began to strike me that way after lying awake and thinking about the nightmares she must be having."

"Norman's words gave very little room for doubt," Christine said. "And her worst fears came true. Or her premonitions, as he said she called them. She'd been stewing for hours while she didn't know where Lachlann was. She'd worked herself into a state. It's not uncommon to expect the worst and then, when it happens, to have 'known all along.'"

"Norman made it sound like she's been in these states before," Janet said.

"I'm not explaining it well, but it's more than that," Tallie said. "She called us because she'd heard what we've done in the past. But we haven't traced missing people."

"We've solved murders and caught killers," Janet said. "What a bizarre thing to roll off my tongue so easily."

"Murders and killers are a step up from a husband who's late getting home," Summer said. "Is that what you're getting at?"

"That's part of it. Lynsey said herself that she didn't think he'd run off. I think she was afraid he wasn't just stuck somewhere or that he'd been in an accident. I think she was terribly afraid he wasn't just missing, and I wonder why. If we discount the premonitions the way Norman did."

"Grasping at any lifeline she could find?" Christine asked. "She *was* in a state, and if she was afraid her husband might have killed himself—"

"Then there are much better options than calling the local meddlers who've adopted the odd pastime of solving murders," Janet said. "I see your point, Tallie. We might think Norman is stodgy porridge and she might think he's a great eejit, but he's—"

"But he's our stodgy porridge and not such an eejit as all that," Christine interrupted. "You're putting the evening into a more peculiar light, Tallie, and it was plenty peculiar to begin with. Lynsey didn't mention suicide as a possibility. But according to her, Lachlann's father thought something was bothering him. And according to the neighbor, father and son had a rammy in the garden."

"You and I wondered if either of them has a gun," Janet said. "But is the cause of death official? The neighbor didn't even seem to know Lachy's dead."

"And we only heard Lachy was shot from Ian, but is Ian's source reliable?" Tallie looked at her phone. "I've taken up the whole meeting with this. It's time to open."

"Tip of the iceberg, tip of the iceberg," Christine muttered. She twirled her hand around her ear. "Thoughts swirling."

Summer had her phone out, too. "Just sent a text to James. He says he has no details." She put the phone away. "Or none that he's telling."

"Would he do that?" Tallie asked. "Have details and not tell?"

"I hate to break this up," Janet said. The others didn't move. "All right, then." She clapped her hands to get their attention. "New proposal. As we have thoughts and icebergs still swirling around, this morning we will institute the 'Walkabout Meeting.' We will continue our discussion, as customers allow, and circulate between bookshop and tearoom, keeping each other in the loop. Agreed?"

"We could just text as things occur to us," Tallie said.

"No, we couldn't," Christine said. "My thoughts are bigger than that and so are my thumbs. And think what happened with Norman last night. We don't need spelling errors or autocorrect sending us in wrong directions. I like this idea, Janet, and I have one word to say to you: WIP."

"Sorry?"

"Walkabout in progress."

They'd discovered that Thursdays were their quietest day of the week. Fewer day coaches rolled into town, meaning fewer tourists bent on spending their colorful Bank of Scotland notes. Janet had heard an explanation for the number of coaches from the owner of a souvenir shop. "Saving their petrol to crush us on Fridays and the weekend," she'd said cheerfully. The lull made Thursdays good for catching up on inventory, ordering, cleaning, and any of other chores so easily shunted aside for customers.

"It's the perfect morning to roll out the walkabout meeting," Tallie said after unlocking the front door and looking up and down the street. "No one waiting out front. No one walking this way."

"We won't roll it out, though," Janet said. "We'll stroll it out. Me first. I have a question for Summer."

"Go for it. I'll put on the strolling music."

To the strains of Gershwin's "Promenade," Janet sashayed down the center aisle and through to the tearoom. Quiet there, too, with only two tables occupied, and she crooked a finger at Summer. Summer crooked a finger back.

"You two have a confab," Christine said, nodding toward the kitchen. "I'll tend the teapots."

"Call if you need me," Summer said, then when she and Janet were in the small galley kitchen she asked, "What's up?"

"A question about James."

"We aren't officially seeing each other."

"Oh." Janet wondered if she looked wide-eyed, like a surprised owl.

"We're only slightly seeing each other."

"Oh."

"I like being forthright," Summer said.

"I think that's wonderful. I appreciate it. That wasn't actually my question, but I'll be forthright, too. I've been trying to figure out if I should be suspicious of James. Tallie's question about whether he might not tell the details he knows reminded me of it. I have been suspicious of him, in the past—wondering what he knows, what he thinks, what sorts of connections he has. All that kind of thing. And I think sometimes he's suspicious of *me*."

"Oh." With her hair pulled neatly into a bun, Summer looked more like a sleek, nonplussed harbor seal.

"So my question is, should I pay attention to these recurring suspicions? Although, now that you're slightly seeing each other, you might feel uncomfortable answering."

"Or I might not be the best judge."

"That too." Janet tried a forthright smile. She felt it flickering.

Summer grinned. "Don't worry about it. Suspicion is what happens to good reporters, and if I told James you're suspicious of him, he'd be well chuffed. He loves a good laugh. But I won't tell him. 'Slightly' doesn't include telling on friends."

"Thank you. How's your aim coming?"

"I discovered a great way to sharpen it. Anger. When I was practicing night before last, I heard some woman talking about Florence. I have no idea if she's met her, but that's beside the point. Florence is a friend of Christine's and she just lost her brother, but that's also beside the point. This woman was talking about her the way Ian did. As if 'old woman' is synonymous with deranged nutter. It just totally torqued me off. You should've seen my game. James made me stop playing because he doesn't want anyone to know how good I am. That cheesed me off, too."

"Were you still mad the next morning?"

"And yelled at you guys about rules. Sorry."

"No need to apologize. Those are excellent reasons to be angry," Janet said. "Keep it up."

"Will do. It's awful about the way last night ended, but I wish I'd been there for the game."

"It had its moments," Christine said, coming to the kitchen door. "You would have been proud of me, Boudicca. I lured Norman to Janet's with the same skill and precision you use in your darts game."

"Is that the same skill and precision you used to lure the cats into the middle of the game board?" Janet asked.

"*That* took skill, precision, and excellent cheese."

Janet returned to the bookshop and, after a drizzle of customers, filled Tallie in on the first leg of the walkabout meeting.

Tallie tossed aside a review journal she'd been flipping through. "While you were in the tearoom, my thoughts went walkabout on their own."

"Where did they go?" Janet asked.

"They were busy. They went a few places. The open window and the hole in Carmichael and Macleod's information, for instance. Anything or anybody could have gone in and out of that window. It's an unknown quantity."

"And the hole?" Janet asked.

"It's up for grabs, too. We have no idea what Carmichael and Macleod are looking for, or how they know to look for it, or if it'll give them answers when they find it."

"We do have some idea, though," Janet said. "It's something small enough I could walk off with it and not raise Norman's eyebrows."

"That could be something Malcolm always carried with him. Wallet, watch, phone. Or something a cyclist would have. Tool kit, water bottle. If you'd picked either one up and put it with your own bike, Norman could miss it."

"I saw a tool kit. Maybe they're looking for something that should've been in it. The other cyclists might know—Rhona or Isla. I wouldn't bother Lynsey with a question like that right now. And something else they might know. Why was Malcolm wearing tweeds and not bicycle kit of some sort? It wasn't a race, but was that how he dressed for rides?"

"I'd forgotten about that. Do you suppose Florence *is* right—that he really did go home after the ride? What if he went home, changed, and went out again shortly after?"

"Does that tell us anything new? It leaves us with the same questions about the open window."

"It makes Florence a little less dithery."

"But after a fifty-mile ride?" Janet asked. "Would he have gotten on his bike again and gone up the same road he'd been on? I'm here to tell you that my knees and thighs are amazed and agonized to think he could or would—with or without the wool suit."

"We know he didn't finish the Haggis Half-Hundred," Tallie said.

"You're right. Knees and thighs calming down. And surely Carmichael and Macleod asked Florence and the other riders how he dressed for the ride."

"That's something we can ask Norman."

"Who might not know, or might not be able to find out, because Sandra and Fergus aren't forthcoming. So," Janet said, taking pen and paper out of a drawer in the counter, "I'll start a list of questions for Rhona and Isla."

"My thoughts went one more place—our cloud files. Much as I love your walkabout meeting idea, virtual walkabout meetings are more efficient."

"Although wouldn't it be nice to think we'd only ever use it for sharing recipes and pictures of the grandboys from now on?"

"And pictures of Butter and Smirr," Tallie added.

"Absolutely. But you're right. Resurrect the cloud file. Create a document with a list of the things we want to know, another with working theories. We'll have to get back into the habit of updating with new information and questions regularly, and we'll share with Norman when appropriate."

"Ahem."

"You know what I mean. There are some discussions and pieces of information he really doesn't need to know. The cloud needs to be a safe place for us to throw ideas and information around—and scream virtually when we need to. But yes, share with Norman. Can you get that started this morning? The office is all yours. I'll call you if I need you."

"A couple of folders and a couple of documents? Mom, it took a couple of seconds for each. I did it while you were talking to Summer. There are folders labeled 'Malcolm' and 'Lachlann' with question and theory documents in each one. Plus documents in each for contact information so we can keep track of who we talk to. Feel free to relabel anything."

"Ooh—fly me to the cloud." Janet pulled out her phone.

"There's plenty of leg room for wandering to new documents any time and at your leisure. Enjoy your flight."

"Let the others know."

"Doing that now."

A short time later, Christine came to the Yon Bonnie sales counter, and quietly said, "Lynsey might have been afraid to say 'suicide' out loud when we made our list of possibilities last night," and then started back to the tearoom. She didn't get far before turning around and coming behind the counter. "Are there customers?" she asked.

"No. Let's not say it's dead, though," Janet said.

"Then if you don't mind?" Christine settled on the tall stool. "I love the return of the cloud file, Tallie, and I'll add that thought about Lynsey to it. The file is a valuable tool in our kit."

"Right, but that's all it is," Tallie said. "It's a good one, but it's just another tool. It doesn't replace real-time discussions."

"The give and take of face-to-face conversations."

"Would you like me to go walkabout and give Summer a hand?" Tallie asked.

"No need. Rab's there."

"Is he?" Janet looked over to the fireplace chairs. "Ranger, too. I didn't see him come in. Did he have any news?"

"You know Ranger. He never lets on." Christine shook her head. "Sorry. In poor taste. But no. Rab hadn't heard anything at all about Lachlann. We told him the little we know and asked him to keep his ears open. His only comment was rather vehement, considering it came from him. He said, 'Never suicide.'"

"I would never want it to be suicide," Janet said, "but the alternative makes me sick to my stomach. And think of poor Lynsey."

"I'm glad she wasn't home this morning for the casserole," Christine said. "Imagine. A casserole in exchange for a husband."

"That's not how it is," Janet said.

"I called it a prop."

"That's not why you took it or how it was meant," Janet said. "What did you do with it?"

"Took it to Florrie and gave the flowers to Mum. She was tickled, I should give her flowers more often."

"How was Florence?"

"She was Florence." Christine nodded and stared at nothing. She sounded and looked as melancholy as Janet could remember seeing her.

"That reminds, me," Janet said. "The thistles along the burn where Malcolm died—I think they're melancholy thistles."

"Apropos of?" Tallie asked.

"People sitting behind the counter feeling blue. Is there anything we can do for you, Christine?"

"I actually came out here to be useful. Summer and I revisited some of those swirling thoughts we had in the doorway meeting. She wasn't there last night and she hasn't met Lynsey, so she can only react to what we tell her and what we try to describe."

"A different perspective," Tallie said.

"Yes, but she's the first to say that being different doesn't make her perspective clearer or more accurate. She was intrigued by your idea that Lynsey knew Lachy wasn't just missing. I think we all found the possibilities behind that idea unsettling, but Summer came right out and said it. Did Lynsey know because she killed him?"

Christine had been speaking quietly, but those words made Janet and Tallie jump and look around to be sure they were still without customers.

"And because she's Summer, and probably reads a dozen newspapers a day," Christine continued, "she backed that up with an article she recently read about the difference between crime fiction killings and, as she said, the real deal. In real life, killings are less about elaborate and secretive plots and more about domestic disputes."

"I'd like to be aghast and say it isn't even fathomable that Lynsey did that," Janet said. "But I can't, so now *I* need to sit down." She prodded Christine and they traded places.

"I wish it were different," Tallie said. "But we don't know her, didn't know him, and don't know what their lives were like, or what she's capable of."

"And if there's one thing we've learned over the past six months," Janet said, "it's to keep an open mind about murder."

16

"This particular facet of an open mind is an unexpected perk to uprooting our lives and coming to Inversgail," Christine said.

"Perk is an interesting way to look at it," Tallie said.

"And looking at things in interesting ways is another perk to having an open mind. So let's look at last night again," Christine said. "We don't really know what Lynsey was thinking before, during, or after she arrived, so let's walk through it."

"And *guess* what she was thinking?" Tallie said.

"Dear," Janet said, "you're the one who opened these minds when you started guessing this morning."

"True."

"Call it educated speculation and probing," Christine said. "ESP. You go first, Tallie. Start with the text to Norman."

"She texted Norman. She didn't text him back when he blew her off. Then she called Mom."

"*Because* he blew her off," Janet said, "and she was frantic with worry. You didn't hear her voice on the phone."

"That's the first you've described it, but she was upset when she got to our house," Tallie said. "I have another swirly sort of thought. What if she put the typo in the text to Norman on purpose?"

"She couldn't know he'd react the way he did," Janet said. "You don't think now you're trying *too* hard to be suspicious?"

"I do. Let's dial it back a bit from her thinking he was dead and from her killing him."

"That actually feels better." Janet patted her heart.

"What's your alternative?" Christine asked. "Why did she think Norman and Reddick were there? What did she think they were going to tell her?"

"That they'd arrested Lachy," Tallie said. "For something stolen."

"The rammy report," Christine said.

"It says something about her and him that she *didn't* think that," Janet said. "She didn't offer that as a possibility last night. Didn't mention an argument or fight at all. If that's what it was."

"Something stolen," Christine said. "Maybe she worried he'd been caught by a householder and stopped. Permanently."

"As a district nurse, he probably visited lots of houses," Tallie said.

"He takes an interest in his patients," Christine said. "Helps them out. Looks around. Sees things they might not need or miss. Things he and Lynsey can't afford. Things he'd like to give her."

"Maybe he goes back and takes them," Tallie said.

"What does he do with them?" Janet asked. "They live in a semi-detached and don't appear to live beyond their means. They only have the one car."

"He might not be greedy," Christine said. "Only takes one or two things from time to time. Or he banks the ill-got gains somewhere. Under the floorboards, for all we know. Maybe all this skullduggery doesn't sit well with his conscience, though, and his father notices. Or his father finds out, or figures it out. He's a philosophizing plumber. He visits lots of houses, too."

"Maybe they're in it together and have a falling out," Tallie said. "Or someone else figures it out. One of his victims. Or a fence. Things go bad and bang. He's dead."

"Maybe Lynsey figured it out and she's been begging him to stop," Christine said. "Maybe she told his dad and asked him to get him to stop."

"The open window," Tallie said. "You wondered if Lachy or his dad had a gun. I wonder if Malcolm had one. Or Florence."

"I'm not sure quiet mornings are at all good for us." Janet got up from the stool. "Listen to what we're saying. I feel like we're assassinating the characters of two people we don't know at all."

"Three, if we include the person who shot Lachlann and if that person isn't his father or his wife," Christine said. "We can't discount villainy just because people tell us how much they liked him. People liked Malcolm, too, but then listen to Florence."

"Let's dial it back again," Tallie said. "Let's consider Lynsey's motive for surrounding herself with virtual strangers last night, instead of trying the logical route—another text to Norman."

"Or a phone call," Janet said. "It's not because she's phone-phobic. She called me."

"She wouldn't have known I was there or that Ian would drop by," Christine said, "or that Tallie was there, for that matter."

"I told her you were there." Janet sat back down. "And the *number* of virtual strangers might not have mattered."

"If some is good, more is better," Tallie said.

"*Mony a mickle maks a muckle,*" Christine said. "It's what you said, Tallie, but alliterative and local."

"She's the one who asked if she could come see us," Janet reminded them. "But she wouldn't have known ahead of time that she could reach me or that I'd say come on over."

"She might have called other people first," Tallie said. "We—you, Mom—might have been second or third choice. Let's think of who else she could've called instead of us."

"We know she talked to Lachy's dad," Janet said.

"We know she *said* she did," said Christine.

"You're right, you're right," Janet agreed. "She said she didn't talk to Isla again, but we don't know that's true, either. Rhona? We don't know how close they are. But *we* aren't close, and she called us."

"What about the person who picked her up last night after the police dropped her off?" Christine said. "Who was that and where were they when she needed someone to convince that she was worried?"

"But really, we might be blowing this out of all proportion," Janet said. "She might truly have been out of her mind with worry. Norman said she has premonitions. If she does, she might believe them."

"Her premonitions might well be real," Christine said. "Who are we to say?"

"If they're real, or only real to her, then that might be why she called us," Janet said. "I think you're right, Tallie, that she *was* afraid he wasn't just missing. But you know, we don't have to wonder about it. If she came to us because she was afraid of something, then we can ask her about that. We can ask her what was going on in her head last night, because she came to us for help."

"And we are nothing if not helpful," Christine said.

"But if we get the chance to talk to her, no one does it alone with her," Tallie said. "And we should find out if Norman knows about the rammy."

"If he doesn't know, then I reckon he'd like to," Christine said.

"Not just 'he'd like to,'" Tallie said. "He *should*. We can't hide information like that from him."

"Absolutely right," Christine said. "He *should* know. You are indeed a valuable asset to the team, Tallie."

"What team?"

"S.C.O.N.E.S. After being such an asset, don't be dim. Remember how Norman claimed he didn't want to spread gossip, when in fact he probably didn't know the answers and just wished he did? There are probably other bits and bobs of information like that out there."

"The rammy, and whatever the Road Policing Unit is looking for," Janet suggested.

"Yes," Christine said. "Do you think he's open to a trade?"

"How do you see a trade working?" Janet asked.

"If we find out X first and tell him, he tells us Y," Christine said. "We can fill in the details of what X and Y are as we go along."

"And if he finds out first, and tells us, then why don't we tell him we'll give him the lovely little *Kidnapped* as a token of our esteem," Janet said.

"A wonderful idea," said Christine.

"A terrible idea," Tallie said. "Look at me, you two." She pulled her glasses down her nose. "I am looking at you severely. There will be no bribing the constable."

"Well, we'll at least think it over," Christine said. "Here comes a whole family to your door. If the children appear to be house-trained, send them our way after they've spent money with you."

The family bought a postcard each and asked if the shop had a public toilet. The woman cast longing looks toward the tearoom, but the children reminded their father he'd promised pizza for lunch and deep-fried Mars Bars after, and she followed them back out the door.

"Mind if I go in the office and try to capture our wide-ranging conversation for the cloud?" Tallie asked. "I'll cast the part about bribing the constable in a good light. Or forget it altogether."

"Forgetting is probably best, dear. When you're finished, I might take a real walkabout and go over to Basant's."

"Do you want to go now?"

"No, get the notes done while everything's fresh in your head."

A spate of customers saved Janet from dwelling on the swirl of questions in her own head, and in between sales she started a grocery list for her trip to Basant's. After adding lentils, she looked up and was happy to see the mother of the deep-fried Mars Bar family return.

"I came back for a book and a cup of tea," she said. "Their deep-fried stupor should hold them for an hour. Two, if I'm lucky. Do you have anything by Ian Atkinson? What a dish. His detective, too."

Janet didn't mind hearing customers gush over Ian in whatever way they wanted. She didn't need to share their opinions. In fact, she and the cash register enjoyed indulging them. The woman bought Ian's two most recent books and sighed her way toward tea, scones, and a helping of dishy crime fiction.

Tallie came back in time to say goodbye to one of the stuffed Highland cows a couple was buying for their newborn grandchild.

"Maybe we should keep it at our house, so he'll have something when he comes to visit," the new grandfather said as he gazed into the cow's hairy face.

"You could buy two, so he'll have one at each house," Tallie said.

The man left the counter and came back with a Hamish under each arm. His wife patted each cow on the head. "Now *you'll* have one at each house," she said, patting her husband on the head, too.

"That didn't take you long," Janet said after the husband mooed and the couple laughed their way out the door.

"Dart points, mostly," Tallie said, and then to Janet's raised eyebrows, "Calling them bullet points sounds a little too close to home right now." She picked a piece of paper up from the counter. "What's this?"

"List for Basant's."

Tallie read the list aloud.

> dish soap
> tea
> lentils
> Lachlann's death: suicide or murder
> mushrooms
> raisins
> rammy: was there one? about what?
> walnuts
> who's gun
> where is Lynsey?
> avoiding inquiries
> helping with inquiries
> hummus

who came to get her?
Who knows habits of Murray household?
Malcolm's death: accident or intentional
ask Florence if anything is missing
marmalade

"Another good reason for the cloud," Tallie said, "is so we don't have to worry about customers wondering what kind of shop they've wandered into when they see a list like this lying on the counter."

"I'd just tell them I'm working on a mystery and they'll think I'm the next Ian Atkinson."

"Unless the person who sees it is local. Then they'll think you're loco."

Janet took the list from Tallie. "Sometimes I feel like you're the parent and I'm the child. That's an observation, not a complaint. I'll put my questions in the cloud when I get back."

She got her purse and sweater from the office. Tallie was with a customer in the travel section when she came back out, or she would have smiled to prove that her observation hadn't made her cross.

The walk to Basant's—formally named Paudel's Newsagent, Post Office, and Convenience—made Janet feel almost completely virtuous. It gave her a boost of midday fresh air and exercise, and she liked shopping local and supporting the other small business owners in Inversgail. She enjoyed the chance to schmooze and exchange news. On a day like this, she hoped the fifteen- or twenty-minute round trip would cool her temper. *Because I might have been observing, but I was most definitely complaining, too, and Tallie knew it.*

Basant's shop, not much bigger than the postage stamps he sold, squeezed itself onto a corner of the High Street. Basant claimed he stayed slim so that he had room to move around behind his crowded counter and could maneuver easily past customers in either of the narrow aisles. He'd emigrated from Nepal and bought the shop as a way to support his younger sisters as they furthered their educations. One sister was now a nurse in Glasgow and the other, reading history and languages at St. Andrews in Aberdeen, planned to teach.

Basant, always reading, looked up from his book when Janet entered the shop. "Mrs. Janet, a pleasure to see you, and because you always ask." He held up the book so she could see the title—*Shadowed Lives* by Annie S. Swan.

"Any good?"

"That's what I asked the librarian. She said young women at the turn of the last century could not get enough of Mrs. Swan's romantic stories. I've only just started and already I'm hooked. I found it on the Bring One, Take One shelf, and very glad I did."

"Then don't let me drag you away."

"Please let me know if you need assistance."

Janet took a basket from the stack by the door and quickly found what she needed. Now for the fun part of a visit to Basant's and the reason she could never feel completely virtuous—taking home something she *didn't* need. She went to the counter and set her basket down.

"The mushrooms look particularly good this week," Basant said as his fingers danced over the cash register keys. "Now, what else can I get you? Or shall I surprise you?"

"Surprise me, and also tell me what you've heard about Dr. Murray's death."

"About that, I have heard two things that surprised *me*. First, there are plenty who still believe he went off the road on his own in a tragic accident."

"Really?" Janet took a string bag from her purse and loaded the groceries into it.

"They believe it, or they wish it, yes."

"What else surprises you?"

"Not everyone has heard the news, and I wonder how that is possible in a village. My experience in my village in Nepal would have me believe otherwise. Or perhaps I am thinking of some of the mysteries I watch on TV, where village life is full of mishaps."

"Mishaps and murderers," Janet said.

"Every week, like enjoyable clockwork."

"The other day, Christine reminded me that just because we live in a village, we're not all idiots."

"Mrs. Christine is wise."

"My addition to her wisdom is that we don't all live with one ear to the ground."

"But those of us who do live with an ear to the ground perform a vital service," Basant said. "So tell me, what have *you* heard about Dr. Murray and what do you know of him?"

"I never met him. I *found* him, but that's—"

"I did not know you found him. I am sorry."

"Thank you, Basant. I can't say, from only seeing him like that, if he was a good man or not, but he looked oddly comfortable."

"Forgive me, but you do not sound comfortable saying that."

"It just seemed . . . it wasn't as upsetting as it might have been. But it was sad."

"Of course."

While they talked, Basant turned sideways to her—still obviously listening, but also looking over the shelves of glass jars on the wall behind the counter. The jars held a wide assortment of old-fashioned sweets.

"Anyway," Janet said, "what we keep hearing is that most people loved and respected him. That he did a lot of good for the community. But we've also heard a few negatives. Did you know him at all?"

"I knew him by that good reputation and by sight only, but to me he looked the same coming and going." He took down two jars—one labeled "Rhubarb Creams," the other "Dolly Mixture." "You and I—and of course your colleagues in the bookshop and tearoom—as business people, we have the opportunity to see and reflect on quite a wide range of human nature."

"Summer describes some of them as the rude, the mad, and the spiritually ugly."

"Tell me about it. I agree with her one-hundred percent. And that is sad, is it not? So often people make the mistake of seeing another person as only this one thing or only that."

While he talked, he scooped some of the rhubarb creams—football-shaped, rosy red on one side and the rich color of pouring custard on the other—into a small white bag.

"But you, your colleagues, and I are lucky enough to know better. We—and I take the very great liberty of speaking for all people because I am that magnanimous—we are rarely just one thing."

He unscrewed the lid from the dolly mixture—an assortment of multicolored fondant cylinders and cubes and sugar-coated jellies—and scooped a small amount into another bag. He twisted both bags closed, put them on his scale, and added the price to her total.

"Because although I am magnanimous, I also must make a living. And one more surprise, but not on your bill. A gooseberry hand pie." He took a crescent-shaped pastry from the case at the end of the counter, wrapped it in grease-proof paper, and slipped it into the string bag. He added a folded piece of paper.

"I'm no good at waiting for surprises." Janet took the paper out and read it. *Once a bossy law professor, always a bossy law professor, but still capable of being an eejit. Gooseberry pie from a silly goose. I'm sorry.* "I just left the shop and this is Tallie's handwriting."

"She wrote the note, scanned it, and sent it to me. I printed it and put the pie on her tab. Magic."

Janet took the bag and he picked up his book again. "One more thing, Basant."

He put the book down. She told him about the box of books on the doorstep and asked if he had any thoughts about where they'd come from. "It's a long shot, I know."

"As much as I enjoy reading, books are your area of expertise. Groceries and deliveries in boxes are mine."

Janet described the Dalwhinnie box, the glued flaps, and the note.

"This sounds like a careful person. Also a person who does not shy away from whimsy. Yet, leaving the box on the doorstep? Above all, this sounds like one of our people who is not just one thing. I have not heard anything to solve this mystery for you, but I will keep an ear to the ground."

Janet trusted Basant's ear as much as she trusted him to choose the right sweeties. So she found it interesting that his ear apparently hadn't heard anything about Lachlann Mòr.

17

Norman Hobbs dropped by Yon Bonnie Books that afternoon. Janet and Tallie, busy with customers at the counter while surreptitiously sharing the gooseberry hand pie, called hello. He touched the brim of his cap, put his hands behind his back, and walked up and down the aisles of bookshelves as though patrolling a beat.

"On the lookout for errant editions," Tallie whispered to Janet.

"After receiving reports of villainous volumes," Janet whispered back.

At one point it looked as though Ranger had decided to follow Hobbs, but when Hobbs came back toward the counter end of the shop, Ranger had disappeared.

"Gone to fetch Rab and tell him their work day has gone on long enough," Janet said.

"Or maybe to fetch Christine," Tallie said, nodding in the direction of the tearoom.

Coming toward them were Hobbs, followed by Christine, followed by Ranger. Ranger went back to his chair, jumped into it, and settled back into his nap with a gusty exhalation that sounded very much like one of Christine's *pffts*. Christine and Hobbs approached the counter, looking very much like opposing counsel approaching the bench.

"I have a good idea," Tallie said before either of them opened their mouths. She swirled a finger indicating the opposing counsels and her mother. "Why don't the three of you troop into the office where you can be comfortable, and the customers won't overhear anything that makes them *un*comfortable?"

Christine took the tall stool with her and winked at Tallie before closing the door. Tallie whispered, "no bribery," but Christine gave no indication she'd heard.

"Why don't we all be seated?" Christine said, waving Janet and Hobbs to the desk chairs.

"Won't you be more comfortable in a chair?" Hobbs asked Christine.

She shook her head, and in extending that courtesy, he lost the chance to sit at the desk with the foundling books. Christine perched on the stool, and when Hobbs sat, she smiled down at him.

"Now," she said, "I want to know if Norman is here as an ally or a spy."

"How do you mean?" Hobbs sounded offended.

"I think she means that *we* know that *you* know that we intended to talk to Lynsey this morning when we returned her bike," Janet said, "and she wonders if you're going to try to winkle out of us what we learned."

Hobbs looked less offended, but Christine looked betrayed.

"This is a situation where we need to cooperate, Christine," Janet said. Her friend looked less betrayed but still annoyed. Janet turned to Hobbs. "Ally sounds better that spy, don't you think? We didn't see or speak to Lynsey this morning. She wasn't home or she wasn't answering her door. Her bike is back at my house again. We aren't playing cops and robbers."

"I am happy to hear that," Hobbs said.

"But we do have a way of collecting information," Christine said.

"I am well aware of that."

"And speaking of robbers," Janet said.

Hobbs had been watching Christine, but whipped his head around to Janet.

"Have you heard that Lachlann Mòr and his father got into a rammy in Lachlann's front garden Sunday last?" Christine asked.

"No, I have not." Hobbs moved his chair so that he could see them both easily, and he took out his notebook and pen.

"We're concerned about Lynsey," Janet said. "There's been nothing on the news."

"A statement is forthcoming. Now, about this rammy."

"Strong language involved and a mention of something stolen," Christine said. "Is Lynsey somewhere safe? With family?"

"Do you know who came and picked her up last night after you dropped her off?" Janet asked. "*Did* you know someone picked her up?"

Hobbs was silent while he made notes, then he looked up. "You understand that I am not part of the Major Investigation Team, and therefore not privy to all their information?"

"That must be frustrating," Janet said. "Lynsey's neighbor stepped outside this morning when we went to return the bike. She mentioned the rammy and someone picking Lynsey up."

"We didn't tell her anything other than there'd been a death in the family," Christine said. "That is correct, isn't it?"

"Lachy?" Janet asked. Hobbs nodded and Janet added, "Shot?"

No one spoke for a few moments. Then Hobbs asked, "Official information has not yet been released. Where did you hear that?"

Again no one spoke. Christine looked at Janet, apparently happy to let her decide what to say, and Janet thought about friends telling on friends. *Rat out Ian? Is he a friend? He probably thinks he is. But friends have to help friends, too.*

"Ian heard last night," she said. "He knew it from a text before you and Reddick drove away."

"Interesting." Hobbs pursed his lips, making his own decision. "Lachlann Maclennan was shot and killed yesterday."

"Shot and killed," Christine said. "Not suicide."

"Do they have anyone in custody?" Janet asked.

"No."

"A suspect?" Christine asked.

"Not to my knowledge."

"*Do* you know where Lynsey is?" Janet asked.

"No. I do know Lachy's father is in hospital, having suffered a possible heart attack after being informed."

"What about his mother?" Janet asked.

"Died some years back. His father has lived alone since."

"The poor man," Janet said. "We'll hope Lynsey is with family or friends and that she and Lachy's father find some measure of peace down the road."

"Time doesn't heal all wounds, does it?" Christine said. "Though friends help."

"I'll call round to Dr. Murray's this afternoon, to follow up on your concerns of last night," Norman said.

"Thank you, Norman," Janet said. "We worry that Florence is a danger to herself or the dog or the house. The books, if nothing else."

"Mrs. Jones, even at this sad time, must appreciate having thoughtful friends."

"Mrs. *Jones.*" Christine pointed at Hobbs. "Forgive me if I remind you, Norman, but I asked you about Florence's husband, and you laid on that song and dance about not spreading gossip. Could you not have seen fit to tell us her married name? How would *that* be spreading gossip?"

"You asked what became of her husband, Mrs. Robertson. Forgive me if I assumed you *knew* her married name."

"You're right." Christine looked near tears again. "Of course, you're right, and what kind of friend have I been? And I won't, I can't, use being away in America as an excuse."

"You don't need an excuse," Janet said. "She didn't keep up with you, either. It happens. *All* the time."

"Mrs. Marsh is correct," Hobbs said. "Please also forgive me if I sounded critical."

"Thank you, both. I will try to focus on going forward and being a friend, if Florence wants that. I'm glad you're going to see her again, Norman. Now let me put my original question—what became of her husband—another way. What else do you assume I know about Florence?"

Hobbs looked at her steadily, imperturbably, until just before Janet thought Christine might launch herself at him.

But Christine didn't. She figuratively dusted off her not-quite-smile and said, "You're very good at your job, Norman. I hope you know that people appreciate that."

Hobbs stood, literally tipped his hat, and glanced at the foundling books. "Any news?"

"Not yet," Janet said. "But the books aren't going anywhere, so there's no particular rush. At this point, knowing who left them might be more for my own curiosity. If nothing else, I'd like to know if there are more where these came from. I don't want lots of donations, but I do like looking at old books and dreaming of finding something special."

"In that case," said Hobbs, "May I suggest that tracking down the owner is a better use of your time than tracking down armed people who might or might not be going in and out of windows."

"You don't really mean that," Christine said. "Because we *do* have a way of collecting information, and if we learn anything useful, you know we'll tell you. You're leaving now with several pages of notes you didn't have when you came in. You're good at your job, Norman, but the fact is, we make you look even better."

"The box might still be a clue," Janet said. "There's more than one place to buy Dalwhinnie and maybe more people who buy it by the case. Restaurants? Small hotels? Or the box might not mean anything. It might have been an empty picked up at the off-license. We could ask Danny, Christine. He might have some suggestions. And maybe the flaps tell us something."

"What about them?" Hobbs asked, reaching for his notebook.

"That's kind of you, Norman," Janet said, "but we can't ask you to spend more of your time chasing this down. It's the glue. The fact the flaps were glued shut, and I mean thoroughly glued to the point of being *fricking* irritating. Pardon my American. Any normal person would tuck the flaps in or tape them. So the glue might be a clue. A fairly useless one, no doubt."

"No doubt," Hobbs agreed.

"Basant is keeping his ear to the ground about the books," Janet said, "and I'll keep an eye out for a fussy fricker with a glue fetish. Again, pardon my American."

"Very good," Hobbs said, and took his leave.

∽

Yon Bonnie Books had a visit from another policeman that afternoon. Inspector Reddick of the Major Investigation Team, generally considered a friendly face, nonetheless prompted the combined staff of bookshop and tearoom to be on their best behavior. They knew Reddick from two previous investigations and the time he'd spent in Inversgail while convalescing from an accident. They also knew his collie, Quantum. They had warm feelings for Reddick, but felt more at ease calling Quantum by his first name.

"Good afternoon, Inspector," Janet said when he came through the front door. "How is Quantum?"

"Up to woof, thank you. He'll be pleased to know you were thinking of him." Reddick turned in a circle, taking in the changes since his last visit, and audibly filling his lungs. "Book air. Nothing like it. Ranger not in today?"

"Oh, yes, he's—" Janet looked over at the fireplace chairs. "I guess you missed him. What can I do for you?"

"Hobbs told me about some books you found."

Janet raised her eyebrows. Tallie raised the question. "Are they under investigation?"

"Sorry?" Reddick appeared taken aback.

"Sorry," Tallie said. "We're a little jumpy after last night. Jumpy and jumping to conclusions. We haven't really let anyone know we have the books."

"Give us an inquiry from an inspector and we'll jump to miles of conclusions," Janet said.

"Understandable. My motives are purely selfish, though. I'm a fan of old books. The few you have in your locked case are a bit dear for my salary. Would you mind terribly if I look at them?"

"Not at all," Janet said. "They're in the—"

Tallie cut in. "Just as easy if I bring them out. Be right back."

She wasn't immediately back, and while he waited, Reddick wandered over to the crime fiction section and picked up Ian Atkinson's latest. Janet waited on a customer and was just wondering what her daughter was up to when Tallie came back with the books stacked back in their box.

"This gives you the fun of discovering them one at a time, like we did," Tallie said.

"Shall I take them over there?" Reddick asked.

"The end of the counter is good. You won't be in the way." Tallie moved a display of bookmarks to make room for him.

Reddick rubbed his hands and took the first two books out. "*Swallows and Amazons* and *The Incredible Adventures of Professor Branestawm*. I read them both from the school library when I was a lad, but these—are they firsts?"

"Some are first editions," Janet said. "Some are early editions. 1940s, '30s, and before. They're all well-loved. That will make some difference when or if we put prices on them."

Reddick pulled out a paperback of *Cold Comfort Farm*. "Not familiar with this one."

"Find it and read it. You'll love it," Janet said. "But not that one just yet. We should probably put it aside where it won't get knocked around."

"Dear?" Reddick asked.

"More fragile than a hardback." Janet moved closer and spoke quietly. "Being such an early paperback, possibly quite dear. If and when they're ours to sell, we'll need to research them before we set prices. But I don't feel we can discuss that until we know more."

"Hobbs told me a little about the mystery surrounding them."

"Any thoughts?"

"Not really. You're the bookseller and should do as you're comfortable and see fit. Are you sure you don't mind me looking? Carefully?"

"Go right ahead."

Business had slowed to a trickle again, as was typical toward the end of a quiet Thursday. Tallie went to straighten and tidy before closing. Janet sat on the stool and enjoyed watching Reddick unpack the box. He seemed most taken with the children's books, stopping to marvel over the early edition of *The Sword in the Stone*. When he found *Records of a Family of Engineers*, he thumbed through it looking almost cross-eyed, suggesting either no affinity or absolute awe for that kind of work.

As he came to the last few books in the box, Janet caught sight of Isla, in her blue nurse's tunic, browsing the gardening section. Or pretending to browse. Janet knew the difference between serious and sham browsing. Bored spouses often performed the latter while they waited. Janet wondered who Isla was waiting for. She must have come in through the tearoom. Janet hadn't seen her come through Yon Bonnie's front door.

Reddick put the last book down on the counter. "Thank you, Janet. Time well spent." Then he looked at the time on his phone. "And now it's time to be away." He started packing the books back in the box.

"It's okay. I'll get them," Janet said. "You go on."

"You're sure? Aye, well, thanks again. Will you let me know if and when?"

"Deal. I'd like to picture you reading *Swallows and Amazons* to Quantum."

Isla waited a few moments after Reddick left and then made her way to the counter, stopping at the postcards and touching the calendar display on her way past. Janet thought that if she asked Isla to describe anything she'd just looked at, Isla would come up blank.

"Hello, Isla. It's nice to see you." Janet spoke a little louder than she usually did. Tallie hadn't met Isla, and if she heard, maybe she'd swing back around to the counter to catch a glimpse.

"Such a jolly American greeting. Nice to hear a shout of welcome."

Prickly as ever, Janet thought. "Did you find what you wanted?"

"Sorry?"

"While you were browsing. Did you find what you were looking for?"

"*Whilst* I was browsing? No, that's all right. No worries. I just thought I'd come in and have a look round. It's my short day and I found myself with time to kill."

An expression I would just as soon never hear again, Janet thought. Aloud she said, "That's fine, then. Let me know if I can help you," and started putting the books back in the box. She saw that Tallie had come to the end of the aisle nearest the counter, behind Isla. Tallie caught her eye and then stayed there quietly doing a bit of sham straightening.

"I should have let you know the invitation stands," Isla said. "To ride mornings. I could phone or text you to let you know where we'll meet next, how far we'll go. If you like."

Is this what Lynsey meant by don't mind Isla? She's just awkward at making friends?

"I'd like that," Janet said. "I might not make it every morning."

"Och, well, no one's asking you to."

Wheesht, Isla, Janet thought.

"What's your number?" Isla had her phone out.

Do I want this prickly thistle to have my number? Wheesht, Janet. She told Isla her number and watched her enter it. Isla hadn't said anything about Lachlann. *Is that curious or does it mean the official statement still hasn't been released?*

"Do you ken who'd like this one?" Isla picked up *The Bell Rock Lighthouse.* "Gerald Murray. Malcolm's brother."

"Do you know him?"

"Do you?"

"No," Janet admitted. "I saw him Monday night in Nev's, but I didn't know him or his brother."

"You met them both on the same day, then."

"I hadn't thought of it that way." *And I don't want to think of it that way, but now I'll probably never get it out of my brain. Thank you, Isla.*

Isla idly flipped the book from front to back on the counter. Over and over.

"May I?" Janet took the book from her and put it in the box. "How do you know Gerald would like it?"

"He's one of our patients. Typical vet. Bit of a head case." She didn't seem to have the same feelings about patient confidentiality as Lachlann, if Lynsey's view of him was accurate. "Does a wee bit of farming. Pictures of lighthouses on his walls. Harmless." Isla pulled the box flaps back and peered in. She let them close again without comment. Then, with no particular expression on her face, she said "Cheers," and left.

"You hesitated before you gave her your number," Tallie said, coming over to the counter.

"It was that noticeable, huh?"

"Probably not to her. She's probably not the best spokesperson for the bike riders club, either."

"I don't think it's a club in any formal sense," Janet said. "Rhona and Lynsey both keep saying 'don't mind Isla.' You can see why."

"You did a good job of not minding, though. And you can always block her if it turns out you need to mind her after all."

"That's what I thought, too."

"I'll finish the straightening."

"I'll put the foundlings back in the office and start the cash register." But first Janet took out her phone and let her fingers run up to their cloud file. She added a third folder labeled "Foundlings," and then created a document called "book clues" and typed a short list:

```
Dalwhinnie
glue
Paddington note
publication dates
variety, mix of titles
timing of drop off
```

Her fingers hesitated before adding one more entry:

```
Reddick's interest purely selfish?
```

∽

"It's been a long day," Christine said, coming through from the tearoom with Summer after they'd closed up and locked their front door. "I'm knackered and famished."

Janet yawned. "That's nothing new, but I'm right there with you."

"Please don't start that," Summer said. "Do you know what a yawn does to my aim? I don't have nearly enough days left to practice before the tournament."

"Boudicca is right," Christine said. "We should make an effort to take our leave on a more positive note. So, what have we learned today? Tallie, you go first. Think upbeat."

"The cloud file is up and running."

"Excellent," Christine said. "That's useful and shows we're working toward a goal. Summer?"

Summer opened her mouth, but her answer disappeared into a sudden word-engulfing yawn.

"We'll come back to you. Janet?"

"I am so cool and capable. I added a folder about the foundling books to the cloud file."

Tallie and Summer immediately had their phones out.

"Reddick's interested in the books?" Summer asked, reading the last item on the list. "Well, I guess I can see that. He's the quiet bookish type, from the David Tennant school of policemanship instead of the academy for musclebound bruisers. How'd he hear about them, though? Is that what makes you suspicious?"

"He said Norman told him," Janet said. "That's probably true. Wondering about his motive is a totally wild projection on my part."

"And yet," Tallie said. "I brought the books out to the counter so he had to look at them in front of us."

"I wondered why you did that," Janet said. "He enjoyed taking them out of the box, and he seemed genuinely interested in the juvenile fiction, but I couldn't help thinking there was more to it. Like he wanted us to judge him by his cover and not wonder what was going on inside."

"That's the way I felt," Tallie said. "I'm willing to believe it's just because of the upright, always-on-the-job cop vibe he gives off, though, because what did we expect him to do? Steal one of them?"

"Oh dear," Janet said faintly. "Something stolen, from the rammy." She looked toward the office. "*A* something? Or a whisky boxful?"

18

The four women looked at each other.

"If Reddick thought they were part of his case," Tallie said, "they wouldn't still be here. He'd have packed them back in the box and carried it away. But I agree, he might have been here with that idea in the back of his mind."

"The *Kidnapped* we have is the only one of a Robert Louis Stevenson set," Janet said. "When I told you that, Tallie, you said something about *it* being kidnapped."

"You think Reddick made this leap because an odd box of books showed up on a doorstep somewhere?" Summer asked. "Sorry. Sounds kind of random."

"Maybe not so random." Janet started ticking points off on her fingers. "Norman told him about the books. He's working on Lachlann's case. We told Norman about the argument and the 'something stolen' so he could pass that information along. And that's if Reddick hadn't already heard about the fight or possible theft as a result of his own investigation." She looked at her fingers, now splayed, then made balls of both hands and tucked them in her armpits. "So maybe our educated speculations and probing this morning were even more educated than we knew. And then there was Isla. Did you see her, Christine? She must have come in through the tearoom."

"And went straight through to you," Christine said. "She didn't even stop to smell the rose hip tea. What did she want?"

"My phone number, so she could let me know where she and Rhona plan to meet for morning bike rides."

"Did you notice she waited until Reddick left before she went to the counter to talk to you?" Tallie asked.

"She didn't want to interrupt, I assumed."

"That could be. Or she was really there to see what Reddick was up to?" Tallie said. "I saw Reddick pass our windows before he came in. I didn't know who she was, at the time, but Isla came along soon after. She turned her head, for a very quick look in as she passed the door, but she kept going. The next thing I knew, she was in here pretending to look at books."

"*Definitely* pretending," Janet said. "But we can't call the police on everyone who does that. She took mild interest in the foundling books, though. She picked up one of them and looked in the box before she left."

"She's a district nurse," Tallie said. "Like Lachlann. Lynsey texted her and the charge nurse when Lachy didn't come home yesterday."

"Okay, so not so random after all," Summer said. "What about this, then? One of the theories you put in the cloud this morning has Lachlann and his father thieving together. Maybe it wasn't them. Maybe it was Lachlann and Isla." She looked at the time. "I need to scoot. Do you want me to take the books up to my flat for the night for safekeeping?"

"I don't know if we need to go that far," Tallie said.

"Book people love looking at old books," Janet said. "They're like old photographs, like magnets. You're drawn to pick them up. Norman had no ulterior motive when he first saw them. He fell in love with that copy of *Kidnapped* as soon as he laid eyes on it."

"But from the way you described her, Isla isn't a book person," Summer said. "And if you start adding up the little connections and coincidences—there's nothing wrong with an abundance of caution."

"Book people who love looking at books also like owning them," Christine said. "One way or another."

"Oh, yes," Janet said. "There are famous cases of people who stole priceless books—lots of them—from libraries and collections. These aren't likely to be priceless, though. Too well-loved over the years."

"Have you looked at them that carefully?" Christine asked.

"Not really."

"Why don't we each take some?" Christine said. "Summer needs to run—"

"Good idea. Split them up," Summer said. "Leave mine in the office and I'll get them when I come back. I haven't really looked at them at all. Who knows? Maybe fresh eyes will see something you've missed. See you all tomorrow."

"Keep your eye on the target and your arm loose," Christine called as Summer let herself out the front door.

Summer relocked the door, mimed taking aim and launching a dart, and took off up the street at a trot.

"I know Summer's careful and capable," Janet said, "and I'm not trying to be the mom. But if we're considering the safety of the books, we should consider our own safety, too. Should we worry about her out on her own after dark?"

"In light of Malcolm and Lachlann, it's a fair question," Christine said. "A fair worry, too. My feeling at this point, though, is no. We have a lot of unknowns, but not much else. Do you feel differently?"

Janet waved off Christine. "What do you think, Tallie?"

"I agree with Christine. Not yet and maybe not at all. But this isn't a majority rule situation. We're still gathering information and evaluating."

"Because none of us likes not knowing what's going on," Christine said. "That's why I don't mind adopting the slur with which the late, not-so-dearly departed Daphne graced us. We *personify* the Shadow Constabulary of Nosy Eavesdropping Snoops. Although I think we're more sophisticated than that."

"Goes without saying," Tallie said. "So, Mom, do you feel differently? What's your evaluation telling you?"

"I do feel differently, but that's all it is. A feeling," Janet said. "It isn't based on anything concrete. Not concrete enough, anyway. Not yet. So I agree with you, and I'm glad we've all reached the same place."

"We've also all been in a place of critical danger," Tallie said. "Traumatic danger."

"I'm sure that's part of the feeling," Janet said. "I'd be daft not to recognize and admit that. The other end of that, though, is letting our questions—all the whys and the wondering—eclipse good sense. We can't let that happen."

"We don't appear to be," Tallie said, "but I'll be happy to snap at the first person who slips."

"The problem with you, Tallie," said Christine, "is that I can't always tell when you're *seriously* being serious."

Janet studied her daughter's face and then nodded. "She's absolutely serious. Thank you, Tallie. The four of us are good at watching out for each other, but having a designated snapper is added insurance."

"I was hoping for the title Snapper in Chief," Tallie said.

"I think that's appropriate." Christine brought out her phone. "I'll put it in the cloud to make it official."

"Cool," Tallie said. "I'll get the box."

"We've made the right move coming here," Janet said to Christine as Tallie disappeared into the office. "We've surrounded ourselves with good people. Well, with the exception of the ones who've turned out to be murderers."

"It happens to the best of people, I'm sure."

"But we have Tallie and Summer. Danny, Rab, Basant."

"Stodgy Porridge and Reddick," Christine said. "Maida, too."

"All of them, and Sharon at the library. And don't ever call Norman that to his face or I'll sic the Snapper in Chief on you. Here she is. Snap those books up onto the counter, Snapper, so we can get home to our tea."

"How do you want to split them up?" Tallie asked.

"Any way you want. Four stacks as they come out of the box or choose the ones that interest you." Janet started taking the books out and spreading them across the counter.

"You take the ones that are most likely to be valuable," Christine said.

"I'll take the *Cold Comfort Farm*," Janet said. "But really, until I do the research, I don't know. Even worn first editions of some books are worth oodles."

"That's secret bookseller slang," Tallie said.

"There's a good sampling from the Kailyard School here," Christine said. "*A Doctor of the Old School* by Maclaren, *A Vexed Inheritance* by Swan, *The Little Minister* by Barrie. Calling them Kailyard or humble kitchen garden novels is just as rude as calling us S.C.O.N.E.S. Literary snobs thought they were overly sentimental, but they probably outsold anything the literary snobs were peddling."

"Genre fiction of the time?" Tallie asked.

"And quite enjoyable, aye. I'll take those in my stack. Mum and Dad will get a kick out of them. I still have the other book at home. The Culpeper."

"Did you say one of them is by Swan?" Janet asked. "Basant is reading a book by her. He found it on the Bring One, Take One shelf at the library. I wonder why our foundlings didn't get dropped off there?"

"Maybe the donor was spreading the wealth," Tallie said. "We should check with Sharon. See if they've had similar donations."

"Oh, joy," Janet said. "But you're right. We should."

Sharon Davis, director of the Inversgail Library and Archives, was very good at her job—in part because she was *so* very good at inveigling community members into donating time to various library projects. "Time" often ended up operating to a loose definition. Janet had learned that the hard way and tried to limit her exposure to Sharon.

"Now, now," Christine said. "I see the look on your face, Janet. We were going for upbeat and that's not it."

"Why don't *you* talk to Sharon, then?" Janet asked.

"Because I know my strengths," Christine said. "Ignoring suggestions like that is one of them." She picked up *The Bell Rock Lighthouse*. "Danny might like this one, if the books end up being ours to sell. Do you know the Bell Rock Light? It's off the coast of Angus. It's the oldest surviving sea-washed lighthouse in the world."

"That's the book Isla picked up," Janet said.

"May I?" Tallie put her hand out and Christine passed the book to her.

"It's one of the lighthouses our statue's grandfather built," Christine said. "RLS, who stands at the harbor, forever gazing at the Inversgail lighthouse and thinking his granddad could have made it look more impressive."

Janet started looking through the stacks of books Tallie had made. "Isla said Gerald Murray would like the Bell Rock book because he has pictures of lighthouses on his walls." She found *Kidnapped* and *Records of a Family of Engineers*. "We have a trio of Stevenson-related books."

"Isla notices the pictures on people's walls?" Tallie said. "No, forget I said it like that. There's nothing wrong and everything *normal* about noticing things about where other people live. It doesn't mean she's casing her patients' houses."

"We're learning that suspicion is like seasoning, don't you think?" Christine said. "Too much, too little, or just right—it can make or break a recipe, or scuttle a line of inquiry. We can call the search for that balance the Goldilocks Quest."

"Who knew being a member of the S.C.O.N.E.S. would be such a folkloric learning process." Tallie glanced at Christine. "I was being serious just then, too, in case you were wondering. Really, who knew?"

"It's another connection, though," Janet said. "Isla knowing what Gerald has on his walls, these books, and 'something stolen.'"

"Not enough seasoning," Tallie said. "Tenuous at best."

"How about this, then," Christine said. "We wondered if the books belonged to Malcolm. What if they belonged to Gerald? Not stolen from him, though. Maybe Malcolm's death made him think about the decades and decades of accumulated stuff in that house they grew up in, and it prompted him to have a clean-out."

"The books showed up here the morning after he was in Nev's," Janet said. "How does that taste to you, Tallie?"

"Better." Tallie pulled *The Sword in the Stone* and *The Incredible Adventures of Professor Branestawm* from a stack. "These and *Swallows and Amazons* are old enough that he could've owned them as a child."

"Easily," Christine said. "*The Bell Rock Lighthouse* is part of a series for schools, so that fits in, too."

"If they'd belonged to him when he was a kid, then you'd think Florence might have recognized some of the titles," Tallie said.

"If she knew what books her brother owned," Christine said. "But after all this time? Maybe and maybe not."

"I didn't list all of them," Janet said. "She didn't recognize the ones I did, so listing more struck me as useless. She said she didn't pack the box or bring it. Malcolm might have packed it, but *he* certainly didn't bring it."

"Does Florence strike either of you as someone who quotes Paddington Bear?" Christine asked.

"Easiest question of the evening to answer," Janet said. "No. Well, let's each take a stack and put one in the office for Summer."

"What are we looking for with our fresh eyes?" Christine asked. "Do you want us chasing down prices for like editions in comparable condition?"

"You sound like a bona fide bookwoman," Janet said. "Sure, you can do that. Or just flip through them and see what you see. We're shy on seasoning at this stage, so any information helps."

"I wonder if that's all the note was asking," Tallie said. "For us to do the digging? Probably not, though. That would have to be someone who's too cute to be efficient." She thought for a moment, then said, "Christine, you never told us what *you* learned today."

"Didn't I? Och, well, mine's more what I *might* have learned while we were *not* bribing the constable."

"Is it upbeat?" Tallie asked.

Christine considered the question, her eyes focusing briefly on the ceiling, then the floor, and then the two waiting for her answer. "In fact, it's a lot of 'mights' and 'could bes,' and regarded in the right light, they can be seen as positive, so yes, let's say it is upbeat. This *could* be something else that moves us forward. Norman *might* have let something slip. Did you catch it, Janet? In his warning about not spending our time tracking down armed people who might or might not be going in and out of windows."

"There's an upbeat image for you," Tallie said.

"I'm not sure I did catch it," said Janet.

"And I might just be projecting my upbeat attitude onto it," Christine said. "But what if Norman, or someone else officially in the know, sees the two cases as one? Malcolm and Lachlann? Norman could have said tracking down armed people *and* people going in and out windows, but he didn't. He left out the conjunction."

"Interesting," Janet said. "Very."

"But we did a boatload of educated speculating and probing about the rammy and something stolen this morning," Tallie said. "And when Norman said that, hadn't you'd just told him about all of that? Maybe he combined everything to be stodgy and efficient."

"We told him the scant bit we heard from the neighbor," Janet said. "A rammy, strong language, something stolen, and nothing more. We didn't elaborate."

"Your mum's right," Christine said. "That possibly inspired, possibly in-the-know combo is down to Norman. We didn't burden him with our ESP about Lachy the thief."

∞

Janet and Tallie walked home together, each carrying their stack of books, feeling like schoolgirls with an evening of homework ahead. As they passed the cheese shop, their noses waylaid them and led them, helpless, inside. They came out again with an aged Dunlop so they could have toasties for tea. Halfway up the hill to Argyll Terrace, their phones alerted them to texts. They stopped and Tallie juggled hers from her pocket first.

"From Summer to both of us and Christine. The official statement's been released. No surprises. No arrest. No suspect mentioned."

Janet didn't say anything and started walking again.

"Mom? Are you all right?"

"Not as all right as I'd thought."

Tallie made the sandwiches when they got home. Janet thanked her and ate hers, and then went into the living room. She'd put her stack of books on an end table. She moved it onto the floor where she couldn't see it with a casual glance, and then she curled up with two cats and a crossword until bedtime.

In the morning, when the cats finally convinced Janet they were seriously starved, the three trooped down the stairs and into the kitchen together. Janet thanked the lads for not tripping her, fed them, and saw a note with a web address that Tallie left before going for her morning run.

Hope this doesn't put you off your breakfast. Streamed interview with Ian.

∽

"I was ready to hand in my S.C.O.N.E.S. membership card," Janet said at the doorway meeting that morning, "until I saw Ian's ridiculous interview. I'm keeping the card now, if for no other reason than to stop Ian's idiocy. The way the interviewer fawned over him upset Smirr, too. The poor cat sneered and left the room."

"Show them," Tallie said. "Do your impression of Ian."

"I have a jolly good theory," Janet said, doing a poor imitation of Ian's accent but an excellent one of him flipping hair from his forehead. "I'm reaching out to the Road Policing Unit and, what ho, they appear to be jolly well receptive."

"The bloody fool," Christine said.

"What's his theory?" Summer asked.

"That's the kicker," Janet said. "He wouldn't tell the interviewer, so I find it hard to believe he really has one. He might be working on one, but in that case, he's nosing around and meddling and who knows what kind of evidence he's screwing up."

"Don't you love it when her dander's up?" Tallie said.

"I'm glad it amuses you," Janet said. "Thank you, though, for finding exactly what I needed to get me going again this morning. With the official statement out, and now with Ian loose, we need to focus. Are there any new insights?"

"I have a new idea about the puzzle of Florence being so sure Malcolm came home after the ride," Tallie said. "It's my earlier idea tarted up. It explains the open window, too. Malcolm didn't come home, but someone else did, someone who knew Malcolm's habits. Someone who might have an interest in going through the books there. Maybe even packed some of them up in a handy box. Maybe Gerald."

"Yesterday or the day before, you wondered if it was an intruder," Janet said.

"From the way Florence talks about Gerald, he's kind of the same thing," Tallie said.

"I like this," said Christine. "A lot of pieces fit together. Florence didn't see *who* came in that afternoon, and we know from our experience at Nev's that Gerald will come and go without a word. We know he likes books. Janet spotted one under his arm that night, and Danny says he always has one with him. Last night we wondered if the foundlings are his. A book about the engineering feat of the Bell Rock Lighthouse is just the kind of thing to impress a boy who grows up to join the Royal Engineers. By report, he has pictures of lighthouses on his walls." She looked at each of the others. "What do you think?"

"It's worth following up," Summer said.

"Sure," Tallie said. "Whether the books are Gerald's or Malcolm's or belonged to both of them."

Janet nodded agreement.

"Good," Christine said. "I think we should call on him."

"Wait." Janet had started to nod again, but stopped. "On Gerald?"

"Who did you think I meant?"

"I—oh, but don't you remember when we showed up that first time at Florence's? It didn't go all that well." Janet pictured Gerald at the bar in Nev's, looking like a grizzled wolf in lean times, with Danny standing guard. Had Danny been guarding the wolf or guarding them *from* the wolf? "I don't know, Christine."

"It'll be fine," Christine said.

"But in his time of grief?" Janet said.

"*Is* he grieved?" Christine asked.

"Why wouldn't he be? Reclusive doesn't mean unfeeling," Janet said.

"Although it might," said Summer. "What else do you know about him?"

"He lives local, but Danny says he lives on his own terms," Christine said.

"And what are his terms?" Summer asked.

"Keeping to himself," Janet said.

"But he was in Nev's Monday night," Christine said, "and that implies a need for human contact."

"Or whisky," said Tallie.

"This isn't a *whigmaleerie*," Christine said.

"As if we'd go in for a *whigma*-whatsit," Janet said. "As if I'd know one if I ever saw it."

"*Leerie*," Christine said. "Whigmaleerie. It's a whim, a fanciful notion, but it's Scottish, thus more robustly onomatopoetic, and it's exactly what this visit to Gerald is *not*. Listen to me, Janet. One of the reasons I was successful as a school social worker, and thoroughly enjoyed my work, is because I looked at every problem as a mystery to be solved. You know I'm a nut—not a *bampot*—but an avid mystery reader. I approached my families like mysteries, knowing that if I could uncover the right clues, and put them together so they answered the questions, then I could help my clients. I particularly enjoyed working with extended families. I've a real touch for connecting with people, and I believe wholeheartedly in the power of intergenerational connections for finding answers."

"It's hard to argue with that," Janet said. *Hard to argue with Queen Elizabeth ever,* she thought. *QE II—the avenging social worker.* Even so, she didn't quite see how intergenerational connections were going to help them approach a lean, lone wolf.

"You'll see," Christine said. "It'll be fine. I'll call ahead this time."

"You have his number?" Janet asked.

"Amazingly enough, he's in the directory," Summer said. "I found him while she was stirring us to action." She held her phone for Christine to see.

"In that case"—Christine tapped the number into her phone—"why wait?"

Janet, Tallie, and Summer watched Christine place the call. All four of them jumped slightly when Gerald answered.

Christine turned her back to them while she talked, and they gave her that much privacy. She didn't move away, though, and they didn't either. From Christine's end, it sounded like a pleasant, wide-ranging chat. She mentioned books in general and the books in the box, Lachlann, Danny and Nev's, remembering him when she was a girl, and a pantomime she and Florence were in. She listened a good deal, too. Then they heard her ask if she could bring him anything and what or who Cyrus was.

"I'll see you this evening, then, Gerald," Christine said. "I'll bring my friend Janet. You and Cyrus will like her. Cheery-bye the noo." She disconnected and turned back around, looking as surprised as she sounded. "He says come."

"And maybe a bit more than that," Tallie said. "You sounded almost like old pals."

"I'm actually quite gobsmacked. There I was, afraid I was blethering on, but he blethered right back and sounded such a lovely man. He said he likes books, Lachy, and Danny and Nev's. He said he was sorry, but he doesn't remember me as a girl, nor does he remember leaving a box of books on anyone's doorstep. He doesn't get many callers other than Lachy. When I asked what I can bring him, he said toffee. No hesitation at all. He says the door will be open and not to mind Cyrus."

"And who or what *is* Cyrus?" Janet asked. "We heard you ask that."

"I think he's a dog, but don't hold me to it. When I asked, Gerald laughed and said, 'Not old enough to be retired like me. He looks after me. He's gentle as a lamb.'"

"I'm glad you had the good sense not to mention your aversion to sheep," Janet said. "It doesn't sound as though Gerald looks the same coming and going at all."

"No, and the visit isn't a whigmaleerie at all," Christine said. "We're doing a good deed. My only misgiving is that he didn't seem to have heard about Lachy and I hate to bring that kind of bad news."

∞

"What and where is this Achnamuck where Gerald has his croft?" Janet asked as they closed the shop and tearoom that evening.

Tallie found Achnamuck for them—a road they could reach by driving out the way Janet had bicycled the morning she'd found Malcolm, and going over the Beaton Bridge, then several miles beyond. They promised Tallie and Summer they'd be careful and would keep in touch. They took the box of books with them and stopped at Basant's before leaving Inversgail.

"I know it is not polite and it is not the correct pronunciation," Basant said when they asked for toffee pudding, "but toffee always reminds me of the poem about the Welshman. Do you know it?

> *"Taffy was a Welshman,*
> *Taffy was a thief.*
> *Taffy came to my house and stole a piece of beef.*

I went to Taffy's house, Taffy was not in.
Taffy came to my house and stole a silver pin.

"The reason I think of that might possibly be because when we were lucky enough to have taffy or toffee when we were children, my small sisters thought they were very clever to steal my share."

"The wee rascals," Christine said.

"So they thought," Basant said. "They didn't know that I would set aside a thieves' portion for them."

"That was kind and generous," Janet said.

"It taught me to remember that thieves live close to home. Is the pudding for your mother, Mrs. Christine? I heard she hasn't been well."

"She's on the mend, thank you. No, this is for Gerald Murray."

"Then you are kind and generous as well," Basant said, and gave them an extra-large portion. "You heard the terrible news about Lachlann Mòr?"

"We did. Did you know him?"

"A friendly chap. His death has shaken me and I am sorry for his young widow. There was none better at tossing the caber, none gentler with those in need."

∞

"Was it just me, or did Basant's rhyme sound a lot like *Lachy* was a thief?" Janet asked when they were back in the car.

"It occurred to me, too."

Soon after, Janet heard Christine humming to herself. "What's that you're singing?" she asked.

"Not singing. Composing," Christine said. "What do you think of this? It's a pastiche.

"Lachy was a nurse-man, Lachy was a thief.
Lachy came to my house and stole my handkerchief.

I went to Lachy's house, just to have a look.
Lachy came to my house and stole a precious book.
I went to Lachy's house and called for Lynsey dearie.
Lynsey came to my house and told a whigmaleerie.

"I used poetic license there at the end. In my rendition, whigmaleerie means something closer to taradiddle. What are you doing?"

"Typing it into the cloud," Janet said. "Sometimes truth is stranger than doggerel."

Christine slowed as they neared the Beaton Bridge, and then pulled onto the verge and stopped.

"Why are we stopping?" Janet asked.

"Just for a moment. I want to do something."

"Do what?"

Christine got out without answering. Janet climbed out, too, her antennae quivering. But Christine did nothing more than stand in the middle of the span and lean against the solid stone wall so she could look along the burn toward where Malcolm and his bicycle had come to rest. Janet went to stand beside her.

"I wanted to pay my respects," Christine said. She pulled something from her coat pocket and dropped it over the side into the gurgling burn below.

"What was that?"

"A piece of juniper. The plant badge of Clan Murray. Something to say goodbye to an old friend. Not really a friend, though. Goodbye to a memory, a vestige of my childhood. Come on, let's go call on another."

When they were back in the car, buckling their seat belts, Christine said, "Did you know that if you ingest juniper, you're more likely to see ghosts?"

"You haven't been drinking gin, have you?" Janet asked.

"I'm not partial to the taste. I'm not partial to the idea of seeing ghosts, either."

Achnamuck Road wasn't much more than a single lane track up and over one brae to the isolation of the next. Gerald's house, when they saw it, wasn't anything more than it needed to be—long, low, and whitewashed, with a door in the middle and a chimney at either end, the snug comfort of smoke rising from the nearer one. The roof, rather than traditional thatch, was corrugated tin the color of a blue Highland sky.

"It looks fresh and well cared for," Christine said. "*Lang* may his *lum reek*."

"I beg your pardon?"

"Long may his chimney smoke," Christine said. "I don't see a car or truck. He must have one, though, to get into town."

A granite barn with a pen alongside stood beyond the house. A ewe and two half-grown lambs watched from the pen.

"In the old days, he might have kept the animals inside with him at one end of the house," Christine said. "I don't see the dog."

"*Is* Cyrus a dog?"

"We're not to mind him, whoever he is."

They parked on a level area where other vehicles had clearly come and gone, and got out of the car wondering who the last person to come visit had been.

"Lachlann or Isla," Christine said.

"Or Norman when he told him about Malcolm," Janet said. "I'll take the box. You bring the pudding."

They knocked and called and found the door unlatched, as Gerald said it would be, and heard an answering woof that reminded Janet of Malcolm's dog.

"Hello, there," Christine said to the collie who met them when she opened the door. "You must be Cyrus. I'm Christine and this is Janet."

"There's something so businesslike about a smooth collie," Janet said. "Like Reddick's Quantum. Hello, dear. I'd offer to shake paws, but I have this box." She held the box so the dog could sniff it.

They'd come into a square entry with enough room for a couple of people to greet a dog, wipe their feet or leave a pair of garden boots, set down a basket or umbrella, hang a coat, take off a hat, tidy their hair.

"Take us to your friend, Cyrus," Christine said. "Come along, Janet."

The dog sat in front of Janet, stared at the box, and growled low in his throat.

"It's all right, Cyrus. It's just a box of books." Janet stepped sideways. The dog growled again. "You go on, Christine. I'll stay here until Gerald calls him."

"Try putting the box down."

"What do you think, Cyrus?" Janet asked.

At the name, the dog looked up at her and then turned back to the box. Janet slowly lowered the box a few inches. The dog watched. She lowered it a few more inches and stopped. The dog looked at her again as though offering encouragement.

"Maybe it's the Dalwhinnie he doesn't like," Janet said.

"He might be more of an Oban or Lagavulin man," Christine said.

Janet lowered the box to the floor. The dog bumped it with his nose and then licked her hand. "Don't keep Gerald waiting, Christine. This is working. We'll be along."

"Righty-oh." Christine left the entry calling, "Hello, Gerald. It's Christine and Janet and lovely toffee pudding."

Janet rubbed the dog's ears and caught the tag on his collar. "You *are* Cyrus. It's good to meet you." Below his name on the tag was written *He who bestows care.* "You're doing a fine job of bestowing care on your friend. You saved him from the unwanted clutter of stray boxes. Let's go see him."

"Janet?" Christine's voice sounded loud in the quiet house. "Janet? *Janet!*"

Janet stumbled over the box, but kept herself from falling, and then she followed Cyrus, running toward Christine's urgent calls. They ran straight ahead, through the narrow house, and into an extension made entirely of floor to ceiling windows that hadn't been visible from the front. A fantastic panoramic view of the sea, from all three sides of the room, drew Janet's eyes first, then Christine's white face and open mouth, and then Gerald Murray on the slate floor, and the pool of blood around him.

19

gain. How can it be again? I don't want to hear that word. I don't want to be here. I don't . . .

Janet was having trouble concentrating, kept seeing the dagger and Gerald. She swallowed and focused instead on remembering the details of the house so at odds with the man who'd walked silently in and out of Nev's.

Had he added the extension himself? Rebuilt the interior of the original house? The place was Spartan, like a man who didn't say much when he went to a pub. Engineered and carpentered. Tight. Neat. Tidy. Precise. Private. Clean. White, white, white. That's why the blood was so shocking. Slate floors. In the room they walked back through to get out, to get away, he didn't have much. But what he had was good. Flat-woven kilim rug, deep upholstered chair. A Charles Rennie Mackintosh chair? Possibly. Photographs of lighthouses, a drawing of a bridge. Two bookcases forming a library corner. If the books in the whisky box were his, had they fit on those shelves?

The outside of the house was like the outside of Gerald. Not much to look at. Deceptive. But only from the front. He and his house were not the same coming and going.

Janet, Christine, and Cyrus waited outside after calling the police. Christine paced. Janet stood next to the car, hugging herself, letting

Cyrus lean against her, staring at the ground. Vehicle tracks marked the area where they'd parked.

"You saw the tracks at the bridge when you found Malcolm," Christine said.

Janet shivered and thought back to the tracks she'd stepped over to get down the slope to the burn.

"Any chance they're the same?" Christine took out her phone and crouched over the tracks.

"What are you doing?" Janet asked.

"Making a record. For comparison to the pictures we took the other night."

"That's useless and you know it. Don't."

Christine continued taking pictures, moving to get other angles, shots of other tracks.

"Stop. Stop it. I need you to stop and behave normally," Janet said, "because any minute I might fall apart and I don't need any help to get there. Please."

Christine looked up.

"Please."

Christine put the phone away, popped the trunk of the car, and took out a blanket. She wrapped it around Janet's shoulders and then stood beside her with an arm around her waist.

"I'm sorry," Janet said.

"Whatever for?"

"You and I process things in different ways sometimes."

"I *do* and you *notice*. We're a good team."

"But I interrupted your doing, so I'm sorry."

"Anyone who's found two bodies in less than a week deserves a friend with a blanket and an arm to hold her."

"Thank you. Don't forget poor Lachy."

Christine held Janet tighter.

∞

They'd expected Constable Hobbs to be the first to arrive, and hoped to see him driving up the track to meet them. He didn't, though, and they didn't know any of the police who did. Police Scotland Major Investigation Teams that responded to suspicious and violent deaths were made up of specialists assigned to go whenever and wherever needed. Janet would rather have seen Reddick on this team, but decided it was good that she hadn't had reason to call so often that she knew more of the officers by name or sight. She was about to share that glass half full with Christine when a sharp-nosed officer opened the door of the police car where they sat.

"Mrs. Robertson and Mrs. Marsh?"

"Yes," Christine said.

"Detective Inspector Russell. A few more questions, if you don't mind."

"Of course not." It hadn't really been a question, but Janet felt obliged to answer anyway.

Another officer opened the door on the side where Janet sat. She rubbed her suddenly cold hands. The officer closed the door, went around to the front passenger side, and climbed in there. After closing that door, he turned sideways to get a better view of them.

"Detective Constable Shaw," he said, and took out a black pen and brown notebook. Both serviceable, but not as inspired as Hobbs's.

"You can't stand?" Inspector Russell asked.

"Created a cross-breeze, sir," Shaw replied. "No need to make them more miserable than they are."

"Are they? Right. I'll ask the questions."

"Sir."

"What brought you here this evening?"

"One of the other officers got that information earlier," Christine said.

"Indulge me."

Christine told him the bare facts—a visit, a pudding, a question about books.

"You knew him?" Russell asked.

"When I was a child. I knew the family."

"What about you?" he asked Janet. "Did you know him?"

"No. I know his sister."

"And?"

"I'm sorry?"

"Who else in the family?" Russell asked.

"No one."

"That's not exactly true, though, is it? You found the brother dead, too."

"I did."

"It's an interesting coincidence."

"I wish I hadn't found Malcolm. I wish we hadn't found Gerald," Janet said. "It might be a coincidence, but it wasn't interesting. It was awful."

She didn't like Russell's voice. It was nasal and unpleasant. But with that dislike to focus on, she thought she might be able to feel neutral about the rest of him.

"Whose car did you come in?"

"Mine," Christine said.

"Yours is not the name on the registration."

"No. That would be my father, David Maclean."

"Why didn't you say so?"

"My parents and I share the car. I meant that it is mine as opposed to being Janet's."

"Do you own a car, Mrs. Marsh?"

"Yes," Janet said.

"When did you last drive it?"

"Why?"

"Just answer the question."

Janet glanced at Shaw in the front seat. She thought she might have caught the tail end of an eye roll. "What's today? Friday?"

"Friday. Yes," Russell said.

"I wasn't asking you. I was asking myself. I drove it Tuesday night."

Janet hoped Russell developed a crick in his back from bending to look in at them for so long.

"How did you get in the house?" he asked.

"I rang ahead," Christine said. "Gerald told me he'd leave the door unlocked and we were to come right in."

"What time would that have been? That you say you spoke to him?"

"Shortly before ten this morning. I have three witnesses."

"Who only heard your end of the conversation?"

Christine shifted in the seat and Janet imagined the rustle of a royal awakening.

"Are you making an accusation?" Christine asked.

"Tell me about these books," Russell said. "Who do they belong to?"

"They were left on the doorstep of our shop," Janet said. "Anonymously. We thought Gerald might have left them."

"Why? You admitted you don't know him. How would you know his books?"

"Books are our business," Christine said, the royal rustle growing louder. "We've been trying, since Tuesday, to determine who brought these particular books. Our inquiries led us to Gerald. We don't know if they're his or not. Now we might never know."

"How much are they worth?"

"We won't know until we research them," Janet said.

"Interesting." Russell looked at them, seemingly without blinking, and Janet guessed he wanted them to look away first. They didn't. He asked another question. "Did either of you touch the dagger or the gun?"

"What gun?" Janet asked at the same time Christine said, "Dagger? There was no dagger."

Inspector Russell's only physical reaction was a bored-looking, slow blink. "Interesting. We'll be in touch," he said, and started away.

Queen Elizabeth issued a command. "Wait."

Russell looked over his shoulder at them. Whether he reacted to the command or simply rethought his exit, he came back to the car.

"A dagger *and* a gun?" Queen Elizabeth asked.

"How did you not see the dagger in the middle of his chest?" Janet asked her.

The Queen stared at her incredulously. "He was shot in the head. You saw the blood."

"I did," Janet said, "but I saw the dagger and nothing much computed after that. Where was the gun?"

"And I suppose I *must* have seen the dagger, but when I saw the blood I immediately looked away. And there was the gun. A handgun. Perhaps you couldn't see it from where you stood. You didn't actually come into the room."

"I couldn't look at anything else once I saw the dagger," Janet said. "It was horrifying."

"Are you finished comparing notes and getting your stories straight?" Russell asked.

"Inspector Russell," Queen Elizabeth said, rounding on him as he bent to look at them in the backseat. "You are speaking to two citizens who are doing their public duty by answering your questions to the best of their abilities. We are shaken by what we saw. We are stricken by the loss of a member of our community. We do not need to apologize for hesitant or muddled answers, as we are not detective inspectors, and we are not crime scene experts. I daresay *you* are not expert in all walks of life either, and I doubt very much that you are burdened with people who insist on hinting that your lack of acumen in other arenas is evidence that you harbor criminal intent. Please extend the same courtesy to us."

Inspector Russell slow-blinked again, unfazed.

"What about our box of books?" Janet asked him. She'd had to sit on her hands so she wouldn't forget herself and applaud at the end of the Queen's speech.

"What about it?"

"We left it in the house. In the entryway," Janet said. "Can we get it? I suppose you don't want us going back in, though do you?"

"How do we know any of it is yours? The box or what's in it?" Russell asked. "That it's the box you claim you found on your doorstep? That you weren't here filling it up with an old man's valuable property?"

"Constable Hobbs can tell you that we've had *those* books, in *that* box, since Tuesday morning," Janet said.

"Constable Hobbs is otherwise engaged."

"Inspector Reddick, then. He saw them in the shop this afternoon."

"He is also otherwise engaged."

Queen Elizabeth was not yet cowed. "Be that as it may, we did find the books, in that box, on the doorstep of our business, Tuesday morning. Two policemen and one customer can attest to that, as can Gerald's sister, Florence."

"She saw the books, too, did she?"

"I told her about them Tuesday night," Janet said.

"But she didn't see them?"

"It doesn't matter if she saw them or not," Janet said. "Constable Hobbs and Inspector Reddick both did. Our fingerprints and theirs are all over them."

"All over them. Interesting. I'll be holding onto them for the time being," Russell said, and walked away.

D.C. Shaw put away his pen and notebook.

"Are we free to go?" Janet asked him.

"Aye, I reckon. Hang on. I'll come round." Shaw got out and first offered his hand to help Christine out of the backseat, and then came around to open Janet's door and help her.

"Thank you," Christine said. "How do you manage to smile like that while working with a man like that? Don't worry, I don't expect an answer."

"The smile is not for present working conditions," D.C. Shaw said. "It's because I know he's taking retirement in a fortnight."

"Congratulations," Janet said. "Do you know what will happen to the dog and the sheep?"

"I'll see they're taken care of. I've an uncle, lives not too far. He'll come."

"Shaw!" Russell barked.

∽

The two women seethed most of the way home.

"He'll be in touch," Christine muttered. "He'll be holding onto them. I'll touch *him* and hold onto *him*."

"He's a nasty little man," Janet agreed.

"Not so little as all that."

"I was describing his shriveled soul. And you were right. He gave the distinct impression that he's suspicious of us. Us! What does he think, we're as good with burglar tools as we are with books? Oh dear, though. I hope I haven't caused trouble for Norman and Reddick over their fingerprints."

"We fumbled it with the fingerprints," Christine said. "And don't forget the bodies, Janet. We've found a few of those. More than a few. *Several.* We're brilliant at bumbling into bodies."

"Where was Reddick when we needed him?" Janet asked.

"On the Maclennan case. Poor Lachlann Mòr. Poor Lynsey. Where's *Norman* when we needed him?"

"Forget Norman, where's *normal*?"

Janet closed her eyes when they reached the Beaton Bridge. She thought she might not want to open them ever again.

"Do you fancy a drink at Nev's?" Christine asked.

"I fancy going home." She wanted the cats. *Wanted* normal.

"Will Tallie be there?"

"I don't know."

"If she isn't, I'm coming in with you. If she is, I'll drop you and get home to Mum and Dad."

They traveled the rest of the way in silence, and Janet opened her eyes again when they made the turn into Argyll Terrace. A quiet, normal street. Lights on at Ian's. Lights on at home.

"Tallie's in," Janet said when they pulled into her driveway. "What are you doing?"

Christine had her phone out. "Texting her to make sure she didn't just leave the lights on and go out." Her phone pinged with an answer almost immediately. "She's home."

"Thank you."

"I need you in my life in one piece," Christine said.

"I will be. For ever and aye."

"I know you can't guarantee that, but if anyone can do it, you can. That's another reason I need you—because you're braver and stronger than I am."

"Havers."

"And because now we have another question to answer."

"We have questions galore," Janet said. "Which one's worrying you?"

"Lachlann and Gerald, both shot. Was it the same gun?"

"The same gun," Janet echoed. "Shut off the engine and come inside."

20

Tallie met Janet and Christine at the door and looked at their faces. "What is it? You both look as though you've forgotten how to blink."

Christine brushed past her and went down the hall to the living room. Janet and Tallie followed.

"I want some answers," Tallie said. "First, are you all right, second, did you see Gerald, third, do you want a drink?"

"We're fine," Janet said. "We don't want drinks. Unless you do, Christine?"

"I wish I did." Christine dropped onto the couch.

Tallie took her mother's purse and jacket. "Can I take your coat, Christine?"

"I won't stay."

"All right, that answers questions one and three," Tallie said. "It leaves Gerald. What happened?"

They told her about the trip to Gerald's croft, taking turns with the story, Christine upright on the couch in her coat and Janet standing in the middle of the room, shoulders hunched and arms crossed. The telling stumbled a bit when they told her about finding Gerald, and Tallie put her hands on her mother's shoulders, steered her to her favorite chair, and made her sit. Smirr appeared, followed by the kitten, and the two jumped up to spread themselves over her lap.

"I'm still surprised we didn't remember the same details," Christine said. "Or that we didn't see them."

"It would have been an interesting experiment, except that it wasn't an experiment," Janet said.

"It was a nightmare," said Tallie. "Sometimes all we remember of them are a few horrible, distorted details. What was Norman tied up with?"

"No idea. It could be anything," Janet said.

"Oh, good Lord," Christine said. "I've just realized that someone will be breaking the news to Florence. I pray to God it isn't the odious Russell who calls on that unhappy house. Here's the awful question that brought me inside with your mother, though, Tallie. Was this the same gun that killed Lachy?"

"It goes beyond that," Janet said. "It goes to what you said last night about Norman slipping. Did he give us a hint about a theory he or the Major Investigation Team has—are Malcolm's and Lachy's deaths connected? Because if they are and if this is the same gun, then Gerald's death is connected, too."

"That's awful and really not so far-fetched," Tallie said. "And now we, but especially you two, are connected to all three deaths. You, Mom, in particular."

Janet took a deep breath. Held it. Let it out, then took another. "No more so than the rest of you. Anyone who knows that we've gotten entangled with crimes—"

"Solved murders," Tallie said.

"Found killers," Janet said, thinking to herself, *deep breath, deep breath, exhale.* "Anyone who knows that will also know that the four of us work together and that we don't keep information from the police."

"It's only the person, or persons unknown, who don't know those details that we'll have to be on the lookout for," Tallie said. "I'm not being sarcastic, just realistic."

"And realistically there's not much we can do about it tonight," Christine said. "I'll go home, kiss my old dears, and make my notes in the cloud. You do the same, Janet, but substitute your young dears. I'm that angry at the nasty man with the shriveled soul, though. I'd spit if it wouldn't upset Tallie and the moggies. And I will spit if he lets anything happen to those books."

"What about the books?" Tallie asked.

"They could easily belong to Gerald," Janet said. "But we don't know, and now that he's gone and they're with Russell, we may never know."

"They're in police custody as evidence," Christine explained, "as possible evidence of possible theft. According to Inspector Russell."

"Well we did wonder if they were stolen," Tallie said. "Does he have more information?"

"Even better, from his point of view," Christine said. "He has suspects. Your mother for one."

Janet pointed at Christine. "And my accomplice."

∽

Constable Hobbs knocked on Yon Bonnie Bookshop's front door before they opened the next morning. He had the whisky box in his arms.

"I called him after you were in bed," Tallie said, and went to let him in.

"It was Reddick," Hobbs said, when Janet thanked him and asked how he'd managed to get the books away from Inspector Russell. "Reddick is younger, but he's senior. Through the grapevine, I've heard that Russell's career plateaued some years back, and he's developed the habit of taking out his disappointment on those he thinks are weaker."

Christine snorted.

"Reddick sorted the fingerprint issue, as well," Hobbs said.

"Thank goodness. I am so sorry, Norman," Janet said.

"You did nothing to be sorry for. Unless you went to Mr. Murray's with ulterior motives."

"We went because we thought the books might be his," Christine said, "and to take him toffee pudding that he asked for when I rang him."

"He had a sweet tooth. What time did you ring him?" The purple pen and notebook came out.

"Shortly before ten yesterday morning. Is there an estimated time of death?"

"I'm sorry. Once again, I do not have full details. Reddick shared a few he heard from D.C. Shaw, about Mr. Murray's dog."

"He was going to call his uncle," Janet said.

"This was before the uncle arrived. The dog took possession of the whisky box and wouldn't let anyone near. Anyone being Inspector Russell. The dog had no problem with Shaw or his uncle."

"Norman, could it be the same gun that killed Lachy?" Christine asked.

"That has yet to be determined."

"*Could* it be?" Christine pressed.

"It is possible."

"Why the dagger *and* the gun?" Janet asked. "You knew about that, right?"

Rather than answer, Hobbs made a note. "What are your other questions?"

Christine nodded at Janet. "You go ahead. If I think of others, I'll add them after."

"Which weapon killed him? Does it matter? And why did the killer leave the gun behind? As a message?"

"What message do you imagine that would send, Mrs. Marsh?"

"I have no idea. That's why it's a question. It might not have been intentional. The killer might've been interrupted. Maybe by Cyrus. Cyrus is the dog."

"Thank you."

"But there's a wee bit more," Janet continued. "Was it a robbery? Is anything missing from the house?"

"It might be difficult to know," Hobbs said.

"I think it could be very difficult. That's all I have. Christine?"

"I do have one question. Hang on." Christine had her phone out and she was swiping the screen. "There. Would you like to see pictures of what I'm sure are the same tire tracks at the bridge and at Gerald's?"

"May I ask why you have these photos?"

"She's a doer, Norman," Janet said. "Doing something helps her work through the stress of a situation."

"She's right. The stress of finding Gerald and then waiting for the police to arrive was almost unbearable."

"Will you send me copies of your photographs?" Hobbs asked.

"Of course."

"Then I'll just put the whisky box in your office and be on my way. I'm sorry that I wasn't within range to answer the 9-9-9 call last night. I located Mrs. Maclennan and the mysterious person who took her away in a car."

"Is she all right?" Janet asked.

"She's at her mother's."

✍

Rab and Ranger came to work that morning. Ranger appropriated his chair. Rab set himself to changing out the front window displays, cleaning the glass, dusting lower shelves, and tidying the area behind the sales counter. He took a shift in the tearoom, shooing Christine into the bookshop for a break. His unusual industriousness had an unusually calming effect.

"Did you give him all these directions?" Christine asked Janet and Tallie.

"Maybe Ranger did," Tallie said.

Janet went over and scratched Ranger between the ears. "You're a good dog, and a smart one." Her phone buzzed in her pocket. Ranger looked at her askance. "Sorry, dear. It sounds like a horsefly, doesn't it?"

Janet looked at the phone's display and jumped. Lynsey. She answered, walking quickly back to the counter to catch Tallie and Christine's attention.

"It's good to hear from you, Lynsey. How are you holding up?" Janet grabbed a pencil and piece of scrap paper and wrote, *wants bike*. "What's the best way to get it to you? What's easiest for you?" Janet wrote, *wants to come get it*.

Tallie wrote her own note, *pick up here not home*.

wants to talk to us, Janet wrote.

Christine took Tallie's pencil and wrote, *invite for a meal*.

Tallie took Janet's pencil and wrote, *meal HERE*.

"And you've already talked to the police?" Janet winced as Lynsey's response hit her ear. "You're right, daft question."

Tallie wrote, *HERE away from Ian's eyes*.

good point, Christine wrote.

Janet, regretting the four-way, bimodal aspects of the conversation she'd introduced, relayed the meal invitation and was somewhat surprised when Lynsey accepted.

"We'll see you about—"

Christine held up six fingers.

"We'll see you at six."

"How will she get here?" Tallie asked after Janet disconnected.

"She's been staying with her mum. She'll borrow her car and put the bike in the back. She said she needs the bike because she never wants to get in Lachy's car again. She sounds quite shattered."

"What does she want to talk to us about?" Tallie asked.

"I guess we'll find out."

Summer took a break after Christine went back to the tearoom. Tallie told her about the meal with Lynsey.

"I'm there," Summer said. "There's plenty of time for darts practice afterwards, and I haven't met her yet." She glanced around.

"No one in earshot," Tallie said.

"We don't have a suspect file in the cloud yet," Summer said. "Is it time for that?"

"Or should we stick with theories for now?" Janet asked. "Refining them might help narrow the field."

Tallie did some quick thumb work on her phone. "We can have both."

"Do you have someone in mind?" Janet asked Summer.

"Not yet, but it doesn't hurt to be ready. I do have a new theory." She glanced around again. "Last night's circumstances—two weapons—strikes me as vicious. It could be retaliation for Lachy. It could be two people."

"We should find out if Lachy's dad is still in hospital," Janet said.

"And where Lynsey was before Norman found her at her mum's," said Tallie. "Where her mum was, as well."

∾

Shortly before six, Summer and Tallie arranged small tables by the chairs at the fireplace. Christine and Janet brought plates with slices of spinach quiche and vegetable couscous they'd sent Rab to pick up at Basant's.

"Shall we have her sit here, so her back's to the windows?" Christine asked.

"No," Janet said. "Facing the windows."

"I thought a bit of privacy for the widow," Christine said.

"Because you're kind," said Janet. "I'm thinking visibility and witnesses."

"It isn't easy to see this far into the shop from the pavement, but I like a good psychological advantage," Summer said. "Is that Lynsey looking in the front door?"

"It's Isla," Janet said. "Now what?"

"Not a problem." Summer went to the door and spoke through the glass. "We're closed now, but we'd love to see you tomorrow."

Isla waved. Summer waved back and pretended to rearrange a stack of books in the window display until Isla disappeared from view.

"Nicely done," Tallie said. "Very profesh."

"Profesh?" Christine asked.

"Lingo of with-it professionals," Summer said. "Like fab and brill. *That* must be Lynsey."

It was. Tallie let her in and Christine took her coat. Summer introduced herself as Janet patted the back of the chair they wanted her to sit in.

Lynsey sat. "But there aren't enough chairs," she said, standing back up.

"Because I claimed the hassock," said Tallie. "I like the perspective from here." She sat on it, cross-legged.

Lynsey sat back down and dropped a small backpack on the floor beside the chair. She didn't quite smile. She had the dark circles under her eyes of sleepless nights and the taut skin over her cheekbones of someone who hadn't been eating.

"We're glad you came," Janet said. "Let's eat and then we'll talk. Or we can talk while we eat."

Lynsey looked at the quiche and pushed it away.

"Or we'll eat and you talk," Christine said. "We're here for *you*, but only as long as you're comfortable and want to stay."

"Thank you. I want to tell you about what's been going on." Lynsey sank back into the chair, her elbows pulled in tight to her sides and her hands twisted together against her chest. "I want to find out what happened. I want to tell you about Lachy."

She told them some of what they already knew. Lachlann Mòr was a big man, a nurse, and well-liked. Quiet, kind, helpful, and strong enough to toss a caber the size of a tree trunk better than most. Lynsey taught three- and four-year-olds at a preschool. They had no children of their own. His mother was long gone. His father was overcome with grief and still in hospital.

"We heard it might be a heart attack," Janet said.

"Aye. Mum spoke to him. I couldn't." She stared at the floor while she talked, and now she twisted her hands tighter. "You've heard of pure luck? Lachy suffered from impure luck."

"What do you mean?" Christine asked.

"No matter how well he did, there was always something to knock him back a bit. He tried to not let it get to him, but then there's his da. 'No good goes unpunished,' his da says. 'Lad, you have to take the good with the bad.' Thinks he's an oracle imparting poetic wisdom from on high and forgets he crawls under sinks for a living. He can't make a compliment without tossing in an insult. That's one of the reasons Lachy liked visiting Gerald Murray. Lachy said he was a sweet old man."

"So you've heard the terrible news about Gerald?" Janet asked.

Lynsey started nodding before Janet finished her question and the nod turned into rocking. She still hadn't looked up from the floor. "That poor old man. Lachy looked forward to his visits there, liked talking to him. Loved hearing his stories about building bridges. I have something here. A book he gave me."

Lynsey pulled a book from her backpack and cradled it in her lap. Janet wanted her to move her hands so she could see more than the faded blue dust jacket.

"Lachy saw it there at Gerald's," Lynsey explained. "He told Gerald how much I'd enjoy reading it, and Gerald gave it to him. He said Gerald wanted me to have it. But it didn't feel right then, and it feels worse now."

"Why didn't it feel right to have it?" Christine asked.

"It's old and all. You can see the cover's a bit tatty." She lifted an edge of the dust jacket to show them a rip. "But even I know it must be worth something. First editions are, aye?" She tipped the book up so they saw the cover—*Excellent Women* by Barbara Pym. "I love Barbara Pym. I don't know if people read her much anymore. This one's autographed, too."

Janet just barely kept herself from saying, *And you brought it here in your backpack? Are you crazy?* Out of the corner of her eye, she saw Tallie tapping on her phone. Tallie paused and her eyes grew large.

"It felt like being given a treasure that wasn't mine to have," Lynsey said.

"But Gerald had grown quite fond of Lachy," Christine said. "An old man might want to give away his treasures while he can see the joy they bring."

"But this belonged to Gerald's mother," Lynsey said. "It's autographed to her. It should stay in the family. It should go to his sister. Will you give it to her?"

"You could give it to her yourself," Janet said.

"I couldn't. I'd be a mess. Malcolm and Gerald suddenly gone. Lachy gone forever—I can't bear it." She handed the book to Janet.

Janet expected Lynsey to break down then, but she didn't. She looked miserable, and the circles under her eyes looked more bruised, but she held herself together. Maybe she'd cried herself out over the past few days.

"We'll take care of it," Tallie said.

"Did Lachy and Dr. Murray work together?" Summer asked.

Lynsey shook her head. "Malcom might have been his doctor when he was a wean, but he retired before Lachy started as a nurse. He was shocked like the rest of us when he died like that. He couldn't believe it."

"Monday night, at Nev's, I think you said he didn't believe it," Christine said.

"Couldn't, didn't, didn't want to—that's all I meant. You don't like to think something like that can happen."

"Could his dad have been right the other night about something bothering Lachy?" Janet asked. "Was it Malcolm's death?"

"It bothered him, aye. He didn't want to think it could happen again, and me out there riding. But no, he knew it was a fluke. He knows Rhona, Isla, some of the other riders. I told him about the Half-Hundred from beginning to end—how careful we were, who rode in groups, our protocol for traffic, all of that. So, aye, he was bothered. We all were. But he thought it through and he calmed down."

"That's a good skill to have," Tallie said. "Was there anything at work bothering him? Anything with the caber tossing events he went to?"

"Not work. Not the heavy events. He hadn't been to competitions in months because he worked too hard. But he loved the job. He was a happy man. His mates at work and the other competitors would be the first to tell you that to know Lachy was to know a friend."

"His dad sounds like a thorn, though, and that's a shame," Christine said. "Did he get into arguments with Lachy?"

"My neighbor told me you stopped by. Did she tell you they'd a rammy Sunday last? She'd no business telling tales. Nosy *clipe*."

"I think she was worried about you," Christine said gently. "Sometimes friends tell more than we'd like when they're worried. It may sound like clipe, but they don't mean to be tattling. And arguments are normal. Do you know what this one between Lachy and his da was about?"

"I wasn't home."

"Lachy didn't tell you after?"

"He didn't like to dwell. And he loved his da the way he loved everyone. If Lachy had a problem, he'd think it through and work it out. He said problems were riddles or puzzles—you sort them and solve them. Over and done and move on, that was Lachy. He never went to bed angry. Sometimes *I* wanted to go to bed angry, mind. But with Lachy, you couldn't."

"Do you know if he heard rumors about stealing?" Tallie asked.

"Stealing what? From where?"

Tallie shrugged. "I was hoping you could tell us."

"He never told me about rumors."

"Is that something his dad could have heard?" Janet asked.

"No telling what his da hears." Lynsey looked up, then, and looked around. "I should go. Sorry about the—" She looked at the quiche and looked away.

"Forget the quiche," Summer said. "We're all so sorry for your loss and for what you're going through."

"Aye," Christine said. "I hope it's a comfort to know he was such a friend to his patients and coworkers."

"I'm sure Isla and the other nurses will miss him," Janet said.

Lynsey picked up her backpack.

"The other night," Tallie said, "when you sent texts to Lachy's dad and the other nurses, it sounded like you didn't want to text Isla again. Why not?"

"Because Isla's Isla. She didn't believe anything was wrong and there's never any arguing with her. Isla's all right, mind. She and Rhona came round to Mum's to see me. I should go," she said again, and stood. "I'll take my bike and let you get on with your evening."

Tallie brought the bike out from the stockroom. Lynsey said goodnight, thanked them, and said it would be easier to put the bike in the rack on her mother's car herself.

"May I give you a hug?" Janet asked, after unlocking the door for her.

Lynsey wheeled the bike out, shaking her head. "I haven't let my mum hug me either."

Janet watched her get the bike on the rack. She waved as Lynsey got in the car, but Lynsey wasn't looking. Janet relocked the door and returned to the others.

"We should go see Florence again," Christine said. "Who else does she have now? *I* should go see her again. Dropping off the unintended casserole wasn't premeditated kindness."

"The casserole wasn't unintended," Janet said, "and it *was* kind."

"But it was intended for Lynsey. Florence was an afterthought. I need to be a more mindful friend." Christine sighed. "Well, so, what did we learn this evening?"

"It was hard not to like Lynsey and feel really awful for her," Summer said.

"But?" Tallie prompted.

"But was she telling us about the real Lachy or was she trying to convince us she was telling us about the real Lachy?" Summer said. "Or trying to convince herself?"

"She did just lose him," Christine said. "She has every right to surround him with a rosy halo. On the other hand, if we're trying to figure this out, we have to look for all the 'buts.'"

"Like the signed Barbara Pym." Tallie held up the book Lynsey had left with them. "Gerald might have given it to Lachy, but Lachy might have taken it."

"She said Lachy didn't tell her about rumors of stealing," Janet said, "but maybe that was a carefully worded, carefully sidestepped answer. Maybe he didn't tell her about rumors because they *weren't* rumors, and maybe he didn't have to tell her because she already knew."

"To know Lachy was to know a friend," Christine said. "That's a lovely thing to be able to say about someone. But in the real world it isn't likely to be entirely true."

"Or it might also tell us that whoever killed him didn't know him," Janet said. "I'm not sure how helpful that is, though."

"When she sat down, she said she wanted to tell us what's been going on," Summer said. "But did she do that?"

"She might think she did," Janet said. "Or she might've lost track of that with all our questions. She isn't likely to be in the most competent state of mind. And I think you can see that I'm having trouble being suspicious of her. I *do* like her."

"This was your first exposure to her, Summer," Tallie said. "Any other observations?"

"This will sound cold, but we should add her to the suspect list. She had access to all three victims."

"Why would Lynsey want to kill Lachy?" Janet asked.

"Are you kidding?" Summer said. "Think how many times a neighbor ends up telling a reporter about how kind, how gentle, how normal the serial killer across the street was all those years. It doesn't feel good, picking and prying at someone and wondering the worst, but the truth is, we don't know what Lynsey is really like."

"Just like we don't know what Malcolm or Lachy or Gerald was really like," Janet said.

"The sooner we figure this out, the sooner we can go back to liking people as indiscriminately as we want," said Christine.

"Here's a what if," Janet said. "What if Lachy took his problem-solving skills and applied them to Malcolm's death? Lynsey said Malcolm's death bothered him. She told him about the ride detail by detail. She didn't say it that way, but that's how it sounded. He was bothered, he thought it through, and he calmed down."

"If he had a problem, she said he'd think it through and work it out," Tallie said.

"What if, in thinking it through, he figured something out, but didn't understand the full meaning or the danger involved, and he confronted the killer?" Janet asked.

"Over and done and move on," said Summer. "Except this time it would be over and done and dead."

"Here's another theory," Christine said. "If the killer realizes Lynsey gave Lachy the pieces he used to solve his puzzle, then that puts her in danger, too."

"She might be in danger, anyway," Summer said. "From some other piece of this we're missing or just not seeing."

"I hate to break it to you, but we're missing or not seeing a *lot* of pieces," Janet said. "It feels like most of them. But if Lynsey is in danger, and if the killer is watching, then we might be, too. We've been down this path before. It's time for serious precautions."

"As Snapper in Chief, I anticipated that and I have it covered," Tallie said, just as they heard a rap on the front door. "Here's the number one precaution now."

21

T allie went to the door, and the other three looked to see who'd arrived.

"Norman," Christine said, turning back around. "Figures. Not that I'm complaining."

"Norman plus one," Summer said, and then to Inspector Reddick, who followed Hobbs to stand in front of the fireplace, "Do you two pal around together often?"

"It's the *norm*, from time to time," Reddick said with an offhand smile.

Several weeks earlier, the women had asked Hobbs if he knew Reddick's first name, as they'd never actually heard it. "Norman," Hobbs had told them, to which Christine had responded, "That won't do. We only have room for one. We'll call him Reddick."

"I let Norman know Lynsey was coming by this evening," Tallie said to the group. "Just in case."

"And Constable Hobbs let me know," Reddick said, "because I want to be sure you understand that *you* do not have a case. However, we do appreciate your concerns and good intentions."

"The information we collect, too, I assume," Christine said. "Shall we fill you in on the myriad of 'what if's and 'but's we spewed out this evening?"

"Please do," Reddick said.

The women took turns recalling the conversation with Lynsey, and their thoughts after she left. Hobbs took notes. And then Janet showed them the book Lynsey had asked them to give to Florence.

"Do you need to take it as evidence?" she asked.

"Not at this time," Reddick said.

"Does that mean you don't think Lachlann stole it from Gerald?" Christine asked.

"My response was neither a confirmation nor a denial," Reddick said, "but your question provides a fine segue into our other reason for being here. We thought we'd try an experiment." He glanced at Hobbs. "Rather, I thought I'd try one. The constable is on the fence."

"The constable is unsure anything will rein in your . . . curiosity," Hobbs said.

"For many reasons, we don't want you under our feet actively trying to uncover the answers to your questions about these crimes," Reddick said. "Here's my deal. You ask *me* your questions. In exchange, I'll answer those I can and ensure the others are given serious consideration. Some we might not have thought of, so you'll be helping us."

The four women looked at each other, and then three of them looked at Tallie.

"This I didn't count on," she said, and then asked the policemen, "Is it a deal or more of an ultimatum?"

"Call it a precaution," Hobbs said.

"Precautionary tales are some of my favorites," Christine said. "Would you like the questions in writing, or did Norman bring a backup notebook?"

Summer raised her hand. "We have them in writing—in a document. Things like: Do you have suspects? Are you looking for cars with wing-dings? Did the same gun kill Lachlann and Gerald? But it'll be more efficient to email the doc."

"Wonderful," Reddick said. "As more questions occur to you, feel free to send them along. Before we go, you might appreciate hearing something I had to learn as a new detective. There's a difference between what might have happened and what is likely to have happened. Or what is possible."

"Thank you, Inspector," Janet said. "We'll keep that in mind, and we won't—how did you put it? We won't get under your feet and actively try to uncover answers."

"Thank you," Reddick said. "For your own safety and to allow us to do our work unimpeded."

"I've one last question," Hobbs said. "Do you know who pointed Lynsey in your direction? Who suggested to her that you've . . ." He hesitated.

"Solved murders?" Janet said.

"If it's any consolation," Christine said, "our minds are boggled as well by this gift we seem to have."

"Rhona told Lynsey in Nev's one evening," Janet said.

"Why?" Hobbs asked.

"We'd been talking about Malcolm," Janet said. "It was the day I found him."

"She's impressed by our track record," said Christine.

"I see what you mean, though," Janet said. "*We* don't go around talking about it. It's not a sideline for us."

"We don't advertise our skills," Christine said.

"Good," said Reddick.

"Formidable though they've become," Christine added.

"She's joking," Janet said.

"She's right," Christine said. "We are amateurs and we know it. We bumble and muddle and we're certainly led astray by red herrings."

"Although, let's not sell ourselves short," Summer said.

"No," said Hobbs. "We wouldn't want you to do that."

"But still, we *are* capable of bumbling and muddling," Tallie said, "and that begs the question—does someone *want* us to fail? To screw things up so *no one* can get at the answers?"

"Is that what you're getting at, Norman?" Christine asked. "Do you see that as something that *might* happen, or as *likely* to happen?"

"It's certainly possible," Janet said. "We have to wonder, then, who wants us to fail?"

"It could be someone we aren't aware of at all. Or it could be Rhona or Lynsey," Christine said.

"Or the other person at that table at Nev's," Janet said. "Isla."

∽

"They were right to rein us in," Christine said to Janet the next evening as they were on their way to Florence's. "For the reasons they gave and others as well, I'm sure."

"It's nice to know they value our contributions, though," Janet said.

"Isn't it? And passively trying to uncover answers, rather than actively trying, is both pleasingly subtle and well within our amateur skill set."

"That was a good tip about staying out from under their feet, too," Janet said. "If we choose places they aren't likely to go, we should be fine. And if they happen to show up, we'll leave. That's fairly straightforward."

Florence and Tapsalteerie met them at the door, both of them looking tired but not uninterested in company.

"I haven't quite been myself," Florence said. "The police have been here again. Norman Hobbs and some others. It's exhausting. I don't suppose they'll be back now Malcolm and Gerald are both gone. Both in a week. Hard to fathom."

"Are you sure you want to sit in here?" Janet asked as Florence and the old spaniel led them into the library.

"Why wouldn't I?" Florence asked. She'd obviously been using the room. She had a fire going and there were plates from several meals, some half-eaten, on a desk that must have been Malcolm's. She'd taken books from here and there on the shelves and left them in stacks with no discernable plan or pattern.

"Last time I was here, you said you don't like this room."

"Times change," Florence said. "Did you know this other man? The other one shot? Malcolm might have. Norman said he was a district nurse. For someone so antisocial, Malcolm knew a lot of people."

"He was quite well-liked and respected," Christine said.

"So I gather. People have been stopping by with an endless parade of indifferent food offerings."

After seeing the dirty plates, presumably with the remains of indifferent food, Janet was just as glad Florence hadn't offered them refreshment. They'd brought with them the Barbara Pym book, though, that Lynsey had given them.

Janet handed the book to Florence. "This belonged to your mother. It was given to us to give to you."

"It couldn't have been," Florence said. "No one had the right to give it to you. It was stolen."

Janet and Christine had only planned to give the book to Florence and glean what information they could from her reaction. They hadn't expected to hear their theft theory confirmed straight out of the gate. They looked at each other, and Janet wondered if Christine would be able to rein in the questions that must be galloping through her head.

"How good to have it back home from wherever it's been and for however long it's been gone," Christine said. "What a relief that must be."

Florence didn't comment.

"The last time I was here, I told you about a box of books someone left at our shop," Janet said. "Since then, it occurred to us they might have been Gerald's."

"Does that matter to you?" Florence asked.

"We're just interested in connections," Janet said.

"Connections are sort of a hobby," said Christine.

"That sounds like one of those useless tips for how to make fascinating small talk," Florence said.

"I am glad to hear that friends have been coming round," Christine said. "Malcolm touched a lot of lives."

"He touched one more often. Isla," Florence said with a snort. "I wasn't meant to know, but I did. I'm not deaf."

"Good heavens," Christine said.

"Is the Isla you're talking about a nurse?" Janet asked. She rationalized asking the question by telling herself it had nothing to do with uncovering answers about crimes. *Because it's nothing more than blatant nosiness.*

Florence snorted again.

Christine gave in to questions, too. "Isla and Malcolm?"

"She didn't get what she wanted," Florence said. "Malcolm's antisocial ways saved him there. Enough of her. Enough of that."

"How long did it go on?" Janet asked.

Enough of that conversation, too, apparently—Florence didn't answer. She gazed around as though mildly surprised by the state of the room.

"Have you been looking for something in here?" Christine asked.

"That's the way it's always been in this house," Florence said. "It's never where you left it or expect it to be."

"Has someone else been looking for something?" Janet asked. Florence didn't answer, and Janet thought she might need to be more specific. She looked around, didn't see any policemen with their tender feet, and plowed ahead. "Could someone have come in and stolen anything, Florence? Books?"

"What is it with you and books?" Florence said. "But there is something. It *is* a book. The *zhen xian bao*."

"Sorry?" Janet said.

"Thread book. Sewing box book. Zhen xian bao. Chinese. It belonged to Mum."

"Is that what you're looking for?" Christine asked. "Can we help? Can you describe it?"

"Beautiful."

"How big is it?" Janet asked.

Florence measured out a rectangle with her hands about the size of a large checkbook. "Not terribly thick."

"When did it go missing?" Janet asked.

"It didn't go missing. They took it. Stole it."

"If someone stole it," Christine said, "why are you looking for it?"

"They stole it and hid it. Malcolm and Gerald. Like they stole this one." She tossed the Pym book on a chair.

"You might want to be careful with that," Janet said. "It's actually quite valuable."

"Worn thing like that? Daft idea."

"When did they steal the books?" Christine asked.

"When they were clever lads. Did you know they were far more intelligent than I?"

"You don't believe that, do you?" Christine asked.

"It's hard not to when that's what you're told by everyone around you."

"There's nothing wrong with your intelligence, Florence. You went off to university."

"That didn't really work out. It's been my experience that most things don't."

"How do you know they stole the books?" Janet asked.

"Gerald admitted it. Not in words. He picked up a new thread book in China and sent it. But it couldn't replace Mum's book, because *her* mother never held it or used it."

"That's so sad," Janet said.

"It's heartbreaking. Those books in your box," Florence said. "When did they land on your doorstep?"

"Tuesday morning."

Florence nodded. "They must be stolen, too."

"When do you think they were stolen?" Christine asked.

"The day Malcolm died."

"I really am sorry now that I took the casserole to Florence," Christine said as she drove Janet home. "Even worse, it was Mum's recipe for stovies—leftovers made into comfort food. An unintended casserole of scraps joining the endless procession of indifferent food—how unfortunate."

"I'm sure your mum's recipe isn't at all indifferent," Janet said. "In fact, I'd like to have it."

"Then you shall. When Florence was talking about Malcolm and Isla, she sounded like the grandmother in *Cold Comfort Farm* who saw something nasty in the woodshed."

"That was one of the books in the box."

"That's what brought it to mind. Do you believe her? About the books, the affair, any of it?"

"I have no idea," Janet said. "This is hardly a revelation, but I think all the Murrays are strange. I really ought to call Maida and see if she can give Florence a hand with the house."

"If there was an affair, and if it was secret, he'd want it kept that way," Christine said. "He had a reputation to maintain."

"Given their professions, it might have been easy for them to connect."

"We could talk to Florence again," Christine said. "It's good to stop by and I think it's doing her some good."

"Yes, but is it good to keep digging things up?"

Christine glanced at Janet. "You can't lay anything to rest without digging."

22

F lorence volunteered the information about the affair," Janet told Tallie the next evening as they walked to Nev's. "We didn't dig or step on constabulary toes in any way to get that gem. There was subsequent digging, yes. So technically we backslid. But we'll work on that. It can be our goal for tonight."

"Nev's is a good place to practice," Tallie said. "I'm feeling a little jaded about our arrangement with Norman and Reddick. Duped might be a better word for it. We've sent them our files. We've sent updates. We got back nada."

"So far."

"So far. Looking on the bright side, the silence might mean we've gotten nearer the solution than we know, and they can't tell us anything without jeopardizing the investigation."

"Then maybe it's almost over," Janet said. "There's Christine's car. Watch this." She went to the car and put her hand on the hood. "Still warm. They haven't been inside waiting long."

Tallie linked arms with her mother. "My very own super sleuth."

Inside, Christine was settling her parents at a long table with some of Nev's other regulars—a group of neighbors, friends, and strangers who'd *become* friends as they'd drifted toward old age over decades of talk and ale and whisky. Janet and Tallie went over to say hello, and then they and Christine went to the bar to order.

"Nice to see your mum feeling better," Danny said.

"Not so nice to see Ian at our table," said Christine. "What's he doing here?"

"It might be your usual table, but Sunday's not your usual night. Sorry, but a numpty's money is as good as anyone else's. I reckon if you want him gone, you can get rid of him faster than I ever could."

"This isn't exactly his natural habitat," Tallie said. "Makes me wonder what he's up to."

"I'll take drinks to Mum and Dad. Then we'll join the numpty and find out."

Christine took the drinks to her parents and exchanged a few laughs. Then she, Janet, and Tallie carried their half pints over to their table where Ian sat alone.

"What a nice surprise," he said, as though he hadn't been watching them since they'd come through the door.

"How's the WIP coming, Ian?" Christine asked. "I see you have a PIP."

"Sorry?"

"Pint in progress," she said.

Ian raised the pint to them and took a drink. "I've back-burnered the WIP while I—" He tapped the side of his nose with an index finger, then made a show of glancing around the room before motioning for the women to lean in. "While I work on a couple of theories. See if they have traction."

"What theories?" Janet asked.

"Mistaken identity. Hear me out." He raised his hand to stop interruptions, although there'd been none. "We have two brothers. Malcolm, the respected doctor, a man of healing. Gerald, ex-military, a vocation that implies a capacity for violence. Violence has a capacity for breeding enemies. Do you see where I'm going with this?"

The women shook their heads.

"What if the killer mistook Malcolm for Gerald? Then, learning of his mistake, he went back to finish the job. That's the first theory." Ian took another swallow from his pint. "The second still needs time with the old synapses." The nose-tapping finger swirled near his temple. "Here's a preview of it. If the brothers looked so much alike, is anyone sure the man on the bicycle was, indeed, Malcolm? Or could *he* be the man dead in the croft house?"

To Janet, the swirling finger implied a capacity for lunacy more than deep thinking. Then she remembered Reddick's advice for new detectives. "Is either of those theories likely?"

"Or possible?" Tallie added.

"That's for my colleague in the force to decide," Ian said. He raised his pint to them again. No one reciprocated. He drank and set it back down.

"I see Rhona and Isla over there," Christine said. "Do you know either of them, Ian?"

Ian stood up to get a better look.

"You want to work on your subtlety," Janet said to him. "Turn your synapses loose on that."

Ian ignored the gibe. "Rhona's an eco-nut. Isla? I don't really know much."

But it was an unconvincing denial, and Janet caught Ian's uneasy glance toward Isla's table. "Of the little you do know, what do you think of her?" she asked.

"Not the warm and fuzzy sort."

"Not that there's anything wrong with that," Tallie said. "You meant to add that, right?"

"Sorry?"

"Never mind," Tallie said. "Who's your colleague on the force?"

"Can't say. Must dash." He tried leaving on a high note—nose to finger again, accompanied by an arched eyebrow. The note was sadly lowered by three sets of rolling eyes.

"He knew the body at the bridge was Malcolm before we heard," Janet said. "His 'colleague' must be someone in the Road Policing Unit. And his theory of mistaken identity could account for the missing item the

RPU is looking for. The wrong man wouldn't have it with him. Lynsey said Lachy didn't believe Malcolm had died. Or was that just a turn of phrase?"

"Are we taking Ian's theory seriously?" Christine asked.

"It's Ian's, so I'm predisposed not to believe it," Tallie said. "But is it any more unlikely than someone killing Malcolm and then the other two?"

"Danny's free," Christine said. "We'll ask him." She waved him over and told him the gist of Ian's theory.

"The killer's a dafty, then," Danny said. "Gerald wouldn't wear tweed."

"Did you know him well enough to be that sure?" Janet asked.

"Who do you know wears tweed? Ian? Malcolm?" Danny looked at his own jeans, bar apron, and habitually untucked shirt. "Gerald wouldn't wear tweed. Fish supper is good tonight. Your mum and dad are having it, Chrissie. Any takers here?"

Christine and Janet raised their hands.

"Not just yet," Tallie said. "When I come back."

"Give the word," Danny said, and went to place the order.

"Where are you off to?" Janet asked Tallie.

"Next door to the Guardian. Check on the DIP—darts in progress."

"Let's check on the oldies and *their* progress while we wait for Danny's fish," Christine said.

Helen and David MacLean, Christine's parents, were slightly deaf and completely devoted. Helen had more trouble hearing in the ambient noise of the pub, and David spent a good bit of his time repeating things into her better ear.

"Have you tried the Melancholy Thistle Gin?" Helen asked as Christine and Janet sat. "That book you brought home says that wine made of melancholy thistles makes you merry as a cricket, so I reckoned gin might do the same."

"Is it working?" Janet asked.

"Och, aye," Helen said. "And puts roses in my cheeks, my laddie tells me." She looked at David. He brushed the backs of his arthritic fingers against one of her papery pink cheeks.

"Speaking of laddies," Christine said, "we were reminiscing with Florence Murray about her brothers, rest their souls."

"The rest?" Helen said. "No, Florrie never looked much like the rest."

A woman, at least as old as Helen, sitting across from them said, "Florrie and two boys, the Murrays have."

"Half, aye," Helen said. "Florrie's half-brothers, Malcolm and Gerald."

"Did I know that about Malcolm and Gerald?" Christine asked.

"Their names? I'm sure you knew them," Helen said. "Florrie's their half-sister. Looks more like her mum than her dad."

"An interesting family," David said. "Their dad and both the mums grew up in China, children of missionaries."

"Airs, aye, Florrie's mum had a few airs," Helen said.

"Strict," the woman across the table said. "She kept those lads in line."

"No, I don't believe it's lime," Helen said, holding her glass to the light. "Made with thistles. Quite lovely."

"As are you," Christine said, giving Helen a kiss on the forehead. "There's Danny with our suppers. We'll stop back in a wee while."

"We've lost our table again," Janet said, "but no matter. Now I don't need to call Maida."

Though cordial with each other, Janet and Maida didn't have much in common beyond their shared, doted-upon grandsons. A short, spare woman, upright in morals and posture, Maida looked out of place in Nev's. Janet thought it interesting that she didn't look ill at ease.

"Hello, Maida. Do you mind if we join you?" Janet asked.

"You look as though you're waiting for someone," Christine said.

"Here for a meeting," Maida said, straightening a file folder on the table in front of her. When the door opened, she looked toward it, then looked back at the table and adjusted the folder again.

"Do you know Florence Murray?" Janet asked.

"Jones is her married name," Maida said.

"I guess you do, then," Christine said.

"Och, *nae*," Maida said. "Only that she came to live here after her husband died." She moved the folder a quarter inch. "They hadn't much."

"You seem to know a lot—"

"Och, nae." Maida looked toward the door. "She's been looking after Malcolm. Taking care of him. They were never close."

"What do you know about Gerald?" Janet asked.

"Not much."

Janet waited for Maida's spare "not much" to expand. It didn't.

"We're a bit worried about Florrie," Christine said.

"Florence," Maida corrected.

"Florence and the house," Janet said, while Christine quietly fumed. "We wondered if you might offer your services. For hire. We're not suggesting you volunteer."

Maida didn't answer immediately, and before she did Danny brought two plates of fish and chips to the table.

"A table in the back's opened up, Maida, or shall I bring you a supper, too?" Danny asked.

"I'll go to the back." Maida tucked the file folder under her arm and stood.

"We can move," Janet said. "We didn't mean to take over."

"You didn't," Maida said. "Our usual's in back."

"What about Florence, Maida?" Christine asked. "Will you call on her?"

"Och, well, I'll see what I can do," Maida said.

"Let us know how it goes," Janet said, then waited until Maida was out of earshot, before saying, "Not exactly enthused, is she?"

"Usual Maida, though," Christine said. "What's unusual is this news that she has a usual table. It makes me wonder. If Gerald's visits were so random and unusual, who did his appearance here Monday night surprise?"

"That could feed into Ian's theory."

"That was not my intention. Here come Tallie and Summer, and there goes James."

James had come in with the other women, but rather than join their table, as he so often did, he made his way toward the back.

Christine turned to watch his progress and then whipped around to Tallie and Summer. "Sitting with Maida? What's this all about?"

Tallie and Summer both shrugged.

"You're of no use," Christine said, "but I know a way to find out. Rhona and Isla are at a table back there. Come on, Janet."

"Again?"

"Bring your fish."

"Or leave it with me," said Tallie. "I'll save some for you."

Janet wasn't sure that would happen, but she left her plate and followed Christine.

"This isn't going to work," Christine muttered, halfway to Rhona and Isla's table. "We'll have to sit with our backs to Maida's table."

"Too late," Janet said through bared teeth. "Be nice."

Rhona waved them into the empty chairs at their table.

"We did this last week under similar circumstances," Christine said, setting down her plate of fish, and sitting. "I'm sorry to be repeating it so soon and for such a sad reason."

"It's almost too horrible to think about." Rhona swirled the ale in the bottom of her pint. "It's as if thinking about it might conjure more, or worse."

"Don't you think 'worse' is already here?" Isla asked. "We're not like America," she said, looking at Janet. "We aren't used to gun violence the way you are."

"Wheesht," said Rhona.

"Hiding from ugly truth never helps," Isla said.

"True enough," Christine said. "What was Lachy like?"

"I used to joke that if I didn't have my own husband, I'd be trying to get him away," Rhona said.

"A round peg in a round hole," Isla said. "A perfect fit for the job."

"The police have their work cut out for them," Rhona said. "Poor Lynsey. Poor lass."

"Is that what you're up to now?" Isla asked.

"Sorry?" Christine picked up a piece of fish and passed one to Janet.

"Sleuthing," Isla said.

"Och, nae," Christine said. Imitating Maida? Janet wasn't sure. "We wouldn't want to get in the way of the professionals."

"Away with you," Rhona said. "You did well with your last case, and there's no police here. Go on and ask your questions."

"All right," Janet said. "There's something we've been wondering—why was Malcolm wearing tweed?"

"*That's* your burning question?" Isla asked. "Why you found tweeds in the weeds?"

"Wheesht, Isla. Respect for the dead, please," Rhona said, and then to Janet, "Malcolm was old-fashioned that way. He said he saw no need to spend money on something that would make him look more like a bean-pole than he already did. He kept a tool kit but had no need for pouches and packs and whatnot. He carried what he wanted in his coat pockets."

"What did he carry?" Janet asked.

"The Road Police asked that," said Rhona. "I wish I could say I know, if it would help catch who did it."

"Aye. The same," Isla said. "On to Gerald? I only know what I've already told you from the few times I filled in for Lachy."

"I didn't know him at all," Rhona said.

"I thought they might have had a falling out, mind," Isla said.

"Who?" Christine asked.

"Malcolm and Gerald. I heard it somewhere."

"Any idea where?" Janet asked.

"From Lachy?" Isla wondered. "Aye. It must have been from Lachy."

A convenient answer, Janet thought. *No way to check it.* Her phone buzzed with a text. "Sorry," she said, "it might be the grandchildren. They like to send me emojis." She looked at the display—not the grandchildren. Summer.

Summer: "just realized isla is the woman making fun of Florence that made me so mad"

Janet: "she was in the shop Thursday. Came through from tearoom"

Summer: "didn't see her. must have zipped through fast"

When Janet looked up from her phone, Isla was watching her.

"You found Malcolm," Isla said. "We were just saying that if it was a car ran him off the road, mightn't there be damage to the bike? You saw it. What do you think?"

Janet pictured the bike's bent fender. "I have no way of knowing how any of the damage happened," she said. It was the truth, but the way Isla continued watching her made Janet think her statement had been as unconvincing as Isla's about the brothers falling out.

"It wasn't the most convenient way of killing," Christine said, drawing Isla's attention from Janet.

"A crime of opportunity, then," Isla said. "Brilliant. You've solved it, and now I'll take this opportunity for the toilets."

Janet only had to wait until Isla had left the table to hear Rhona's usual excuse and dismissal of her friend's attitude. Janet thought she sounded like someone who didn't want to tell tales on a friend. *But at what point does a friend go ahead and tell on a friend?* she wondered.

"We're riding tomorrow morning," Rhona said. "A group of four or five of us. We'll do an easy ten miles. You should come along, Janet."

"Is your idea of easy the same as mine?"

"You won't be the slowest in the group. Eight o'clock at the Stevenson statue."

"I'll see you there," Janet said, "unless it's bucketing down."

"You already sound like one of us," Rhona said. "You'll be grand."

Janet and Christine headed back to their table, arriving in time to see Danny take a plate from Summer and reach for Tallie's—empty but for five chips.

"Oops," Tallie said, saving the plate at the last minute. "These chips have Mom's name on them."

"You can have my plate," Christine said, "if you sit for a minute and answer a question or two." She and Janet sat down, and Tallie pushed Janet's plate back to her.

"One minute, two questions," Danny said.

"What do you know about Rhona and Isla?" Christine asked.

"Rhona's married to a bloke works at the recycle center," Danny said.

"And Isla?" Janet asked.

Danny glanced over his shoulder. "Has bit of a reputation. Nothing more than some of the lads. What I've always said? Isla has her wily ways." He reached for Christine's plate and started to get up.

Christine put her hand on his. "One more. Did Malcolm take part in those wily ways?"

Danny looked as though he wanted to glance around again, but instead looked at Christine's plate and nudged a crumb. "You want to be careful, aye? Ask the wrong person a question like that, and you'll get a story going it'll be hard to stop. But no, if there was anything, it was a better kept secret than many." He stood and wiggled an eyebrow at Christine. As Danny returned to the bar, Janet had the rare opportunity to see Christine blush.

Rab came through the door, giving Christine a focus to overcome the blush.

"Evening, Rab. Have a seat," she said. "We were just talking about you."

"Oh, aye?" Rab took the seat Danny had vacated and put a file folder on the table.

"News to me, too, Rab," Janet said, "but it's nice to see you. Is Ranger—? Oh, hello, Ranger. Can he have a chip, Rab?"

Ranger looked interested. Rab shook his head. "He's slimming."

"They're cold, anyway," Janet said to Ranger, who'd turned his back on them.

"Playing darts tonight?" Summer asked.

"Meeting." Rab nodded toward a table in back.

Christine, having followed the nod, turned back to Rab and his folder. "With Maida and James?"

"Creative writing group," Rab said. "Fledgling. Called Pub Scrawl. Maida's quite good with sonnets. Something else—" He took a piece of scrap paper from his folder, handed it to Janet. "Zhen xian bao."

"Whatever that is, we've heard it before," Christine said.

"It's what Florence called the missing embroidery book she's looking for," Janet said, letting Tallie take the scrap of paper from her fingers.

"Embroidery book, aye," Rab said thoughtfully. "A wee bit more than that, mind." He stood to go and then bent closer. "It's a book of infinite mysteries."

"How did you know—" Janet started to ask, but Rab and Ranger were already on their way to the table in the back. "How did he know about the ginseng bow—"

"Zhen xian bao," Summer said, staring at her phone. "They are *fabulous*."

"He found a website," Tallie said. "That's what's on the scrap of paper. Take a look." She passed her phone to Janet and Christine.

The website showed a handmade book that, when opened, revealed a sort of pop-up book made of folded boxes, each box made of a different piece of patterned paper—boxes within boxes, boxes that flowered into multiple boxes, boxes containing threads, needles, embroidery scissors—all folded into something slightly larger than a checkbook.

"I immediately want one," Christine said, "and I don't do needlework."

"But how did Rab know we'd heard about zhen xian bao?" Janet asked.

"Because," Christine said, "he's a MacGregor of infinite mysteries."

23

"A re you trying to prove something?" Tallie asked her mother the next morning. "Again? You could tell Rhona you aren't ready for ten miles of hills. Or say you have a subsequent engagement."

"I could say something's come up and I only have time for five miles this morning." Janet unlocked her bike and turned it toward the garden gate.

"That's believable and reasonable. You can call it the Forfar Bridie Five."

"But I'm not out to prove anything to anyone except myself," Janet said. "Again and as often as I can. I don't plan to ride for speed or glory, but when I finally ride in the Haggis Half-Hundred, I *will* finish the route, no matter what banks and braes I'm asked to climb."

"Braes are for climbing," Tallie said. "Banks are where you'll want to take a break and dangle your feet and soak your aching knees in the cold, cold water of a burn."

"Precisely why I'm planning ahead. Think how good I'll feel when I do ride fifty miles."

"And celebrate with haggis?"

"There's nothing wrong with haggis. Or goals, or getting in shape." Janet looked down at herself and poked her midsection. "Nothing wrong with working at it, anyway. You want me around for a few more years, don't you?"

"Decades, at least," Tallie said.

"Good. Nothing wrong with seeing what Isla's like within the context of a different group, either."

"That's what gives me pause," Tallie said. "But it's an opportunity, and at least it's a group."

"So far she's just prickles." Janet straddled her bike. "It shouldn't take me more than an hour. Add another half to shower and change and I'll see you at Yon Bonnie before we open. We'll call this the Treacle Tart Ten."

"Be safe," Tallie said.

"I'll ride with the utmost care and sanity." Janet rapped her knuckles on her helmet. "High-impact polycarbonate and impact-absorbing polymer foam." Neither she nor Tallie brought up that a helmet hadn't saved Malcolm.

The Stevenson statue was downhill from Janet's house. *A coast to the coast*, she thought, enjoying the breeze from the harbor brushing her face. It was another morning that reassured her they'd made the right decision coming to Inversgail. She didn't need bright sun and brilliant blues. Seas and skies the color of seals and smoke were just as appealing. When the statue came into view, only Rhona and Isla stood with their bikes at Robert Louis's feet.

"Let's go, then," Isla said when Janet braked to a stop.

"What about the others?" Janet asked.

"You were going to let them know, Isla," Rhona said.

"Was I? Sorry."

Janet wondered if the breeze might oblige with a sudden bucket of rain. It seemed to be scouring some of the gray away, though. A patch of blue had opened.

"Come on, Janet. We'll make it an easy ten," Rhona said.

I can still back out, Janet thought, but aloud she said, "It looks like I'll be the slowest, after all."

They took a wending way into the hills, Isla in the lead, then Rhona, then Janet. Isla occasionally spurted ahead and then turned and rode back toward them to take her place in the lead again, not looking bothered by the extra effort or miles. The colors of the morning changed around them to a tartan of browns and greens with highlights of blue. Janet thought it should smell like wet wool. As they climbed another hill, she knew the real essence would be sweaty Janet. The backside of that hill took them down toward the Beaton Bridge. When they reached it, Isla and Rhona stopped.

Janet reluctantly stopped, too, and looked along the burn to where she'd found Malcolm. She could still imagine the air smelled of wet wool, but this was a tweed landscape. Gray sky, gray stone bridge, brown thistles, brown tweed.

"We haven't been back since the Half-Hundred," Rhona said.

"I want to go down there," Isla said. "To where you found him."

"I don't," Janet said.

"Nor do I," said Rhona. "We all have places to be. Come on."

"He had places to be, too, but all right."

Rhona and Janet started away. Rhona looked back toward the bridge, and Janet chanced a look over her shoulder, too. Isla, still on the bridge, dropped something over the side into the water.

"What did she drop?" Janet asked.

"Her good sense," Rhona said. She shouted at Isla, "Littering! What are you doing? You know better. What *was* that?"

Isla pedaled calmly toward them. "A memorial."

"Christine did the same thing with a bit of juniper," Janet said. "Badge of clan Murray."

"Aye, that was it."

"It didn't look like juniper from here," Rhona said.

As Isla rode past them to take the lead, she said, "I can't help what things look like to you from a distance."

⁊⁊

"From a distance," Christine said after Janet recapped her ride at their morning meeting. "I don't like the way that reminds me of Ian's mistaken-identity theory. Malcolm from a distance might have looked like Gerald. I don't like that Isla thought to throw juniper off the bridge, either."

"If it wasn't juniper, I'd love to know what it was," Summer said. "Any point in going out there to see if we can find it?"

"I doubt it. The water's fairly wide and flowing fast," Janet said. "Where do we go from here?"

"On a business day? About the only place we can go," Tallie said. "The cloud file. Make sure it's up to date. Add your questions and if you have any thoughts on someone else's note, add those, too. Maybe we'll be lucky and one of us will have a flash of brilliance."

Janet leaned against the door frame and rewarded her hill-riding knees and thighs with an almost soundless groan. Not soundless enough.

"I shouldn't have said 'again,' should I?" Tallie pulled her glasses to the end of her nose.

Janet did the same. "Christine says I don't look as severe as you when I do this."

"She's right, but for the moment I'm being sincere and apologetic. When I said 'again,' it just egged you on."

"Your 'again' isn't why I rode up two dozen hills and only seemed to come back down one of them. You don't have that kind of power over me. I am the captain of my own bicycle. Tenacious enough to complete my inaugural Treacle Tart Ten."

"In honor of which—" Christine flourished her hand toward the tearoom.

Summer had momentarily disappeared into the kitchen, and now came back with her hand behind her back. "Your well-earned reward," she said. The plate she brought forward held a wedge of treacle tart.

⁂

Business was brisk that Monday—good for their bottom line, but difficult for sustained detecting. Janet was glad when she heard the bell over the door and saw Maida come in. Maida waited patiently while Janet finished with a customer and then stepped up to the counter and told her she'd been to see Florence.

"She's more peculiar than I thought," Maida said. "I heard she was looking after Malcolm. That might have been, but she did not look after the house. You could stir some of the rooms with a stick. *Stoor* and *oose* under the beds so thick you could make yourself a whole warren of dust bunnies. It was probably like that when she moved in. Malcolm never had a cleaning service that I know of, and when would he have had the time to clean?"

"But he expected her to clean it up?"

"I don't know that. I don't know anything about their ways," Maida said. "But what has she been doing with all her time since she's been there?" She left with a dour sniff.

Tallie came to the cash register with a customer. Janet stepped back to check the cloud for the hoped-for brilliance. It looked more like a collective brain fizzle and an accumulation of dead ends. She added a note about Isla dropping something, possibly juniper, off the bridge. Then she went to straighten the shelves where two small children had entertained themselves while their parents browsed. *Some people will always have Paris,* she thought, *but I will always have books.*

Hobbs found her mourning a ripped page in a book of fairy tales.

"It happens," she said, tucking the book under her arm. "Are you here for the box?"

"Sorry?"

"Now that Florence says the books are stolen. You did read the update I sent, didn't you?"

"I did, but Mrs. Jones has not called or otherwise made a report, so no, I'm not here to take the box."

"Huh."

"Aptly put," Hobbs said, "but as you've noted, she appears to be confused from time to time."

"Kindly put."

"I came to give you answers to some of your questions."

"That's wonderful."

"The Maclennans' neighbor claims she only noticed the rammy when she heard the objectionable language. She did not hear what it was about. It was a believable statement. As for the missing item, as you call it, the Road Policing Unit says it is most likely something that fits an inside coat pocket."

"Like money? An ID? Sensitive information?"

"They don't know," Hobbs said. "It remains missing and unidentified."

"But it's something he carried in his pocket. Interesting."

"They used the pocket for scale. They didn't say it was *in* his pocket."

Janet nodded and waited, expecting more, but Hobbs had started browsing the shelf beside him.

"That's it?" she said. "Norman, that wasn't *some* answers. That was two."

Hobbs sighed and started to say something, but the bell over the door rang and they heard Ian call hello to Tallie. Janet started to say something, but checked herself. Instead she waved to Hobbs and went to the counter.

"Good! Janet! Excellent!" Ian said. "Glad to see you both. I can kill two birds, as it were."

"Please don't kill anything on our behalf," Janet said.

"Er, no, of course not. I thought you'd like to know that my theories *have* gained traction. My colleague reports the crime specialists are taking them seriously. Following up, and all that."

"That's very interesting, Ian," Janet said. "Your books should be here in the next day or two. We'll give you a call. Thank you for stopping by."

Ian saluted and left, and Janet turned to Tallie. "Thank *you* for not saying anything rude."

"You can thank me, as well," Hobbs said, stepping from the aisle where he'd overheard the conversation. "I've my doubts about his theories, although my doubts no doubt illustrate why I'm yet a P.C. and not a specialist."

To Janet, that sounded more like a source of pride than an assessment of shortcomings.

Just before the four women left Yon Bonnie Books for the evening, Christine's father phoned to say they'd cracked the code. Christine, bewildered, relayed the call for the others. "What code are we talking about, Dad?"

"Two of them, actually. In the Culpeper herbal. Quite ingenious, but not so difficult once we caught on. You did your mum a world of good. Says she's ready to join the women at Bletchley Park and wonders do you have another book like that for her?"

24

Christine brought the Culpeper back the next morning. The four women had arrived earlier than usual, and rather than meet in the doorway, they gathered in the office with the box of books.

"It's a substitution code based on words underlined on page 180," Christine said. "That's the page where Mum read about the merry benefits of melancholy thistle wine." She handed the book to Summer. Tallie reached for paper and pencil.

"I saw the margin notes," Janet said. "Some in ink, some in pencil, different hands. They looked like they'd been added over generations—the kind of notes you'd make after trying recipes. *Next time less salt*, that sort of thing."

"A lot of them are like that," Summer said. "But some read like lines from a drunk bard, like this, *Merry that cricket, decoction merry thistle wine.*"

"That's what Mum noticed. And then she saw the underlined words on 180 and her dear old brain started whirring. Dad is right, a simple substitution code isn't difficult to break, but for a couple of boys, leaving notes for each other, it must have felt subversive and oh so clever."

"*Merry that cricket, decoction merry thistle wine* translates to *Our code*," Tallie said. "And here are their names. Malcolm is *Makes for body decoction merry body makes*. Gerald is *Drank wine cricket for body thistle.*"

"It sounds like a drunken poetry slam," Janet said.

"The other code is even easier," Christine said. "Do you see the small dots spattered across some of the pages? Each dot is under a letter. String those letters together and they spell words."

"We should check the other books for dots and underlines," Tallie said.

"May I?" Janet took the book. "Poor old thing." She ran her hand over the slight depression in the pages that she'd noticed that first morning. "Someone closed something up in it. You can see its impression, so it might have been here for years. It helped split the text block."

"You know what would fit right there?" Summer said. "Probably a bit too thick, so it would split the text block? The zhen xian bao."

Janet looked at the book and then at the others. "I wonder what else those boys got up to and what their notes are about?"

Tallie and Summer started leafing through the other foundling books.

"It's time we thought these books through more carefully," Janet said. "Florence is saying now that they're stolen. It's easy to dismiss that, because she hasn't called the police or asked to have them back. But, if a thief or thieves are at the center of all this, and if the books are stolen, then we have an interesting clue."

"Or a red herring," Christine said. "We can call it a whisky herring. But let's go on the assumption they're stolen. To simplify things, let's call the thief 'he.' He stole them, and then dropped them here. Why?"

"He felt safe," Summer said. "He didn't think we'd make a big deal out of them."

"They weren't what he was after," Tallie said, "but why take a chance by leaving the note?"

"He feels safe and values books," Janet said.

"He might feel safe because he knows Florence," Christine said. "That she wouldn't recognize them, care about them, or know that we have them. He might know she doesn't go in the library."

"He might know about the open window," Tallie said. "Lachy could have learned those things from Gerald. He could have told a partner. Isla could have learned them from Malcolm, Lachy, or Gerald. She could be a partner."

"She could be working alone and Lachy found out," Janet said.

"Or the books have nothing to do with the deaths," Summer said. "Gerald could have taken them the night he came to town. Is it stealing if they're family books? But again, why take them and then drop them here?"

"What if our thief stole the *box* because he thought he was getting whisky?" Janet said. "But who wouldn't know a box of whisky from a box of books when they pick it up?"

"Kids," said Tallie.

"Maybe he had a general idea what he was looking for and maximized his thieving time by grabbing options," Christine said. "He looked through them at his leisure, kept what he wanted, and then dropped the rest here."

"Like first editions in better condition with no codes or margin notes." Tallie patted *The Sword in the Stone*. "That's not this one. Dots galore. It was Gerald's book."

"This was Malcolm's." Summer put *Swallows and Amazons* beside *The Sword in the Stone*. "If the thief didn't want these, maybe he was looking for the zhen xian bao."

"I wonder if Florence made any notes," Janet said.

"Too young, I should think," Christine said, "or told she wasn't clever enough."

"Mean big boys," Janet said. "I'd like a chance to tell them what I thought of that."

⁊

Ian's books arrived that morning. He arrived that afternoon to sign them and brought disquieting news with him.

"Something I thought you should know, Janet. I've seen a car stopped in front of your house several times. I believe the driver is a woman, although I haven't had a good look. It was there again this morning, and I thought I'd do you a favor—stroll outside, pretend I'd just seen her, tell her I thought she was someone I knew—that sort of thing. Let her know she's been seen and will be recognized."

"Thank you, Ian," Janet said.

"Didn't do any good. Broke my concentration, and as soon as she saw me step out the door, she drove off."

"Can you describe her at all?" Tallie asked. "Old? Young? Hair color?"

"Sorry, left my specs inside."

"You wear glasses?" Janet asked.

"Only in the privacy of my study. My vain little secret."

Twit. Janet hoped she hadn't said that out loud. "What kind of car?"

Ian stared blankly. Then he looked interested. "That would have been useful information, wouldn't it? Sorry. If it helps, it was a sort of metallic. Gray. Silver. Possibly gold."

While Janet thought about unidentifiable cars lurking in Argyll Terrace, Tallie told Ian he reminded her of an OED. He thanked her and left, looking pleased. Tallie looked pleased, too.

"Wait, OED?" Janet said.

"It's a simple substitution code," Tallie said. "Instead of Oxford English Dictionary, it's old enormous dic—"

"Wheesht!"

Tallie bit off most of the last sound, and went to shelve the signed books, still looking pleased. When she returned to the counter, Janet had her phone out and her thumbs were busy.

"Text?" Tallie asked.

"To Norman about the books. And the car. Not that he can do anything about that."

"Drive by more often? But if this was someone with nefarious motives, it wasn't very subtle or nefarious."

"That's true," Janet said. "That makes me feel a little better."

"Good. And here comes someone who's a real mood-changer."

The door opened and a smiling Sharon Davis breezed in. Breezing and smiling were good signs. At other times, the director of the Inversgail Library and Archives had pounded the sales counter as she'd ranted about inconvenient authors or roped Janet into volunteering for a committee without giving an accurate picture of the commitment.

"How did you like the books?" Sharon asked.

Janet tried to remember getting a book recommendation from Sharon any time recently, but knew her face must be as blank as her memory. "Sorry, Sharon. What books?"

"Don't tell me someone poached them from your doorstep."

"From my door—oh my *gosh. You* left them?" Janet looked at Tallie. "*Sharon* left them. Oh my gosh."

"I'd no idea they'd cause such a stir," Sharon said. "A box of old books like that?"

"But the library has book sales, doesn't it?" Janet said.

"Quite successful, too. We had one a fortnight back," Sharon said. "But these arrived after, and we're firm about not accepting donations until we put out the call. We've no room for storing boxes and boxes of castoffs."

Janet felt a moment of panic. "Please don't bring them all to us."

"Well I'm sure I didn't mean to create a *stramash* over them," Sharon said, pulling in her chin. "I certainly won't in future."

Good, Janet thought. Aloud, she was placatory. "It's just that we don't sell many used books, and we have the same storage issues."

"The anonymous note had us guessing," Tallie said. "You created a mystery more than an uproar."

"Didn't I sign the note? Och, I didn't mean to be *that* mysterious."

"Do you know who brought the books to the library?" Janet asked. "Did they arrive in that box?"

"They did. Believe me, if I knew who brought them, I'd have phoned immediately and told them to come collect them." Her tone implied knuckle rapping, too.

"We wondered if it might have been one of the late Murray brothers," Tallie said.

"Was that not a tragedy?" Sharon said. "A double tragedy. Gerald didn't often come in the library. Malcolm did more frequently after he retired. Not much of a joiner, mind. Worn out from all those years of caring, I suppose."

"His sister, Florence, says he was always antisocial," Janet said.

"Doctors do have to kill their feelings. That allows them to work. That's according to my brother who is one, but perhaps not a happy one. Malcolm did a lot of good in his life."

"Do you know when the books arrived?" Tallie asked. "What day?"

"Saturday, so Malcolm might have brought them. He hasn't before, though. Sorry for the confusion, but I know you like mysteries, so I don't feel too bad. I'd best get back. Cheerio."

"Before you go, out of curiosity, why did you glue the box flaps shut?"

"I didn't."

⁂

Tallie sent the latest information about the foundling books to the cloud. Christine and Summer had both read the update when they came through from the tearoom at the end of the day.

"Our box is both more and less mysterious," Christine said.

"Basant called it, though," Janet said. "He was closest, anyway. He said the person who left the box was many things. Instead, several people were involved. It's *Murder on the Orient Express* except without the train or the murder. Well, murder, yes—"

"Murd*ers*," Christine corrected.

"Are all our theories about the books out the window now?" Summer asked.

"I don't think so," said Tallie. "We still don't know why or how the books got to the library. And at least some of them belonged to the Murrays."

"We don't know who glued the flaps, either," Janet said.

"Someone at the library and Sharon wasn't aware," Christine suggested.

"Well, it was irritating," said Janet. "Summer, your theory about the zhen xian bao being stuck in the middle of the Culpeper is still good."

"If young Malcolm and Gerald took it, I bet they put it there," Christine said.

"I bet you're right," said Janet. "But who took it out and where is it?"

"What about Ian's theory?" Tallie asked. "Can we throw *it* out the window?"

"I don't see how we can," Janet said. "Especially if the police are taking it seriously. When Gerald came into Nev's last week, he looked like Malcolm to me. Anyone who didn't know them well might make the same mistake."

"Lynsey might," Christine said. "It's harder to believe Isla or Lachy would, but seen at a distance, who's to say?"

"Who's to say there isn't a suspect we know nothing about?" Tallie said. "Someone we have no resources to identify or follow up on?"

"That may be, but if Norman or Reddick knew that Lynsey or Isla were in the clear, they'd tell us," Christine said. "There'd be no reason not to, and very good reasons to do so. Now, we've considered theories about thieves and mistaken identity. As well, we need to consider the jilted lover."

"Isla," Janet said.

"Aye. Florence says she and Malcolm had an affair, but it ended without Isla getting what she wanted. Depending on what she wanted, that could have been quite a blow and a motive."

"I'd love to believe murders don't happen for those reasons," Summer said, "but I spent too many years reporting that kind of story."

"But how did she manage to run him off the road, if she was on her bike?" Tallie asked.

"She didn't. She had an accomplice," Summer said. "Someone who saw an opportunity and took it. Someone who spilled that terrible secret to Gerald, and then both of them—the accomplice and Gerald—had to be silenced."

"Or an accomplice who's still out there," Janet said. "Remember, Lynsey thinks Lachy figured something out and that's what got him killed. Isla doesn't have to be the killer; she might have someone killing for her."

"So many theories, so few hard facts," Summer said. "We might as well be throwing darts to identify the villain."

"It's not a perfect method," said Christine, "but there's something I learned during my years as a school social worker—it doesn't have to be perfect, it just has to work."

Summer shrugged. "Then here's another dart and another less-than-perfect way to identify the killer that I've been thinking about. Sudden violent death is shocking. It's jarring. So if *you* took that life, if *you're* the one who jarred everyone else, how do you react? If it's someone like Lynsey or Isla, you've undoubtedly jarred yourself, too. Are you able to cope, or if we watch, can we tell something's off-kilter?"

"We know from personal experience that some killers manage quite well," Tallie said. "Personal experience with killers—talk about jarring."

Christine raised an imaginary glass. "'And if He doesn't turn their hearts, may He turn their ankles, so we'll know them by their *hirpling*,' to borrow Norman's word."

"*Slàinte mhath*," Janet said. "To our own good health. Not theirs."

∽

Norman Hobbs phoned Janet the next morning as the doorway meeting finished up. At his first words, she asked him to wait. "I'm turning up the volume so Christine, Summer, and Tallie can hear. There. Sorry, can you start again?"

"They've made an arrest," Hobbs said. "I thought you'd like to know. Put your minds at ease."

"Who?" Janet asked.

"I'm not at liberty to say just yet."

"That doesn't put our minds at ease," Christine said.

"I am sorry, Mrs. Robertson. An official statement is forthcoming."

"Norman," Tallie said, "was Ian involved in the arrest? Because he just showed up at our front door and he's gloating. And limping."

25

Janet hesitated before unlocking the shop's front door, but only because she wasn't up for listening to Ian. On the other hand, Hobbs didn't know if Ian had been involved in the arrest, and if he had, they just might hear details before the constable did. Also, it was time for Yon Bonnie Books to be open. Summer said she would open the tearoom so Christine could stay to hear what brought Ian so painfully to their door.

"Morning, Ian," Janet said. "What have you done to your ankle?"

"Twisted it." He limped to the counter. "Doing my duty."

"What duty would that be?" Tallie asked.

Ian glanced around. "Are there customers?"

"You just saw me unlock the door," Janet said.

"They might have come through from the tearoom."

"I'll check." Tallie made a quick circuit of the shop and came back. "Clear. What duty?"

"The apprehension and arrest of Lynsey Maclennan for the murders of Malcolm and Gerald Murray and her own husband. The crime specialists and I joined forces last night. I sustained an injury, but I'm not in too much pain, I'm happy to report. She used you, by the way, the night she came to your house. Creating a sympathetic audience."

Janet wanted to wipe the smugness from his face and the condescension from his voice. Christine opened her mouth but closed it again, and her fingers curled into fists.

"She couldn't have done it without an accomplice," Tallie said. "Not possibly."

"Her husband," Ian said. "She killed him when she found out he'd talked to Gerald, and then she took care of Gerald. We were ahead of you on that, too."

"We weren't in a competition, Ian," Janet said. "This has never been a game."

⁓

Summer alerted the other three to the official statement when it was released later that morning. It told them nothing beyond Ian's news. It made no mention of the police being assisted by a bestselling crime writer. Even that official snub of Ian's role didn't lighten the mood in the bookshop or tearoom.

During a lull in business after lunch, Isla called Janet. "You've heard? About Lynsey?"

"Yes. It's awful. I'm stunned."

"I couldn't comprehend it at first. Rhona's shattered."

"How are *you* doing, Isla?"

"I don't want to believe it, but I think I do. Rhona's shattered. Did I tell you that? It's hard to keep it all straight. But that's why I called. To tie up loose ends. I've got one. I have what you've been looking for. The zhen xian bao."

"You have—how did you know—"

"I'm going to throw it off the bridge."

In her head Janet shrieked, *What?* But she forced her voice to be calm. "Why?"

"Malcolm never wanted it found."

"Then why are you telling me?"

"Loose ends. So you'll know the answer. I know what it's like to not have answers."

"What question will it answer?" Janet asked.

"Police thought something was missing, aye?"

"Have you called them?"

"I'm not an eejit."

"Why do you trust me not to call them?"

"It'll be your word against mine that I ever had it, and it's long gone."

"Don't throw it off."

Isla said nothing.

"May I at least see it before you do?"

"I'm at the bridge. Not for long."

"Wait for me." When Janet disconnected, Tallie stood in front of her. "Will you be all right here by yourself for a while?" Janet asked her.

"You aren't going anywhere by yourself," Tallie said. "Not even for a little while."

"I'm not. Call Rab—"

The bell above the door jingled. "He's shimmering in even as you speak," said Tallie.

"Rab, good. Can you help out in the tearoom? Tell Christine I need her and the car."

"Do you need Ranger?"

"I don't think so." *I hope not.* "That's an incredibly kind offer, though." *And if anything happened to him I would never forgive myself.* "Tallie, call Norman. Tell him we're making a welfare check on Isla. At the Beaton Bridge." Janet thought for a moment. "And call Rhona. Make sure she's okay."

"What's Isla throwing off the bridge?" Tallie asked.

"The zhen xian bao. We're going to get it back for Florence."

∽

"What are the chances the police got it wrong and Isla's the accomplice or did it all on her own?" Christine asked as they got in the car. "What are the chances this is going to end badly?"

"Tallie's calling Norman."

"You're awfully calm."

"It was her voice," Janet said. "It reminded me of the kids when something would happen—fell off a bike or cut a finger. They'd teeter at the edge of tears and panic, watching my face, trying to hold on. If I stayed calm, sometimes they could back away from that edge."

"You hate edges."

"That's why I asked you to come with me. If *I* start to panic, I'll look at you."

When they came over the last hill before the bridge, they saw Isla and her bike in the middle of the span. She leaned against the stone wall, propped on her elbows, looking down the burn toward the rocks where Malcolm died.

"We'll keep the panic out of our approach, too," Christine said, slowing down. Nearer the bridge, she pulled onto the verge and stopped. "There's a liquor bottle on the wall beside her elbow. Looks like whisky. *That* might be what you heard in her voice."

As they walked toward the bridge, Isla straightened, putting one hand behind her back. With the other, she took a drink from the bottle. When she put the bottle back on the wall, Janet saw that it was Dalwhinnie.

"Two against one?" Isla said.

"Let's say it's three together," Janet said. "How are you, Isla?"

"Rhona and Lynsey and I were three and now that's gone. Malcolm and I were two until Florence moved in. It would have ended anyway. That's my luck. And now he's gone, too."

"But you have the thread book—the zhen xian bao," Janet said.

"He said he'd leave it to me in his will. I knew he never would. I doubt he *could*. It meant too much to him." Isla mimed tucking something in the inside pocket of a jacket. "He always carried it with him."

"But you have it now," Christine said.

"I shouldn't." Isla looked over the stone wall then looked at them out of the corners of her eyes. "I worried, during the ride, when I rode back and didn't find him with the stragglers. He was fit for seventy." She trailed off for a moment, then shook herself and went on. "Fit for an old man. I sent the stragglers on their way and rode back farther. I stopped here. And found him."

"I saw him when I stood here on the bridge," Janet said.

"He loved this bridge. Loved the views. Loved the thistles." She pointed down the burn. "I saw him and went down. Couldn't do anything for him. He was already dead. I took it from his pocket."

"But you didn't tell the police," Janet said.

"And be accused of stealing? I knew how it would look."

"But you didn't call them?"

"He was gone."

"I've heard the thread book is quite pretty," Christine said.

"Not pretty. *Beautiful*." Isla took another drink of the Dalwhinnie. "I haven't had much that's beautiful in my life. I had him. He had a beautiful life."

"I'd love to see the book," Janet said.

"What do you mean?" Isla squinted at them. "I don't have it."

"You might be holding it behind your back," Christine said. "You were holding it over the edge of the wall when we got here."

"When you phoned, I asked if I could see it," Janet said. "We were hoping to convince you not to throw it off the bridge."

"You saw me throw it off the bridge Monday morning. Did you not wonder what that was?"

"You said that was juniper."

"Did it *look* like juniper? Some detective."

Janet knew her calm was slipping and looked at Christine. Christine put a hand on her shoulder.

"Throwing it in the burn was an interesting choice," Christine said. "Why did you do that?"

"He never wanted it found."

"What *are* you holding?" Christine asked.

Isla brought an envelope from behind her back. She looked at it as though she'd forgotten why she had it, then handed it to Janet. "It must be for you."

"It hasn't got my name," Janet said, turning it front to back.

Isla shrugged.

The envelope contained a folded sheet of paper. Janet took it out and held it so Christine could read, too.

What's the good if all that's good is gone?—Isla

When Janet looked up from the note, Isla hadn't moved, but tears streamed down her face.

"The world's a dark place when we lose good people," Janet said. "I'm so glad you called, Isla. We're here with you and for you."

"Calling was a good thing to do," Christine said. "We can get you help."

Still crying, Isla dug for something in her pocket. "You should take this. It was in the zhen xian bao and belonged to his mother. Malcolm said he'd leave it to me in his will, too."

"You didn't throw it in with the book?" Janet asked.

"It didn't belong in the book. He only kept it there to keep it from Florence. The book is just folds of paper. It has a chance to disappear in the water. But this is silver." She handed Janet a small pin in the shape of a thistle. "He loved thistles. *He* was a thistle."

"Were you going to jump?" Janet asked quietly, looking at the pin cradled in her hand. When Isla didn't answer, Janet glanced at her and then back at the pin. "The pin is beautiful, too, and you're right. It didn't belong in the book or down there in the water. But you don't belong down there, either."

"I thought I belonged with Malcolm," Isla said. "I thought I belonged with friends. What kind of friend kills?"

"Do you believe Lynsey's guilty?" Christine asked.

Isla curled her hands around each other. She held them against her cheek and then her mouth, breathing hard for a few moments before speaking again. "I've been a district nurse, in and out of people's houses, for twenty-three years. I see the worst in folk, and the best, and all of it turned upside down and backward from what you see and hear when you're chatting with them down the pub. I've learnt I'm no judge of character or other people's lives."

"That's a lesson we have to learn over and over again, aye?" Christine said.

"And sometimes it's bloody discouraging," Janet said. "But I always hope I'll find more good in people than bad. And more hope than discouragement. If you'd already thrown the zhen xian bao into the burn, why did you call me, Isla?"

"You were my second choice. Rhona and Lynsey would tell me *wheesht* for saying that. But I called Rhona, and she was that shattered over Lynsey I couldn't see adding to her misery. And I thought you might come to save a book. I wasn't sure you'd come to save me."

"Hope," Janet said, and she and Christine held their hands out to Isla.

❧

"We got her to call Rhona again," Janet told Hobbs on the phone as she and Christine drove back to the shop. "Rhona came to collect her and her bike and told Isla she's staying with them for a few days." Janet listened for a moment, asked Hobbs to hold on, and then muffled the phone against her chest. "He wants to know why we agreed to meet her at the bridge."

"Hold your phone so he can hear me." When Janet turned the phone, Christine shouted, "Norman, if you trust that your colleagues arrested the right person, then you've no need to *fash yersel* over who we choose to meet and where. Or you could have intervened."

Janet put the phone back to her ear. "You're right, Norman, reporting a welfare check isn't the same as reporting an emergency. It was a fair question, though. Do you think they arrested the right person?" Janet pointed at the phone and shrugged for Christine's benefit. "Pardon me,

Norman, but we've been *extremely* careful to avoid interfering, and if you want our continued cooperation, you'll watch your tone."

"He doesn't think it's Lynsey?" Christine asked after Janet disconnected.

"He said he hasn't been privileged to read all the reports."

"A stodgy porridge answer if ever I heard one. This outcome, this case, they're weighing down on me, Janet."

"Not on me. They're making me boil. When I found Malcolm, I didn't know anything about him. I judged him by his age and his clothes as much as anything, but I can think back and imagine I saw goodness in him and felt sad at his passing. Now, the more I hear about him, the angrier I get. He was a bully as a child, and a mean-spirited man, and instead of compassion for him, I'm angry and I blame him for Lachy's death and Gerald's. *He's* the villain who limped through life and I want to know why."

"What will we do with the thistle pin?" Christine asked.

"Give it to the lawyer handling his estate. Will you hold onto it for now, though? It makes me angry just to think about him hiding it and teasing with it, and I don't want to take my anger out on it. It's another innocent bystander."

"What will we do with your anger?"

"I'm going to take it and those books full of secret messages home. Maybe I'll find some answers. Maybe I'll find a more useful frame of mind."

∽

Janet sat at the kitchen table with paper, pencil, the Culpeper, Gerald's *The Sword in the Stone*, and Malcolm's *Swallows and Amazons*. Tallie put a mushroom omelet and salad in front of her for supper, a cup of tea sometime later, and a glass of sherry before saying goodnight and reminding her not to stay up too late. The cats took turns sitting on her lap.

The coded notes in the novels read like short diary entries. They covered a range of activities—games, hiking, other books, school. There was nothing so neat as a list of mean acts or gloating over clever stunts. Notes in the Culpeper were more like a dialogue between them, but sporadic at best. A message in Gerald's hand read, *false accusation!* Below it, Malcolm had added a quotation, *Calumny is a little wind, but it raises such a terrible tempest. Hall Caine.* There was nothing to tell her, though, if they were real complaints, or brotherly banter, or barbs.

The lack of context for the messages made Janet angry, too. She wanted obvious clues and a despicable boy, but found neither. She found no mention of Florence, either, and that made her even angrier.

But there's nothing wrong with going to bed furious, unless it upsets the cats, she decided. She fell asleep listening to the tempest of Butter and Smirr purring, curled beside her, and a little wind beginning to blow in from the sea to the west.

26

The night's sleep left the cats hungry and Janet feeling resigned rather than angry. "I can't change the past, lads, but I can look forward and *move* forward. And you can look forward to a delicious breakfast."

Tallie had started the coffee before going out for a run. Janet had a cup with her own breakfast. She put the three books in a backpack, the pack on her back, and pedaled to Yon Bonnie Books, determined to look forward. The wind coming in off the sea made that chillier than she'd expected as she coasted down toward the harbor.

"You've roses in your cheeks this morning, Janet," Christine said at the morning meeting.

"The sign of vigor and a healthy attitude," Janet said. She told them about her evening with the books and the disappointing results. "I thought I could nail the son of a—" She counted silently to five. "I am going forward. Moving beyond my anger."

"Good." Tallie kissed her. "We should find out if Florence wants the books back."

"I should give her a ring anyway," said Christine.

Summer moved beside Janet when the meeting broke up. "Getting past the anger probably *is* good, but keep in mind what anger did for my aim."

"My aim is to immerse myself in the panacea that cures, nourishes, and brings joy—books."

"I thought you meant tea and scones."

"They work, too."

※

"Florence rang me before I got around to calling her," Christine told Janet later that morning. "She invited me round for a meal this evening, along with a few others."

"Inviting friends in sounds like an improvement."

"Yes and no. She said it's a way to use up some of the endless parade of indifferent food offerings."

"How jolly."

Christine left work half an hour early, promising to tell them all about the experience, and threatening to arrive at Janet's door afterward if indifferent turned out to be inedible. Fifteen minutes later she called Janet. "Apparently I misunderstood the invitation. The others joining us are you lot."

"Fine with me. I'll ask the others." Janet relayed the invitation to Tallie. "Tallie says yes, and she's gone to ask Summer."

"There's more," Christine said, sounding as though she might now be muffling the call behind her hand. "Apparently she ate all the indifferent sweets. She asked if you're bringing the pudding."

"I am now. What should I get?"

"I'd better ask, in case her definition of indifferent extends to anything else."

Janet heard the question and the answer—toffee pudding—and told Christine when she came back on that she would see if Basant had any.

"Biscuits or ice cream will do if he doesn't. Oh, and Ian was here yesterday spreading the glory of his crime-solving ways. He told Florence we think we're super sleuths. She's quite taken with the idea. Also, she wants the books back. I told her you'd bring them."

"You two covered a lot of ground since you got there," Janet said.

"She's rather like the old Florrie, a definite improvement."

"Good. See you both soon."

Janet rang Basant, who told her he'd have fresh toffee pudding if she didn't mind waiting twenty minutes. She said she didn't. When she disconnected, Tallie told her Summer hadn't made up her mind yet.

"She's conscientious about darts practice."

"Why don't you go on ahead with the books, then," Janet said. "I'll try to convince her while I'm waiting for the pudding."

Summer settled on a compromise—the meal first, and then practice. Janet left her bike in the stock room for the night, and they went together in Summer's used Mini, stopping first at Basant's where Janet ran in. Basant had the pudding ready for her. Janet had a question for him.

"It's hypothetical," she said. "Why does a man keep something in his inner coat pocket?"

"That depends on how long he's kept it there. When I'm waiting to board a plane or a train, it's where I keep my ticket. But I keep two photos there, as well. One is of my sisters and one of my parents. This way they are next to my heart, wherever else they might be. Can I get you anything else this evening?" Basant nodded toward the jars of sweeties.

"Not this evening, thank you. We might be in more of a hurry than we thought."

When Janet slid back into the Mini, she asked Summer, "Can you drive and theorize at the same time?"

"As long as you can theorize and give me directions."

"Go two blocks, take a left, and let's rethink the theory of mistaken identity. Not two people mistaken for each other, but one person who's seen two different ways."

"Who?" Summer asked.

"Stay on this street. We'll turn right in a mile or so. It's Malcolm. Seen one way, his patients mourn him, Isla loved him, and he took Florence in when she needed him. Seen another way, he makes us angry for the way he treated Florence. He was a mean boy who stole a treasured keepsake, and he was a petty man who kept that keepsake hidden. Turn at the next corner, go three blocks and then left. We know this other side of him because Florence showed it to us. The brothers are gone, so we can't see it for ourselves. Other people only tell us how beloved Malcolm was. The secret margin notes don't clarify anything."

"But maybe they do," Summer said. "What if you didn't find the mean boys because they didn't exist?"

"That's what I'm finally wondering. A couple of the margin notes were about false accusations. What if they were a record of Florence's accusations? False accusations?"

"False then and now? But it's a huge leap from false accusations to murder."

"True. So what if Florence has been trying to change the past? It's her version we've been listening to. She told us the zhen xian bao belonged to *her* mother. Maybe it belonged to Malcolm and Gerald's mother, and that's why Malcolm kept it hidden—and next to his heart. Basant said Malcolm looked the same coming and going. Maybe there was only one Malcolm and the wretch I've been so angry at didn't exist. Next driveway on the right."

Summer pulled in and shut off the engine. "Wicked stepmother, wicked half-sister? Does Florence seem wicked?"

"She seems inconsistent."

"So what's the plan?"

"Hope I'm wrong and be prepared to face a plate of indifferent food. And—" Janet took out her phone. "A quick text to Christine. I'm saying, 'just arriving, how's Florence?'" She hit send and they waited. When the phone buzzed they both jumped and Summer laughed. Janet read out, "'Florence in fine fettle, see you soon.' Good enough. In we go."

Florence opened the door before Janet knocked. "I'm not sure I expected four of you, but come in, come in."

"Florence, this is Summer," Janet said, but Florence had turned away.

"Thank you for having us," Summer said to Florence's back as they followed her down the hall. "Can I help you with anything?"

Florence stopped. "Now that's a good idea. You're very kind. And you brought the pudding, did you? Take it on through to the kitchen. It's this way." She opened the door opposite the library. "Through here and through the pantry. Can't miss it. Big room with a cooker," she said with a dimpled smile. "I'll be in directly."

Janet handed the bag with the toffee pudding to Summer. "What can I do for you, Florence?"

"Not a thing, *ta* very much. I've laid a fire in the library. Go in and sit down. After a long day at work it will be lovely, and we won't be long."

"Were you glad to get the books back?" Janet asked.

"Books? Och, aye. These mementos mean so much as we get older. You go on in."

Janet sniffed the air. "Does your chimney smoke, Florence?"

"A wee bit when the wind's out of the west. That's what you can do for me. Can you get the window open, do you think? Careful of your back."

"I'll see what I can do. Are Christine and Tallie—?"

Florence, already on her way to the kitchen, called over her shoulder, "Fetching the dog from the back garden."

Janet could just picture Christine stalking the desultory Tapsalteerie through the garden. She opened the library door and coughed. *Good Lord. No wonder Malcolm opened the window.* She started toward it, but caught movement out of the corner of her eye, and turned in time to see Florence coming at her with a shinty stick, raised like a club, over her head.

"What are you—?"

Janet leapt backward, tripping and falling as she did. But the fall saved her from the stick, and she scrambled like a crab to keep it that way, coughing from the smoke.

Florence raised the stick over her head again—then she screamed in pain and grabbed her right shoulder.

"Florence!" Summer stood in the doorway, right arm cocked and ready to throw a dart. *Another* dart. Janet saw the one already stuck in Florence's shoulder. "I *will* throw again, and it *will* be a bull's-eye. Drop the stick."

Florence whimpered and started coughing. "Let me out."

"Absolutely not." Summer reached behind her and slammed the door. "Do not move."

"Eejit!" Florence screeched. "Now it's locked and we're trapped."

And then Janet heard someone else cough—trying to cough.

"Tallie!" she shouted. "Oh my God, oh my God. Christine!"

They lay on the floor behind the desk, bound, gagged, and both of them trying to cough. Janet's head was beginning to swim. All of them were coughing now. Janet staggered to her feet and went for the window. It was locked or jammed. *Break it*, she thought. *Throw something.* She threw the first thing that came to hand—or, rather, the second. The first was an enormous dictionary on a wooden stand. She set the dictionary aside and sent the stand crashing through the glass, letting in the blessed west wind. After taking great gulps of it, she went to Tallie and Christine.

Florence made her move, rushing for the window. As she threw her right leg over the sill, Summer's second dart bit into the back of her left calf. Florence howled, slipped, cut her right leg on broken glass still in the window frame, and howled some more.

"Tell me what you put on the fire," Summer said.

"I'll bleed to death."

"I have another dart. What are we breathing?"

"Wolf's bane. For Malcolm and Gerald. Not you."

"Summer," Janet called. "Stop the bleeding with these and tie her up." She tossed Summer the cloth strips she'd unknotted from Tallie and Christine. Tallie and Christine were sitting up now, both dazed. Janet gave them each a hug. Then she called 9-9-9.

While Janet tried to explain that the police might have to come in through the broken window, that no one was actually dead, and no, she didn't know what wolf's bane was, she heard Christine regain enough of her wits to become indignant. Janet told the call handler to listen and held the phone so she could hear.

"You tried to kill us, Florrie," Christine said.

"*I'm* the one suffering," Florence said in a pathetic voice.

Janet wanted to smack her for whining, and then felt bad for not feeling guilty about it.

"Wolf's bane," Summer read out from a search on her phone. "Every part of the plant is poisonous, including the fumes when you burn it. You *did* try to kill us."

"Smother what's left of the fire with the dog's bed," Tallie said.

Christine felt the back of her head. "You *hit* me, Florrie? And you hit Tallie?"

"You're not the one bleeding and stuck all over with darts."

"Two darts," Summer said.

"Head injuries are not trifling matters," Christine added.

"The last thing I remember is putting the box down and saying hello to the dog," said Tallie.

Janet looked at what she'd tripped over. "The Dalwhinnie box. I tripped over it and Florence missed me with her stick. Saved by books and Boudicca. I wish you two had seen her. She appeared in the doorway, rising out of the smoke, dart gleaming like a spear."

"Are you *sure* Florence didn't hit your head?" Tallie asked.

"She gave it an almighty try," said Janet. "Summer, how did you know to come to the rescue?"

"I texted Christine on my way to the kitchen, to see where they were, and didn't get an answer. So I texted Tallie, and heard her phone—from the dustbin. Her purse was in the bin, too, so it seemed like a good idea to check on you."

"*Why*, Florrie?" Christine asked. "And how did you think you'd get away with this?"

Florence looked at the four women staring at her. "You're ganging up on me."

"Ganging up like Malcolm and Gerald?" Janet asked. "Is that how you always saw it? It wasn't true, though. Almost nothing you've told us about them is true."

"It's all true," Florence said. "Everyone called Gerald Malcolm's shadow. *I* was the real shadow. Living in their shadows while they shone. Do you know what else lives in shadows? Hate."

"Why did you come back here to live if you hated them so?" Christine asked.

"Things always work out for some, and for some they never do. I thought phoning Malcolm to ask for a roof over my head was the last humiliation—until Malcolm told me how little he was leaving me in his will. And then Gerald—when I went to see him, he said he wasn't leaving me much more. How was I *meant* to react to that? Of *course* I wasn't thinking straight on my way back here and saw Malcolm on his bike. I *told* him a ride like that was dangerous for a man his age. How was I to know he'd panic and go off the road and come off the bike? *None* of this would have happened if he'd listened or kept his head. None of it. Not to him, nor to Gerald after."

"You shot Gerald *and* stabbed him?" Christine said.

"He knew I'd been on the road. He made his guess about what happened. Said he knew it was an accident and trusted me to tell the police. *I* knew he'd come in for a hug, and he did. He was the softer of the two, but it was like a dagger to my mother's heart that they didn't love her even half as much as they'd loved their own. Gerald liked knowing things, so I let him know how that felt. I didn't like to see him suffer, mind, so I brought the gun from the car."

Janet realized her shoulders had risen, while she listened. She'd forgotten about her phone and the call handler. Had no idea if she was still connected. She looked at Tallie, Christine, and Summer. They'd all wrapped their arms around themselves. Florence, though, except for her bonds and bandages, might have been sitting at a bus stop.

"What about Lachy?" Janet asked.

"Who?"

"Lachlann Mòr," Christine said. "Lachlann Maclennan."

"The great git who came with his condolences and blethered on about Malcolm and Gerald? *I* didn't ask him to tell me Gerald said I'd been there the day Malcolm took his tumble. Three foolish men."

"Florrie, you're not right in the head," Christine said.

"It's *Florence*. The boys were allowed their strong names. They were never Gerry or Mal or Calum, but I was not allowed to be anything but Florrie or Ducks. Even the dogs don't get called by other names. And someone should do away with Gerald's dog. He growled and tried to bite me."

"After you killed Gerald?" Janet asked.

"Aye."

"Good."

They heard a sharp rap on the window frame and Constable Hobbs's voice calling, "Police." He and Reddick appeared in the window. "Are any of you in need of immediate medical attention?"

"I'm bleeding," Florence whined. "I've been attacked and I'm bleeding."

"Eventual but not immediate," Christine said to Hobbs. To Florence she said, "*Haud yer wheesht.* You aren't dripping."

"Do you have a spare key to the front or back door hidden anywhere outside, Mrs. Jones?" Reddick asked. "If not, we'll be obliged to make entry as best we can."

Florence didn't answer. She'd turned her head away from everyone else, as though watching the scenery slide past the windows of the bus that had finally arrived. Janet thought she might be humming.

27

T here's a hole in the back garden she must have been digging at for days," Hobbs said. "The dog was standing in it and couldn't get out." He looked down at his uniform. "We'll both need a bath."

"Where will you take him?" Tallie asked.

"D.C. Shaw rang his uncle. He's amenable."

The four women sat at the table in the Murray kitchen, each with a cup of tea that Hobbs had made. After discovering the pudding, he offered them that, as well.

"I've lost my appetite for toffee pudding," Christine said. "It will always be associated with horrifying events."

Hobbs cast a look of poorly disguised longing toward the bag.

"Take it home with you, Norman," Janet said. "Or share it with Reddick and Shaw. But don't open it here, please."

"How much did you and Reddick hear before you knocked on the window?" Summer asked.

"From the point she talked about living in the shadows. Reddick sends his compliments for your excellent aim with the darts, by the way."

"I've lost my appetite for *them*," Summer said. "If James doesn't understand, too bad."

"Are you free to tell us anything Florence said after Reddick cautioned her?" Tallie asked.

Hobbs looked toward the kitchen door, and scratched the back of his neck, considering. "She referred to 'the boys,' making it difficult to know if she was talking about two days ago or fifty years. She spoke fondly of punishing them by hiding things and accusing them of stealing."

"A lifelong pattern?" Christine asked.

"She mentioned boxing up books of theirs, books she'd not been allowed to touch as a child. She wants to press charges against the four of you for stealing the box from the library, where she took it as a donation. She wondered, as well, if you found and subsequently stole a book she's been looking for since the boys hid it from her."

"The zhen xian bao. We know something about that." Janet raised her eyebrows at the others. They nodded. "It doesn't exist anymore. There's no proof of that, and only Isla's word, but there were more reasons for her to keep quiet than to tell us."

She told him Isla's story, watching Hobbs's eyes growing narrower throughout—until she pointed her finger at him.

"Knowing this information, as late as we learned it, would not have made a bit of difference to the police investigation. If the police had heard it, and asked Florence about the zhen xian bao, she would have lied and sent them in some other disastrous direction. It's been disastrous enough for Lynsey. I cannot imagine what she's been through, or imagine putting Isla through that."

Hobbs had the good grace to agree. "One more thing Florence said—she left the gun and the dagger at Gerald's because she didn't need them anymore and they disturbed her."

"They disturbed her," Christine echoed. "They didn't appall? Or horrify? She didn't feel sorry? She got hold of wolf's bane to use on them and used it on us. She isn't doddery or dithery; she's diabolical and deranged."

"Was it Gerald who came in after Malcolm died?" Tallie asked. "Did *anyone* come in?"

"We found no evidence," Hobbs said. "But that neither proves nor disproves it. Her stories and the truth will be hard to disentangle."

"Another lifelong pattern," Janet said. "Taking the truth and turning it tapsalteerie."

~

Isla, Lynsey, and Rhona organized a memorial ride in honor of Lachy, Malcolm, and Gerald for the next Saturday morning at ten. Planned as a short ride along the High Street, from the Stevenson statue to Yon Bonnie Books, it would be an easy distance for anyone on wheels, afoot, or on a leash. The Council agreed to close the street for half an hour to accommodate the memorial.

The day dawned brisk and clear and stayed that way. Janet and Tallie hung a sign on the bookshop door, and Christine and Summer hung one on the tearoom door, and the four women went to join the crowd already spreading along the harbor and spilling into the street.

"How many?" Tallie asked Hobbs when they saw him.

"I lost track at several hundred. And more on the way."

Lynsey called to Janet and the others when she saw them. "Here! Up front with us!"

At ten o'clock they started to move, and it was less a bike ride or procession than a surge washing along the street.

"Washing away the wickedness," Isla said to Janet.

When the women in front reached the bookshop, they stood on the steps and waved as those behind them streamed past.

"A lovely tribute," Christine said when the crowd, at last, began to thin. "Will you come in for tea?"

"Not today," Lynsey said, wiping her eyes. "It's been a bit overwhelming. Soon, though."

A community atmosphere prevailed for the rest of the day, with people visiting in and out of shops. Rab lent a needed hand in the bookshop, and Ranger accepted compliments from his chair near the fireplace.

Hobbs brought the Dalwhinnie box back to the shop as things slowed down later in the afternoon. "That's finally cleared up, then. As they were a donation to the library, and from the library to you, they're yours to sell."

"Wonderful," Janet said. "We'll work up prices and let you know about *Kidnapped*. There's still a mystery, though. Who glued the box shut?" she looked at Hobbs, and then looked more closely. "I've seen that look on your face before, Norman Hobbs. You're hiding something."

"Mrs. Marsh—"

"Tell me what you know."

"I saw the box on your doorstep whilst on my rounds the night before you found them. Out of the ordinary, I thought, so I took a look to be sure it wasn't rubbish or something worse. I saw the books, and didn't like to leave them overnight, should it rain." He'd taken the box home, he said, intending to bring it back shortly before the women arrived to open the shop. As they weren't his, he hadn't looked through them. "I thought to seal it, mind, so no one else could rummage and maybe nick them before you arrived. But I'd used the last of my packaging tape when I sent a unicorn to my great-niece."

"So you glued it. That was thoughtful, Norman, although you could have saved us both some trouble by bringing it back, *without* glue, after we opened."

"I didn't like to disrupt the normal way you do business."

Reddick stopped in before Hobbs left. "I've an answer, of sorts, from the Road Policing Unit."

Janet, immediately worried they'd discovered Isla's role and her own belated knowledge of it, didn't trust herself to say more than, "About?"

"About how they decided something might have been removed from the scene. They found a piece of paper inside Malcolm's jacket, *near* the inner breast pocket, but not in it. They didn't see how it hadn't fallen out of the jacket during the ride. They guessed that it *had* been in his pocket and had slipped out when someone pulled something else out—the infamous missing item. It remains a loose end, however, with no leads. In fact, I think it's entirely possible the paper was not securely in the pocket, so that it came out during that rough ride down the slope."

"Thank you for letting us know," Janet said. "This isn't meant as a complaint. It's just an observation. But I didn't think they questioned me as carefully as they should have."

"Ah, but they complimented you. After a fashion. They told me you're a believable witness. You irritated them, but they believed you."

"That seems fair. They irritated me, too."

"I can also tell you how Ian Atkinson injured his ankle," Reddick said.

"He already told us," said Tallie. "He sustained an injury during the apprehension and arrest of the wrong suspect. Don't tell me that's an exaggerated account?"

"Somewhat," Reddick said. "Fell off the curb, running to his car, after being ordered to leave. His 'colleague' received a transfer."

"Poor Ian," Janet said, after Reddick left, and heard Tallie and Rab snort behind her.

James Haviland came through from the tearoom and accepted condolences from Hobbs and Rab for losing the star member of the paper's darts team. "There's always next year," he said. "You might find this interesting. I've had a letter from Gerald Murray's lawyer. It seems he left his money in trust to go toward helping veterans."

"Very generous," Hobbs said. "Why did the lawyer send the letter to you?"

"Exactly," said James. "This is the interesting part. Gerald named three people to oversee the trust. Ian Atkinson, me, and another lawyer—William Clark."

"Have I heard that name?" Janet asked.

"I have," Rab and Hobbs both said.

"Exactly," James said again and, without further explanation, left.

"Who's William Clark?" Tallie asked.

"And what are those odd looks passing between you two?" Janet asked Hobbs and Rab.

"I'm sure you're imagining them," Hobbs said, answering Janet's question and ignoring Tallie's. "Let me know about *Kidnapped*, will you?" And he was gone.

"That leaves the explanation to you, Rab," Janet said, but too late. Rab had shimmered away. They heard a whistle near the tearoom. Ranger heard it, too. He hopped down from his chair and trotted after it.

"Rab left a box and a note," Tallie said.

"A box and a note? Again?"

"It's addressed to the four of us."

"Then it can wait the half hour until we're closed. Christine says she and Summer have something to show us, too."

The last half hour was quiet. That suited Janet, and she yawned as Christine and Summer came to join them at the bookshop counter after locking the tearoom door for the night.

"We've been working on Tallie's recipe booklet idea," Christine said, "but with a twist."

"Here's a prototype," Summer said. "Postcard recipe cards. We'll have the recipe in the middle, a small photo of the food in the upper left corner, and a small scenic shot of someplace in Inversgail in the lower right—bookshop, tearoom, harbor, Stevenson statue, that kind of thing. What do you think?"

"Perfect," said Tallie.

"Aiming her camera instead of darts," Christine said. "Is she not brilliant?"

"Absolutely," said Janet. "Now for Rab's surprise." She handed the note to Christine and let Tallie and Summer open the box.

"Books. A couple of dozen." Summer took four out and handed one to each of them—slim, slightly larger than checkbooks, with covers of brightly patterned paper.

"Not just books," Christine said, reading the note. "Zhen xian baos. He made them and wants to know if we'd like to sell them."

They opened the books, revealing the first folded boxes within, each box made of a different patterned paper and blossoming into another and more boxes.

"Of course we'd like to sell them," Tallie said. "I don't think there's any question."

"None whatsoever," Janet agreed, gazing at the wonder before her. "Think of all the little things you can hide inside. It could be a whole book full of secrets and clues." She looked up at the others. "I do love a mystery."

ACKNOWLEDGMENTS

Help in writing a book comes from lots of people in so many ways—some of them unexpected—and for all of them I'm grateful. For this book, I owe Susan Meinkoth and Peter Davis thanks for the Haggis Half-Hundred, inspired by the Cherry Pie Ride they organize each year. Ann Campbell tipped me off to the word tapsalteerie. PJ Coldren gave me whigmaleerie. Pat Crowley saved me from mistakes in Scrabble scoring. Cammy MacRae provided invaluable Gaelic consultation. Thanks to Linda Wessels for introducing me to Swedish Death Decluttering. Thanks to Janice N. Harrington and Betsy Hearne for reading and editing, but especially for your friendship. Janice also dazzled me with zhen xian bao. James Haviland and Sharon Davis have again lent me their names (and let me add quirks to their personalities and put words in their mouths). Marthalee Beckington let me borrow her marvelous collies Quantum and Cyrus. This book wouldn't have gotten anywhere at all without my agent, Cynthia Manson, and everyone at Pegasus Books. And I certainly couldn't have finished it without my husband's unfailing help. Thank you, Mike, for keeping the house and everything else together so I can keep writing.